"My place is just around the corner."

Miranda seemed to read his mind with those words. "Interested?"

Jeremiah wanted to shout *hell, yes* but a sliver of reserve had him counter, "Not that I'm not interested, but how about you? Didn't your father ever warn you about taking off with strange men from bars? I could be a pervert or a serial killer."

She slid from her barstool and graced him with a dazzling smile that was a bit menacing as she said, "My daddy taught me to shoot a gun, gut a fish and break a kneecap if need be. Strange men in bars don't scare me."

She slung her pack onto her back and headed for the door. She shot him a single questioning look, then kept walking. The message was clear: *Come or stay, it doesn't matter to me.*

D1413304

Dear Reader,

As a fan of the rugged beauty of a forest landscape, the startling vibrancy of Alaska's wild frontier seemed a natural choice for my next series. It was easy to find inspiration in the endless photos of this gorgeous, untamed state, but it wasn't as easy to find the perfect characters to build a series around. But as they say, nothing worth enjoying comes easily, so I am more than excited to invite you to step into the lives of the Sinclair family as they struggle to find their way to healing and, ultimately, love, while navigating the harsh conditions of their breathtaking state.

Miranda and Jeremiah's love story is no soft climb to paradise—it's fraught with danger, grief, emotional healing—but I hope you find their journey all the more satisfying for their struggle.

Hearing from readers is a special joy. Please feel free to drop me a line via email through my website at www.kimberlyvanmeter.com or through snail mail at Kimberly Van Meter, P.O. Box 2210, Oakdale, CA 95361.

Happy reading,

Kimberly Van Meter

KIMBERLY
VAN METER

That Reckless Night

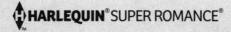

HARLEQUIN® SUPER ROMANCE®

Recycling programs
for this product may
not exist in your area.

ISBN-13: 978-0-373-60811-9

THAT RECKLESS NIGHT

Copyright © 2013 by Kimberly Sheetz

Printed in U.S.A.

HARLEQUIN®
www.Harlequin.com

ABOUT THE AUTHOR

Kimberly Van Meter wrote her first book at sixteen and finally achieved publication in December 2006. She writes for the Harlequin Superromance and Harlequin Romantic Suspense lines. She and her husband of seventeen years have three children, three cats and always a houseful of friends, family and fun.

Books by Kimberly Van Meter

HARLEQUIN SUPERROMANCE

HARLEQUIN ROMANTIC SUSPENSE

*Home in Emmett's Mill
**Mama Jo's Boys
***Family in Paradise
^Native Country

Other titles by this author available in ebook format.

I would like to thank Antoinette Ryun for her invaluable insight into Alaskan living. Without her, I would've been unsure where to start, where to inquire, and ultimately lost in pages and pages of research. Thank you, girl!

To my family, twenty books in and you're all still my biggest fans.
I'm a lucky girl and I will never forget how blessed I am.

To the residents of Alaska, you are so lucky to live in such an amazing place. Please forgive my poetic license regarding certain areas of the landscape. My creative vision of Homer is a pale imitation of this vibrant and thriving place!

Lastly, to my sister Kamrin, who in spite of becoming a new mom, acquiring her first home and still being a newlywed, agreed to become my assistant to help keep me (a flighty creative type!) on track.
Thank you, Kikikins! I love you!

CHAPTER ONE

MIRANDA SINCLAIR TOSSED the tequila popper to the back of her throat, relishing the burn as the liquor warmed her in all the right places, loosening up the tension in her shoulders from a craptastic day in the field and an even crappier anniversary.

"Keep 'em comin'." She motioned to Russ, a hard-bitten man with cheeks made ruddy by countless years spent in the harsh Alaskan air, who owned and bartended The Rusty Anchor. She offered a grim smile as he slid the shooter across to her in a practiced move, and after she'd dispatched it in the same efficient manner, she swiveled on her barstool to survey the prospects for the night.

That was right—tonight she was going to take home one lucky SOB, ride him as if the world was going to end tomorrow, and then when the first tender rays of light hit the windowsill, she'd send him on his way with a cup of coffee and a boot print on his hindquarters.

It was a helluva plan.

"Killing yourself with booze and bad choices isn't going to bring her back," Russ said.

Miranda scowled. "Play bartender psychologist with someone else, Russ. I'm not interested in your counsel right now."

Russ shook his head. "Always so filled with piss and vinegar. Girl, someday you're going to have to rein in that acid tongue of yours."

"So they say," Miranda quipped. She had plenty of people telling her she needed to try tact once in a while; she didn't need her bartender to join the chorus, too. "But not tonight. Come on, Russ. Stop crashing on my buzz. I need this." Besides, contrary to Russ's opinion, Miranda thought her plan of action was far better than the alternative—curling up in her worn recliner, nursing a bottle of Jack. "Today has to be up there as one of my worst days in a long time."

"Yeah? What made it so bad?" Russ asked, polishing a glass, his dark eyes serious. Russ knew about the anniversary—for God's sake, the whole town knew and never let her forget, seeing as it was everyone's favorite go-to gossip topic—but he was asking about the less-obvious reason she wanted to blot out her brain with booze. She almost waved off his question, not sure she wanted to share, but she did anyway.

"I didn't get the job," she answered, her chest tightening again as bitterness followed. "Apparently, I'm not management material." She tapped the bar with the shot glass for another round. "So, whatever."

"Did they say why not?"

"Nope. I was just thanked for my interest in the position and politely informed that the department had chosen to go in another direction." She looked pointedly at Russ and waggled her glass at him. He sighed and refilled it. Yep. This was a much better plan.

Done talking, she swiveled her chair away from Russ and surveyed the bar. Slim pickings to be sure. The bar was filled with the usual nightlife but the place stank of fish, which meant the men probably had wet socks and frozen toes because they were all in port from their commercial fishing outfits scattered throughout Alaska.

She recognized a few familiar faces, Johnny, Macho, Heff—all working on the halibut fishing boat *The Arctic Maiden*—and certainly not contenders for her purposes tonight. Miranda scanned the room and found a decided lack of options. So much for cutting up and losing herself in a night of debauchery she'd likely regret when she sobered up. For a brief—nanosecond-brief—moment she considered Luke Prather, but the last time she'd taken him to bed for a one-nighter he'd fallen head over heels in love with her and it'd been no fun whatsoever trying

to scrape him off her doorstep for weeks after-
ward. That had been awkward *and* irritating. *No,
thanks*. Her personal brand of misery did not include ducking the lovelorn. She mentally crossed
Luke from her list.

What happened to all the raw, randy men built
like cedar trees with big, beefy hands that were
worn and tough like old shoe leather from working hard since the day they were big enough to
swing an ax or cast a line? Too bad the *AnnaMarie*
wasn't in port this month. The *AnnaMarie*'s cap-
tain was always down for some unattached wild
times.

Well, maybe getting laid wasn't on the agenda
tonight but getting stone-cold drunk certainly
was. She turned to Russ with a morose sigh. "And
it just keeps getting better and better," she murmured in frustration. "Another round and stop
skimping on the tequila."

"You've got that look in your eye, kid," Russ
said with knowing. "Maybe you ought to just go
home and watch television."

"I don't have a television," Miranda said,
motioning for her fourth round, which Russ
plainly ignored. She made a face. The last thing
she needed was Russ passing judgment on her
choices. She had her mother for that. "Come on.
Are we going to play that game? I'm no kid and

I've earned the right to get snot-faced drunk if I please."

"Go home," Russ said, bracketing the bar on either side of her.

"Are you saying my money's no good here? Last I heard you needed the cash. Am I wrong?"

"You're as stubborn as your old man and just as mean," Russ said, setting up her drink. "Why do you do this to yourself, girl? It ain't gonna bring her back, and before you start spouting off about some desk job you're plainly not suited for, there ain't a person in Homer who don't know why you drown yourself in booze every year on this night. Ain't it time to start a new tradition?"

Miranda stilled, the subtle tilt of her lips freezing as her heart rate stumbled beneath the shelter of her breastbone. "Not allowed, Russ," she warned him quietly. "Not allowed." Today was the anniversary of her sister's death. And no one was allowed to bring up Simone's name. Not today. This, Miranda thought as she stared at the refilled shot glass, was how she chose to cope with Simone's death and no one was going to convince her otherwise.

What did they know anyway? They didn't know of the bone-crushing guilt that Miranda carried every day or the pain of regret and loss that dogged her nights and chased her days. And they certainly didn't know of the recrimination

Miranda saw in her mother's eyes for a falling-out over a damn sweater that had kept Miranda from picking up her sister that night in a fit of pissed-off ire. Nobody knew. Nobody understood. And that was just fine. Miranda wasn't inviting anyone in to take a look and offer their opinion.

Russ heaved a sigh and shook his head. "One of these days you're going to realize this isn't helping."

"Maybe. But not today," she muttered as she tossed the shot down her throat, her vision swimming nicely as the alcohol began to do its job. The sudden blast of arctic air chilled the closed-in heat of The Anchor, chasing away the stale smell of fish, beer and good times, and Miranda gave a cursory glance at who had walked through the front door.

And suddenly her mood took a turn for the better.

Hello, stranger. A smile settled on her mouth as she appraised the newcomer. The liquor coursing through her system unhindered by anything resembling food made her feel loose and wild, and that broad-shouldered specimen shaking off the snow from his jacket and stamping his booted feet was going to serve her needs perfectly.

"Hey, Russ…who's he?" she asked.

Russ glanced up but shrugged after a speculative look-see. "Never seen him before. Looks too soft to be a fisherman. By the looks of him, probably a tourist who got lost on his way to Anchorage."

A tourist? Here today, gone tomorrow. "He'll do," she murmured.

JEREMIAH BURKE ENTERED the raucous din of The Rusty Anchor, practically the only place in Homer, Alaska, to get a drink at this hour, and headed straight for the bar. He was well and truly screwed and looking at spending the night stuffed inside a storage closet if he was lucky, and his mood wasn't what one would call warm and fuzzy.

Maybe if he drank enough he'd forget the fact that his hotel had somehow given away his room for the night and none of the other hotels had any vacancies. His options were slim seeing as he didn't know a soul in his new zip code and he was looking at bedding down at his new office, on the old, lumpy couch that looked as if it'd been salvaged from a trash heap after spending a few nights in the elements. Hell, he'd been tempted to try his luck in his rental truck after taking one look at the couch. No telling what vermin had made their residence in its old springs.

He sidled up to the bar and signaled for the bartender.

"What's your poison?" the man asked.

"Whatever's on tap," he answered just as his gaze found the leggy brunette regarding him with open interest. Talk about bold. He couldn't say he wasn't flattered but he was surprised to feel equal interest spark to life. "Would you be offended if I said you looked out of place in this bar?" he said, accepting his beer from the bartender.

"Depends on why you're saying it," she countered, swiveling around to give him a full measured stare, a slight smile playing on her lips. "Tread carefully. I was born in this town."

He chuckled, enjoying the husky timbre of her voice. "And by making that statement, I just cemented your assumption that I'm not from around here, right?"

She laughed, her green eyes lighting with amusement. "Honey, I knew that before you opened your mouth but I won't hold it against you."

"Thanks. I'd hate to think I've already made a bad impression."

At first glance, she had indeed appeared out of place in the rough bar with her long hair tucked into a ponytail and a warm woolen scarf wrapped loosely around her neck, but upon a closer look he realized that beyond that pretty face was a woman who could probably take care of herself. There was something hard as glacial ice about her even though her curves were soft. Her tight jeans left nothing to the imagination, something his own mind immediately jumped on with all kinds of scenarios, but it was her eyes that knocked him back for a second.

Green as summer moss with flecks of brown that reminded him of a Wyoming meadow in the spring, her eyes were framed by long, black lashes that dusted her cheekbones, and he had to remember not to stare. Hell, she was gorgeous.

"Careful—you keep staring like that I might get the wrong impression about you," she teased.

"And what impression would that be?" He didn't know how to play this game anymore and he'd never been particularly good at it in the first place. He was already out of his element—new place, new job—why not chat up the prettiest woman in the bar and see where it took him?

She responded with another throaty laugh and his groin tightened, warming in places he'd nearly forgotten about in the past year, but she switched gears, saying, "So, I'm guessing you're not a fisherman.... What brings you to Homer of all places?"

Jeremiah hesitated, not quite sure how much he wanted to share about his personal life. He smiled, going for a variation of the truth. "A change in scenery," he answered, taking a swig of his beer. "What about you? What's kept you in Homer?"

Her smile faltered the tiniest bit but she recovered within a blink, returning to her previously bold assessment of him without being the least bit coy. "Are you married?" she asked. He lifted his left hand, showing her his ringless finger, and she scoffed. "That doesn't mean anything. Half the men in this town don't wear rings—that doesn't mean someone isn't waiting for them to come home at night."

"No one is waiting for me," he said. No one at all. He shook off the pull of sad memories and focused on the woman smiling at him. "And how about you? Beautiful woman in a small town? I find it hard to believe someone hasn't laid claim to you already."

"I don't like to be tied down...*unless* I'm the one in charge of the rope."

Another flush of arousal heated his groin at her suggestive answer and he nearly choked on his beer. He'd always found couples who claimed they'd felt an instant chemistry with one another to be exaggerating. How could you be instantly, insanely attracted to someone you'd only just met? Seemed the stuff of fairy tales and rom-com movies that he usually avoided, and yet, his blood was moving at a fine clip with just one look from this beautiful stranger. How did a woman like her get stuck in a fishing village like Homer without getting snagged by a local? He tipped his beer back, intrigued. "So, what's your name?" he asked.

"Where are you from?" she countered.

"Wyoming." He grinned. "Your turn. Name?"

Her smile deepened and she leaned forward far enough for him to get a nice whiff of her perfume. "Are names really necessary?" she asked. "Here's the thing…. I think you're pretty easy on the eyes and I'm ready to get out of here. Catch my drift?"

"Are you asking me to go home with you?"

"I am." She swigged her beer like a woman who was used to playing poker with the guys and taking all their cash at the end of the night. There was something about her that pulsed like a live wire—dangerous and hot.

And he wanted to feel the burn. Desperately.

"No names. No personal details. Should I be worried?"

"You should be very worried," she said with a mock-solemn nod that only served to make his heart rate triple. "Didn't your mama ever warn you not to pick up strange women in bars?"

"She might've missed that one," he said, sliding his tongue along his bottom lip, mimicking her own subconscious gesture. He knew a little about human nature. He'd taken a course in college on body language when he'd been considering a career in law enforcement. He hadn't become a cop but he'd found the course had been beneficial nonetheless. And right now, she was throwing off major "come and get me" signals from the way she was angling her hips toward his and the tiny dart of her tongue along the seam of her lips, teasing him with the slow, wet slide, practically sending out a gilded invitation to throw her down on the dirty floor. It was hard to remember that he wasn't a randy college kid but a grown man with responsibilities, especially when he was looking at ending a yearlong celibate streak.

"My place is just around the corner," she said, reading his mind. "Interested?"

He wanted to shout *hell yes* but a sliver of reserve had him counter, "Not that I'm not interested but how about you? Didn't your father ever warn you about taking off with strange men from bars? I could be a pervert or a serial killer."

She slid from her barstool and graced him with a dazzling smile that was just a bit menacing as she said, "My daddy taught me to shoot a gun, gut a fish and break a kneecap if need be. Strange men in bars don't scare me." She slung her pack onto her back and headed for the door. She graced him with a single questioning look, then kept walking. The message was clear: *come or stay, it doesn't matter to me.*

He grinned ruefully and tossed a few bucks on the scarred wooden bar. Either he was about to make the biggest mistake of his life or he was going to have a heart attack from the wildest night of sex ever imagined.

He hoped it was the latter.

At least he'd die happy.

And he didn't have to worry about where he was going to spend the night.

Things were looking up already.

Perhaps this gig in Homer was going to work out just fine.

CHAPTER TWO

MIRANDA FELL BACK on the bed, winded and sated, sweat dampening her hairline as her chest rose and fell with the same harsh breaths as her temporary lover. She was thankful he wasn't a chatterbox—she just wanted to enjoy the blissful nothing, the wonderful blankness of her mind that was the aftereffect of a damn good romp in the sack. And oh, yes, it'd been good. Better than good, in fact.

A satisfied sigh rattled from her chest as the sweat drying in the chill air caused goose bumps to pop along her skin. She swung her legs over the edge of the bed and padded silently through the darkened room to the restroom, where she slipped a robe over her nude body and made her way to the kitchen for water.

As she guzzled her glass, she leaned against the old fridge, listening as it clunked and hummed its way through the night as it always did. The wind whistled through the trees outside, whispering of the coming storm, promising a deluge with the season's first snow. Her body hummed and tingled, even protesting with a show of soreness as muscles that hadn't been put to use for a while reminded her that they were still there. But it was a good feeling, even if she had to suffer through the awkward conversation later. Perhaps with some luck he'd already crashed out. A smile curved her lips. The man had stamina, that was for sure. Gotta give credit where credit was due. Unwelcome, her mother's voice in her head crashed her buzz and stomped her good feelings.

When you going to stop whoring around and settle down like a normal girl? Don't you think your son needs a man around? It's bad enough you chose to shack up with a criminal just to prove a point.

Jennelle Sinclair's strident tone had dripped with disapproval and disgust, leaving no room for confusion as to where she stood on her remaining daughter's choices. But that was nothing new. If disapproving of Miranda's choices were an Olympic sport, Jennelle would win the gold.

Miranda closed her eyes and pushed away her mother's recriminations just as she always did when they came back to jeer at her. Tonight would have been difficult no matter how many men she lost herself in or how many drinks she downed.

All because of one damn sweater. Hard to believe given her current penchant for wash-and-wear convenience that there'd ever been a time when she'd cared about something as frivolous as a cashmere sweater.

Miranda couldn't even remember what it looked like any longer, which was a surprise given that it had ruined so many lives.

Simone and her flighty sense of responsibility, her ability to laugh off anything that didn't adhere to her sense of fun and fancy... Miranda's chest trembled with the repression of a sob that felt trapped behind her ribs. "Damn you, Simone," she murmured, adding with a shake of her head, "Damn that sweater."

Would there ever come a time when she didn't obsess on the past? If the fact that she was standing in her darkened kitchen at midnight, rehydrating after a night of alcohol and one-nighter sex was any indication, the answer was distressingly obvious. She blew out a short breath as an ironic chuckle chased her thoughts, and she returned to the bedroom with quiet steps.

"Is that for me?" a deep male voice asked from the darkness. The only source of light, a pale sliver of moonlight shining through the partially parted window drapes, illuminated his profile and glanced off a powerfully built shoulder. She allowed her stare to linger over, savor even, the view and then handed him the water glass with a shrug. He downed it with a good swallow and returned the glass. "Thanks," he said, his voice warm with a smile that she couldn't exactly see but she could imagine. "You really know how to make a man work for his reward. I like that in a woman."

"Yeah, well, right back at you. I value a man with a strong work ethic," she said, placing the glass in the bathroom before shucking her robe and returning to bed. She slid between the covers and made a show of giving him her backside to communicate that she was ready for some shut-eye rather than small talk but it seemed he wasn't quite ready to sleep. A strong arm hooked itself around the front of her stomach and pulled her against him, his nose nuzzling the back of her neck. Her first reaction was irritation and she let him know it as she flipped around to stare up at him as he positioned himself above her. "Listen, fun times are fun times but I have to work in the morning, so unless you want to find yourself sleeping on my old sofa, I suggest you settle down and keep your paws to yourself. Got it?"

He surprised her with a sexy laugh that set off a trip wire of crazy shivers shaking down her spine and she had to fight to remember that she was ready for sleep. "Going by first impressions, I didn't take you for such a lightweight," he teased, moving to caress her neck with the soft touch of his lips traveling across her skin. "A one-and-done kind of woman."

Lightweight? "I am no lightweight," she said, indignant. "I could wear you out in a heartbeat and ruin you for other women."

"Strong words." His tone was faintly disbelieving, but before she could offer an argument, he took away her ability to remember why she was irritated in the first place. His tongue delved deep in her mouth, tangling with hers, sliding in and out in a practiced move that kindled a fire as surely as a spark ignited dry tinder. Within moments she was gasping against his mouth, lost to the wonder of this beautiful, talented stranger as he coaxed pleasure from her body in ways that she never imagined possible. For the first time, she was the one left gasping and babbling, as every muscle tightened in a wonderful chorus of mind-bending sensations. By the time she crashed back to earth, she was wrung out like a washcloth after a sinkful of dishes.

A satisfied sigh sounded from her left and she smiled at the irony that she may have found her sexual match in a man she was destined to never see again by morning. Ah well, that was life, she supposed. She couldn't help the welcome drag on her eyelids as every ounce of her strength fled in the warm wake of her extreme sexual satisfaction. She didn't even protest when he pulled her close, manhandling her in a way that she never allowed, much less enjoyed, but somehow, when done by this man…it was okay. Actually, it was more than okay; it was sublime.

SLEEP DIDN'T FIND Jeremiah as quickly as it did his gently snoring partner but he wasn't complaining. There were worse things than to be cuddled up to a beautiful naked woman on a frigid cold night. But his mind was moving in dizzying circles even as his body was heavy with sated pleasure. The tension that continually corded his shoulders and kinked his neck—no matter how many times his chiropractor back in Wyoming had tried to pull it out—was gone, and for that, he was inordinately happy.

However, no matter how sated his body, his mind refused to give up the images he was doing his best to run away from. Maybe he should've picked a tropical climate instead of a place where it snowed like it did in Wyoming, only ten times heavier.

Tyler had loved the snow; the kid had been fearless on his snowboard. The memory of his eleven-year-old son shredding the slopes elicited a brief smile that faded almost as quickly as it came. Fearless…maybe that had been the problem.

Maybe if he'd cautioned Tyler to be *less* fearless, the boy wouldn't have been crushed beneath his ATV in a rollover that had happened faster than a rattlesnake strike. Maybe. *Maybe*. God, he hated that word.

Shake it off, Jeremiah. Nothing you say or think is going to bring him back. His own counsel always sounded so pathetic in his head whenever he tried to pull himself from that ledge of depression and grief. It'd been a year since Tyler died. Eight months since his wife had left him. Seven months since he'd been served divorce papers. A lot could happen in a year.

The woman in his arms stirred and curled her arm around his stomach, pulling him closer as she buried her nose against the side of his chest. She fit against him as if she were made to.

He touched her hair lightly, enjoying the texture of the dark strands against the pads of his fingers. He didn't know how a woman like her wasn't attached, but for selfish reasons, he was glad. He couldn't imagine a better person to break the seal on his self-imposed celibacy than a hot stranger who wanted nothing more than a dirty, sweaty good time.

He sighed and allowed his eyelids to slowly shut. He was here in Homer for a fresh start with a new job. Tomorrow, he'd put a clean brush of paint on the old and battered walls of his life.

But tonight…he was going to just enjoy the simple pleasure of the feel of a woman's body pressed against his and sleep.

MIRANDA NEVER SLEPT in on a workday and she was never late.

Except today.

She opened her eyes blearily to find the pale watery light of the morning filtering into her bedroom and for a moment she was disoriented by her surroundings. *What the...?*

"What time is it?" she muttered, her mouth tasting like the bottom of a dirty boot. Why had she drunk so many tequila poppers last night? Major mistake. Her head was splitting. With all the sharpness of a dull ax blade, Miranda pulled the memory of last night from her mental cache and glanced around in surprise to realize that her temporary lover had done her a solid by letting himself out before she woke.

And he'd even left her a note. She grabbed the folded paper and focused on the masculine scrawl.

Homer has one hell of a welcome party. Way better than a gift basket.

Miranda dropped the note to her nightstand and fought the growing disquiet churning her insides. On one hand, she ought to be happy that he'd saved them both from any awkward, stilted conversation exchanged in the harsh morning light, but on the other hand, it didn't sit well with her ego that he'd been the one to simply slip out the door while she'd been dead to the world. However, the bigger issue was far more upsetting than a bruise to her ego. Her temporary lover wasn't a tourist.

And by the sounds of it…he was taking up residence right here in Homer.

"I'll be damned," she said, barking a short, irritated laugh, and headed to the shower. The town was too small to hope they wouldn't run into each other at the grocery store at some point, but Miranda wasn't above hoping and praying Homer simply wasn't to his liking and he would leave.

Why? Because there'd been a moment when lying in his arms had felt completely natural—almost as if she'd been waiting to find herself in those arms since the day she was born—and Miranda didn't want any part of *anything* that resembled that.

Besides, she already had her plus one—her son.

And she sure as hell wasn't auditioning anyone for the role of daddy anytime soon…if ever. Much to her mother's chagrin, of course.

With a mild shudder at the very idea, she dropped any lingering thoughts about her overnight guest and, after double-checking with her son's paternal grandmother that the older woman had gotten Talen to school on time this morn-

ing, Miranda rushed to shower away the night's
activities and get ready for work.

Today was a big deal, which made her over-
sleeping a major screwup and only added fuel
to the argument that she hadn't been ready for
the position the new guy had managed to snag
from beneath her nose. She wanted to look the
new boss in the eye and see for herself if he was
up to the job because there was no better tracker
in the department than Miranda, aside from her
brother Trace, of course. And no one knew the
surrounding area better than Miranda.

Miranda pulled into the slushy parking lot, the
crunch of dirt and thin layer of snow beneath her
knobby tires a familiar and welcome sound, but
as she walked up the stairs she couldn't shake the
feeling of disquiet that dogged her steps. Sour
grapes and disappointment, that was all it was,
she told herself.

Talen's paternal grandmother, a Yupik Native,
had always praised Miranda's intuition, saying it
was that inner knowing that helped her to navigate the dangerous Kenai Mountains when tracking the hapless lost. As Miranda pushed open the
door to the Fish and Game Department field office to stride inside, it was then that she knew her
intuition had been spot-on.

Oh, shit. She wanted to die. Or at the very least
sink through the floor and disappear.

Standing there addressing the office, dressed sharp as a tack, looking fresh and starkly handsome, was her one-night stand—and apparently, her new boss.

Hell, she didn't even know his name but she vividly remembered what he looked like naked in the pale moonlight.

Somehow, she didn't think that information was going to be helpful.

Well, her mother had warned her that her bad behavior was going to catch up to her someday.

Guess today was the day. And it felt every bit as wretched as her mother had probably hoped that it would.

Yay me.

CHAPTER THREE

JEREMIAH ADDRESSED HIS new team, looking at faces that he would soon learn to know and personalities he would learn to understand, but part of him couldn't help but wonder if he'd made the right choice as he stood before strangers, especially when he knew for a fact he was running away from a particular heartache.

He had no doubt he could do the job. It wasn't that he was having a sudden attack of inadequacy fears, rather he knew he should have been a bit more adult about his decision to leave everything he knew in Wyoming to start fresh in a town where he knew no one and felt even more isolated than ever.

Wyoming had been good to him until it wasn't, taking the one thing from him that he'd loved the most—his son.

The sound of the door opening and the wind whistling through the open doorway caused him to pause midsentence and turn.

It was then that any misgivings he'd had about taking the job coalesced into a big ball of certainty. It was *her*—of all the people who could've walked through that door in this little fishing town, why did it have to be her? He couldn't believe his dumb luck—some might even say it was painfully ironic but he was in no mood to appreciate the wry humor—but there she was in all her glory, only this time…she was clothed and *in a fish-and-game uniform.*

He swallowed and hoped his shock wasn't plainly evident to his entire team as he stared at the woman he'd buried himself in several times only twelve short hours ago.

And he didn't even know her name. Hadn't that been the stipulation she'd set? And he'd been only too happy to play along. Of all the stupid moves…

Their stares collided, a combination of dismayed surprise and horror, as both processed the reality of the situation. *Yeah, talk about awkward.* It was his first day, and he'd already slept with an employee. It didn't matter that he hadn't known; all that mattered was that now they had history and it was likely to become even more complicated, which was the worst way to kick off a fresh start.

"Everything all right, Miranda?" asked a woman named Mary Calhoun, who had introduced herself the minute he'd crossed the threshold. "We were starting to worry. Is Talen okay?

cook a fish than you can shake a stick at. You'll learn to love it."

"I didn't realize that Homer was such a big halibut outlet. As far as loving fish, I'll just have to take that on faith because I'm probably the only guy in Wyoming who didn't enjoy the sport."

Miranda appeared stymied as he made small talk in the hopes of putting everyone at ease. He was relieved when she was appropriately cordial, even a little on the stiff side. "Welcome to Homer," she said, meeting his gaze for the briefest of moments before quickly moving on.

The statement was appropriate to the situation but he couldn't help but wonder if she was referencing his short little note that had been meant to be witty and tongue-in-cheek, which frankly made him want to clap his hand over his face for leaving a note in the first place.

"Miranda is the best tracker in the state," Mary offered with pride, but Miranda seemed uncomfortable with the compliment and actually murmured something to the contrary to which the woman immediately disagreed. "Now, don't let her tell you that she's not. She's going to tell you that her brother Trace is the best tracker, and don't get me wrong, he is good, better than good. But Miranda has a gift and if I were lost in those mountains I'd want her looking for me."

He lifted his brow at the praise and the way

Miranda seemed discomfited by it and wondered what had happened in this woman's life to make her the way she was. It was a mystery that he didn't want to figure out but it pulled at him just the same. He pushed on. "Your previous director shared his admiration for Miranda's skill. I'm pleased to have someone with such talent on my team." And he left it at that. The previous director had also shared that Miranda was hard-headed, at times difficult, and downright ornery. One thing the previous director hadn't mentioned was how mind-jarringly gorgeous she was. *Stop going there.* Was this going to be a problem? He refocused again. "I promise I'll do my best to lead this team as well as your previous director. I know I have big shoes to fill. Or should I say snowshoes." Gahhh…now he was just disintegrating into bad comedy because his brain had turned to mush. The polite chuckles that followed made him want to assure them that he wouldn't be that guy who was always cracking jokes and trying to be the office card. But Miranda saved him by interjecting.

"Are we finished with the introductions…?" she asked. She was clearly impatient to get on with her day and he didn't blame her. There was plenty of work to be done that had nothing to do with the awkwardness between them.

"Miranda, don't be rude," murmured her friend with a mildly worried tone. "There's nothing wrong with getting to know our new director."

Miranda's face blanched and Jeremiah thought she might actually say something that would reveal their inappropriate encounter, but she recovered well and simply shrugged as if to say *this is me—take it or leave it*. He had to respect the way she was handling things and was happy to take his cue from her.

"No, she's right. We all have plenty of work to do and I'm keeping you from it to blather on about my past when what's really important is the future. I'll trust you to get to your regular schedules and I will work to catch up. So for now I'm going to lock myself in my new office to try and get my bearings. We can reconvene at lunch. Sound like a plan?" There were murmurs of assent as everyone began to disperse, and Miranda wasted no time in disappearing. The fact that his stare wanted to follow wherever she went was troubling but he had bigger issues to deal with and that included establishing himself as the new director of the Homer Department of Fish and Game, above and apart from his personal dilemma. Work had always had the power of distracting him from whatever was happening in his life. This new complication would be no different.

MIRANDA WANTED TO puke. She'd never been so wretchedly embarrassed by an encounter with a one-night stand and that included the unfortunate nuisance of Luke Prather trailing her like a love-sick hound after their one night together. If her mother had been counting on karma to bite her in the ass for all of her past bad behavior it was coming to pass right at this moment. Miranda couldn't disappear into her office fast enough but, of course, locking herself away to wallow in her misery wasn't on the agenda. Mary, the office mate who had been singing her praises so embarrassingly to Jeremiah, was quick to follow.

"Girl, you are running like the devil is on your heels. What's gotten into you?"

Miranda wiped the dot of sweat that beaded her brow as her adrenaline raced through her veins and wished she could get a do-over for the past twenty-four hours. She should've listened to Russ when he'd said to stop drinking. She should have chosen to stay home instead of dropping Talen off at his grandmother's so she could drink herself stupid. She should have read a book, watched a movie, dug a ditch—anything that would have kept her from bedding her boss. But it wasn't as if she could tell Mary that. It wasn't as if she could tell *anyone*. In fact, the one person she could talk to about this was the one person she didn't want to talk to about it. "I'm just not excited about meeting the person who took my job." Well, that was half-true. She'd thought for sure the director position had been hers and it'd been a nasty surprise when she'd learned that she had, in fact, not been selected. "What do you think of him?"

Mary, a middle-aged woman who liked to consider herself hip and cool because she tweeted on her phone every five seconds like the teenagers did even though half the time she did it wrong, considered the question for a minute then nodded decisively. "I like him."

"Why?" The question popped from Miranda's mouth before she could stop it and Mary graced her with a quizzical expression for her sour reaction. Miranda tried to do some damage control. "I mean, how do you know that he's good for the job? I can't imagine anyone would do a better job than me. I know this place like the back of my hand, and that's saying a lot considering how big Alaska is." She was babbling, throwing out excuses for her odd behavior, but Mary didn't seem to notice, which didn't say much for her usual behavior. "I'm just saying, just because he's nice on the eyes doesn't mean he's the right man for the job. You know what I mean?"

Mary frowned. "I think you should give him a chance. I know you're disappointed that you didn't get the job, and you would have been a great director, but the fact of the matter is, unless you want to start job hunting, you'd better start getting on board. You're not going to make any points by cheesing off the new boss."

Miranda fought to keep her expression from revealing the turmoil churning her brain but she felt off-kilter, which was something that rarely happened to her. If only Mary knew how many points she may have made between the sheets last night, not that those points could help her now. Crap. What a mess. Why couldn't the new boss have been a troll? Someone more like their old boss. Virgil Eckhart had been a short, squat, balding man with a barrel chest and a fondness for cheap cigars that he only got the opportunity to smoke when he was ice fishing because his wife hated the smell. There was no way in hell Miranda would've ever wanted to sleep with him. Not even if it had meant a promotion. But then, Virgil had become something of a father figure when her own father simply checked out emotionally. She slowly refocused when she realized Mary was waiting for a response. "Don't worry," she said, trying to put Mary at ease. "I'll make nice with the new boss." *Cringe.* "I have no interest in job hunting anytime soon."

Mary's relief was evident in her wide smile. "Thank God. I was worried that you were going to be a bit of a pill with the new boss. I should have known you'd be mature about it. I'm sorry for not giving you the credit you deserve. Honestly, I don't know what I was worried about now that I think about it. You're not the hotheaded kid you used to be. You're a mother, for crying out loud. Sheesh. Sometimes I embarrass myself. Jim is always telling me to stop being so dramatic."

Miranda laughed, the sound hollow to her ears, yet Mary remained oblivious to her distress, thank heaven. "You worry too much, Mary. Now, don't you have work to do?" she teased. "Go on, get out of here."

Mary left the office and Miranda expelled an audible sigh. "Of all the rotten luck…"

Was karma kicking her in the ass for everything she'd been doing over the past years? It hardly seemed fair when karma had already kicked the shit out of their family.

Laughter rang in her memory, pulling her away from her present pickle and into a time before her sister had died.

"Your snowboarding skills are about as good as your cooking skills," Wade had teased Simone as he slowed to a stop beside her with a laugh. She'd landed on her rear for the third time as she'd tried unsuccessfully to slow down properly and instead simply tumbled to her behind in a spray of snow.

"Stop laughing and help me up," Simone grumbled, then wobbled and lost her balance, falling again. She slapped the snow and pouted. "I hate snowboarding. I want to go back to skis."

Miranda pulled up alongside her baby sister as Wade and Trace followed on their boards. They'd all switched from skis to boards except Simone, and she was having a difficult time making the transition. "Don't give up, Simone. We all fall when we're learning. Are you going to be a quitter just because it's hard?" she asked. "Give it a chance. Besides, if you don't want to be left behind, you need to learn."

"Come on, klutz," Trace said as he and Wade helped Simone to her feet. "You got this. Try again. It'll get easier."

"It won't. I suck at it."

"It's true. You kinda do," Miranda agreed, earning a black look from her twelve-year-old sister as Simone wiped the snow from her snowsuit. "But," Miranda added with a wink, "at least you look good doing it."

At the small compliment, Simone broke out into a reluctant smile, which seemed to bolster her courage and firm her determination. "Okay. I'll try one more time but that's it." She sighed and looked to Trace and Wade. "Show me again how to stop...."

But Simone wasn't a quitter in spite of her complaints, and after plenty of ribbing, lots of laughter and more than a few tumbles, Simone finally caught on. After that the Sinclair family had been unstoppable on the slopes. In fact, in time, snowboarding had become Simone and Miranda's favorite pastime together.

Miranda smiled as she remembered their times at Olson Mountain as teens. Miranda had been eighteen and getting ready to leave for college while Simone had been a know-it-all fifteen-year-old who'd been prettier than any young teen ought to be.

"If you did something more with your hair than just throwing it up in a ponytail, you'd probably get more dates," Simone had advised as they rode the tow rope up the mountain. Miranda cast her young sister a derisive look and Simone laughed. "No, I'm serious. You're so pretty but no one would ever know because you're always acting like a boy. Try a little mascara once in a while, you know?"

"I don't have any problem getting dates."

"Okay, well, how about a boyfriend?"

"I don't need a boyfriend right before I leave for college."

"Good point," she said as if she hadn't thought of it from that angle. "Don't want to be tied down. College is filled with yummy college boys."

"Ugh, kid. You're too boy crazy. Focus on school. Have you thought of what you want to do with the rest of your life?"

"Miranda, live a little, please. Right now I'm focused on my next dance recital and my cheer competition in Anchorage. Anything above and beyond that is way past my interest level."

"You mean that and your unusual interest in my love life," Miranda quipped.

"Well, what are big sisters for if not for introducing their hot college friends to their cute little sisters?"

Miranda laughed. "Glad to know I'm good for something."

Simone smiled brightly and it was hard not to love the kid to distraction. She just had a way about her that was plainly adorable. Simone had been born with magic in her veins.

Miranda closed her eyes, waiting out the echo of grief that followed the memories, until she could safely open her eyes without tears.

How would their lives have been different if Simone had lived?

She supposed it was human nature to wonder, to travel down a road that she knew was a dead end, but when she found herself walking that path most times she became irritated. Simone had died. End of story.

The minute she'd successfully shut down thoughts of her sister, a different sort of unwelcome thought crashed into her mind that was equally irritating but hard to ignore.

If the situation were different, and Miranda had met Jeremiah under completely different circumstances, maybe… *No, don't go there. That's not how we met. That's not our story. Stop trying to rewrite the ending.*

But even as she stamped down any flicker of wistfulness, there was a part of her that refused to let it go. There was a moment last night when wrapped in his arms she'd felt at home, relaxed. Of course, this was completely at odds with how she usually felt after spending an evening with a man. What a fantasy.

She'd come to the realization that whatever essential component was required for a long-lasting monogamous relationship was utterly broken inside of her. If she were being petty, she would blame that on Talen's father, but that was being weak. Fact of the matter was, even though Johnny hadn't known the meaning of the word *monogamous,* she hadn't been blind to that from the beginning. Hadn't expected it, either. So when word came back to her that he'd been messing around, she hadn't been surprised when she felt nothing for the betrayal. Inside Miranda's chest where her heart should have been was a lump of ice that, apart from her love for her son, was deeper and colder than the oldest glacier. And every man who'd had the misfortune of mistakenly trusting her with his heart and feelings had left the relationship soured and disillusioned. Miranda just wasn't the type to settle down and play house.

And a part of her hated that about herself. But if there was one thing she knew, it was that you couldn't run from whom you truly were and so she didn't even try.

One hidden blessing in all this mess was that she wouldn't have to worry about Jeremiah mooning over her, hoping for a relationship out of their torrid encounter. He looked just as ready as she to completely forget last night.

And Miranda was more than willing to play along. As far as she was concerned, they never happened.

CHAPTER FOUR

JEREMIAH SURVEYED HIS new office, taking time to note small details. He didn't much care that it wasn't fancy or the epitome of a corner office—he'd never been one to put much value on those sorts of things—but he did appreciate his own personal coffeepot in the office. He went to the machine and attempted to make a fresh pot of coffee but found himself stymied when he plugged it in and no signs of life happened. He was so busy trying to make the coffeepot work he didn't realize someone had entered his office.

"It doesn't work," Miranda said. "Virgil never drank coffee."

Jeremiah straightened. "So if it doesn't work, and he never drank coffee, why is there a coffeepot in here?"

"Because it was a gift from a relative who didn't know Virgil hated coffee. And because Virgil was such a good guy, he could never bring himself to get rid of it."

"Oh." Were they really going to have this stilted conversation over a coffeepot? He supposed they had to have a normal conversation sometime but the conversation they were having hardly seemed a good start. "Miranda…about last night…"

Miranda waved away his attempt. "I didn't come in here to talk about that. In fact, I'd be really happy if we never talked about that night ever again. I don't need my coworkers to know what a colossal mistake I made on this grand of a scale. I came in to talk to you as an employee."

Jeremiah considered her request. He could understand the urge to ignore the intimate details between them. However, he found it impossible to forget the memories that were seared into his brain and he wasn't so naive as to believe that time would dull their clarity. "As much as your solution to our problem would be the easy way out, I'm not that kind of man. We need to talk about what happened between us. We both acknowledge that we made a mistake. And we need to be adult about it and move on. And I agree— the information should not leave this room."

"Permission to speak freely?"

"Of course."

"Listen, you're new here and so you don't know everyone's back stories, their personal little tragedies or idiosyncrasies, so I'm going to do you a solid and let you in on mine. I'm not a girl who snuggles. I'm not looking for a man to save or protect me. I take my fun where I can find it and I don't apologize for it. You came along at the right time and fulfilled a need. I'm sorry if that sounds crass or unladylike or vulgar, but the bottom line is I had an itch and you were there to scratch it. I do my job well and, contrary to what the admins thought, I would've been a hell of a director. So, what I came in here to say is what I would've said regardless. This is my town and I care about the people who live here. I will hold you to a higher standard and just because you're the boss doesn't mean that I won't tell you exactly how I feel about any given topic regarding my people."

Jeremiah absorbed her statement. On one hand, he could appreciate her stark honesty. On the other hand, he could tell why she hadn't been selected as the director. The administrator didn't have the luxury of saying whatever he or she felt or believed at any given moment. Tact, patience, knowing when to keep your mouth shut were valuable assets that Miranda apparently didn't value. "I've read your file. I know you're a damn fine tracker. I know you come from this town. Though what I don't know is why you have a reckless streak and a dangerous problem with authority."

Miranda's mouth tightened, clearly irritated by the information that'd been shared with him. "Who said I was reckless?"

Jeremiah shook his head, not interested in playing a "he said, she said" game. "Not important. What is important is the intel. The fact that you grabbed a stranger off the street to have sex, without knowing a thing about me, proves the information valid."

"Are you judging me?" Miranda's eyes flashed, revealing a hot temper. "What kind of man goes home with the first woman he lays eyes on in a strange town?"

"A man ending a long self-imposed celibacy with a beautiful woman who openly propositioned him." He shifted, mildly irritated at being drawn into a fight. His point was rapidly becoming lost. "Miranda, if you don't want to tell me your reasons, then don't. But I would advise you not to pick a fight with your superior on the first day."

His advice seemed to hit home. Miranda looked away, and he could tell she was mentally biting her tongue. Perhaps something she wasn't used to doing. "Duly noted." She drew a deep breath and retrained her focus. "In addition to being the best tracker in the area, aside from my brother Trace, I'm in charge of keeping on top of the poachers in the area. If you'd like I can send you a couple of the files I've been working on."

"That would be appreciated." His mind should've been on business, but there was something about her that made it difficult to stay focused. He wanted to know what compelled her to pick up strange men. He wanted to know how many men there had been before him. All manner of questions that he had no business thinking or wondering. "Poachers are everywhere. Same scum, different day. You say you've been keeping track of a few? Anyone else on this?"

"No, it's sort of my baby. My passion, if you will."

"Send me some of your files and I'll give them a read. I can't promise I'll get to them today but I will definitely try to look over the data by the end of the week."

She accepted his answer. "Good. I look forward to your thoughts. Welcome to the team."

Miranda didn't waste any time with chitchat or idle conversation. She blew out as quickly as she blew in. Jeremiah wondered just how complicated his relationship was going to be with the woman. He'd give anything to forget that last night had ever happened. But he'd long given up wishing that he could change the past. His intimate connection with Miranda Sinclair was just one more thing he would learn to deal with.

MIRANDA SAT HEAVILY in her chair and realized her hands were shaking. Damn, why couldn't she just push him from her mind like every other man? She talked a good game, but everything was too fresh, the memories too vivid to simply move on as if it'd simply been another encounter. As if the sex had been mediocre. That probably would have made things a lot easier. A crappy one-and-done certainly didn't compel a girl to chase after another round.

But that wasn't the case. He'd certainly known his way around a woman's body. He had skill. Which, of course, begged the question, why was he single? Not that she cared. But she was naturally curious. She sensed a bigger back story behind those soulful eyes. *Don't dig.* She shouldn't care what his story was.

She placed her fingers behind her head and leaned back in her chair. Maybe she needed some target practice. The familiar weight of a gun in her hand always seemed to soothe the ragged nerves. She liked to imagine she was putting that laser sight right between the eyes of the bastard who'd killed her sister. Of course, she didn't know who that person was because Simone's killer had never been found. So in her imagination there was always a blank face staring back at her.

The phone rang, interrupting her dark thoughts, and she picked up the receiver almost gratefully. That was until she heard her mother's voice on the other end.

"What is wrong with you?"

"That's a loaded question, don't you think?"

Miranda answered with just enough sarcasm to really piss her mom off. "What's the problem?"

"Don't play innocent with me. I know it was you who called that lady. Now I've got these strangers in my business."

Miranda withheld the sigh. The organizer must have paid her mother a visit. "Mom, you need help. I thought Paula could help you get things started." She took a deep breath, fighting the urge to slam the receiver down in her mother's ears. "No reason to get all pissy about it."

"Watch your mouth. And I don't appreciate you sending nosy people into my house to tell me how I should live. And your father isn't happy about it, either," her mother added for emphasis. "You're scaring away business."

Miranda felt a flare of familiar anger bubble up in her chest. "What business? Are you talking about the nonexistent business he makes from his carvings? Or his thriving pot business?"

"You know damn well your father only uses marijuana for medicinal purposes. Stop making him sound like a criminal."

"Mom, you know he sells his pot for money. That is illegal. And I'm not having this conversation with you. Particularly while I'm at work. In case you've forgotten I work for a federal agency."

"I never asked for your help. I don't need an

organizer. And I wish you'd stop foisting your ideas onto me."

"Fine, Mom. I was just trying to help."

Her mother, slightly mollified by the muttered apology, moved on to a different subject that was equally controversial in their family. "I don't like Talen spending so much time with that woman."

And by *that* woman, her mother was referencing Talen's paternal grandmother, Ocalena. "You should take your own advice and stop poking your nose into business that isn't yours. Talen loves his grandmother and she's a good woman. You need to stop ripping on her."

Her mother sniffed, "Well, we all have our opinions now, don't we? Forgive me if I am uncomfortable with my only grandson spending so much time with a loony Indian. It can't be healthy that she fills his head with all sorts of stories about that father of his."

Ah, the familiar argument about Talen's father. One of her mother's favorite topics. "There's no need to pound it into my head how much you hated Johnny. I am well aware of your feelings. However, Johnny was Talen's father for better or worse. Now drop it."

"When it's a subject you don't want to talk about, you're happy to shut me down. When it's a subject I don't want to talk about, you needle me into the ground. Miranda, you've become a raging hypocrite as you become older."

And you've become an even bigger pain in my ass than you ever were. "Was there something you needed to talk to me about?"

"Yes, actually there was. Aside from that horrid little woman intruding on our personal space, I needed to tell you that I heard gunshots on the back forty. I want you to check it out."

Poaching of Alaska's resources was a major problem for the state, and the fact that her parents lived on a very large parcel of land that backed up to the Kenai Mountains made their property a popular trespassing point. "I'll take a look. Did you call Trace?"

"Of course. He's unavailable."

Miranda tried not to take offense. The fact that she was her parent's second choice never felt warm and fuzzy. But she supposed that was something she ought to be used to by now.

"Have you met your new boss yet?" her mother asked, quickly changing the subject.

"Yes." Miranda didn't add details. "Why?"

"Because I know how you'd set your heart on getting that job. However, don't do anything that will put you out of a job. Good jobs don't just fall out of the sky."

Was her mother giving her advice? Surely, that was the sign of the apocalypse. "And what, pray tell, could I possibly do that would put me out of a job?" *Aside from sleep with the new boss?*

"You're like an old bear with something caught in its paw. You know how you get when things don't go your way. I just don't want you to do something stupid."

Something stupid? Such as pick a fight with her baby sister over a sweater that ended up getting her killed and destroying the family? Miranda would try to refrain from making such an epic mistake again. "Your concern is touching, Mom. But I think I've got it handled. You know, would it kill you to acknowledge that I'm not the same reckless kid I used to be?"

"Miranda, I would go to my grave with a smile on my face if I thought you could change. I pray for my grandson that he won't be scarred by your parenting skills."

"Excuse me? What are you talking about?"

"I know why you let that Indian woman take care of my grandson…because you were out trashing the Sinclair name with your loose ways. Don't think that you're not the topic of every whispered conversation, because you are. I can only hope that you've run out of men to sleep with by now."

"Just because I like to have a good time doesn't make me irresponsible in every other way," she said, hurt by her mother's censure, though why she cared, Miranda didn't know. "If you can't tell how I've changed, then you never paid much attention in the first place."

"See it how you will. Doesn't change the facts. Good girls don't take home the first man they lay eyes on and that's a fact. What kind of example are you setting for Talen? No father, no man around to teach him how to do all the things a boy should know…"

"Such as?" she demanded to know. "I can hunt, shoot, trap, track… What exactly is a man going to teach my boy that I can't?"

"I'm not going to argue the point. I've said my piece and I'll leave it at that."

"Well, thanks for sharing," Miranda said. *God, help me now and end this conversation.* "I have to go. Was there anything else that you needed?" *Like the knife stuck in my back?*

Miranda could sense her mother's irritation at her abrupt end of the conversation. Jennelle Sinclair loved having the last word. "I see there's no sense in talking to you when you're going to act like that. Don't forget to look into those poachers above the property line."

The line went dead and Miranda shook her head. Unbelievable woman. Weren't people supposed to mellow out with age? Apparently, her mother hadn't received that memo. She'd like to say they were close at one time, but that would not be true. Jennelle had reserved all of her happiness, her pride and her ambition for her youngest daughter, Simone.

Miranda had simply been the one in Jennelle's way. At least that was the way it'd always felt. If it hadn't been for her dad, teaching her how to track along with her brothers, her childhood would have been depressingly bleak.

At Miranda's lowest point following Simone's death, she'd often believed her mother would have been happy if Miranda had been the one found dead on that mountain rather than her beloved Simone.

And frankly, there were times that fear remained.

CHAPTER FIVE

HE HAD PLANNED to wait a few days but Jeremiah ended up spending some time looking over the poaching reports that Miranda had prepared. The reports were thorough and showed a commendable attention to detail. Even if Miranda hadn't told him that catching poachers was a passion of hers, he would've been able to tell by the nature of her reports. A wry smile lifted his lips. Miranda was a passionate woman, apparently in all things. He wished their relationship hadn't been contaminated by their one-night stand. He suspected they could have become strong allies, maybe even friends. Now their relationship would forever be tainted by what they'd shared intimately.

And about that…what he wouldn't give to get the memories out of his head. It wasn't that the memories weren't enjoyable; no, quite the opposite. The memory of last night made him yearn for more. And that was absolutely not happening. Maybe, with a fresh start, it was time to start dating again. After his son had died and his wife divorced him, the usual appetites for companionship simply died. Ending his celibacy with someone like Miranda had certainly left its mark. *Literally*. Jeremiah shifted as the pull of Miranda's scratch marks on his back caused him to wince.

He rubbed the grit from his eyes and finally shut down his computer. Everyone had long since gone home but he'd stayed behind to further acclimate himself to the new surroundings. He didn't want to seem like that guy who simply punched the clock and didn't care about the job. Back in Wyoming, he'd been accused of being a workaholic. He couldn't deny that charge. That'd been one of the many hatchets his ex-wife had flung at him, screaming that he hadn't been around for their son so he shouldn't grieve for him. That'd been a low blow. Maybe that was why he'd been so ready for a fresh start. He couldn't stomach the memories—both good and bad—that he was leaving behind.

He closed his eyes as one particular memory eclipsed his ability to hold it back.

"How dare you cry for him! It's your fault he's dead." His ex-wife, Josie, stared at him with red-rimmed eyes brimming with hatred. "I told you he was too young for an ATV. But you went out and got him one anyway."

"That's a new low, even for you, Josie. For you to insinuate that it was my fault…you're lucky you're a woman. If a man had dared to say that to me I'd knock his teeth down his throat."

But Josie was wild in her grief and in her belief that Jeremiah had caused the death of their son. "There's nothing that you could do to me that would rival the pain I'm suffering right now. Go ahead and do your worst. He was only eleven, Jeremiah! What kind of idiot allows an eleven-year-old to drive an ATV? It's not even legal!"

"I made a mistake," he admitted, feeling sick in his gut. But Tyler had pleaded with him, using the excuse that nearly all his friends had been riding around on ATVs since they were nine. It had seemed a small thing to allow since he'd only be using the ATV on their property and most of their land was fairly gentle terrainwise. But he should've stuck to his guns and turned the boy down. "I'd do anything to take it back. You know that, right?"

But Josie simply stared, as if it were possible that he'd deliberately made a choice that he knew was going to hurt their son. That was worse than ludicrous; it was downright repugnant.

"What does it matter? He's dead," she retorted dully, refusing to look at him, as if the very sight of him made her want to retch. Well-meaning folks had warned them that the death of a child could rip apart a marriage and they'd need to support one another to get through the crisis.

Jeremiah was fairly certain Josie wouldn't throw a glass of water on him if he were on fire. So much for supporting one another through the storm.

Jeremiah stared at the woman he had thought was the love of his life, the mother of his children, and wondered why he'd never noticed the cruel streak that ran through her like a river. "I think we need a break," Jeremiah said, attempting to slow the runaway train of their marriage. "I can get a hotel room for a few days."

Josie sniffed and wiped the remnants of her tears from her cheeks. "Don't bother," she said, her voice hardening. "I'm leaving you."

On some level Jeremiah must have known things might've been heading that way but when Josie actually voiced the words he couldn't help feeling sucker punched. "That's what you really want?"

Josie didn't hesitate. "Yes."

"Don't you think we should work on it?" Jeremiah wasn't a quitter even if he could see the writing on the wall. "Do you want to see a counselor?" He was really grasping at straws. Although he didn't know why. Their marriage was over.

"I never want to see your face again."

His jaw tensed. There was nothing left to say. "Then get the hell out."

"Gladly." Josie shouldered her purse. "I hate

you. I hope you never sleep again. I don't care how you justify your actions—the fact remains if you hadn't bought that ATV our son would still be alive."

Jeremiah's eyes burned with the pain of his grieving heart and in that moment he desperately wanted to take out his pain on the woman standing before him. By the grace of God, somehow he managed to turn away, but he'd been a heartbeat away from killing her.

The echo of a slamming door reverberated in Jeremiah's memory. Damn, he had to stop traveling down memory lane. That neighborhood had been demolished. He sighed and shook off the morose bent of his thoughts. Sometimes he was just plain tired of feeling bad. Last night with Miranda had shown him that it was possible to feel good again. It sucked about the circumstances… he had a feeling that he and Miranda could've made some beautiful sparks together.

MIRANDA RAPPED THREE times on the solid door of Ocalena's house but didn't wait for an answer and simply let herself in. She knew she was always welcome in this house. Johnny's mother loved her like a daughter, possibly even more than she'd loved her son when he'd been alive. But then, Johnny had been a two-bit criminal who took advantage of every single person who crossed his path, including his own mother. So it wasn't a stretch for Miranda to stand out and gain points with the old Yupik woman.

Miranda's eight-year-old son, the light of her life and the reason she got up in the morning, ran into her arms. "Mama!" Miranda forgot about everything else that was going wrong in her life and simply embraced her son and inhaled the scent of her wild boy.

"Were you good for your *mamu?*"

"Yep," Talen said, breaking the embrace to show Miranda what he'd made. He held up a rudimentary carving and beamed at his handiwork. "*Mamu* said I'm a natural. Do you think so, Mama?"

"Absolutely. Carving is in your blood, sweet cheeks. Remember, your poppy is a carver on my side, and it's on your dad's side, too. It's in your heritage."

Talen giggled and bounded off to continue his next project while *Mamu* and Miranda caught up. Miranda didn't know why the old Yupik woman made her feel more at home than her own mother, but when Miranda walked through that familiar door, all the tension simply dropped from her shoulders—which given the anniversary of her sister's death was a grace she desperately needed.

"Thanks for keeping him," Miranda said, suddenly feeling very fatigued. She didn't need to explain herself to Ocalena, but the words started to flow anyway. "I know I should find a better way to deal with Simone's death, but my good intentions never seem to go very far when it comes down to the actual date on the calendar. It still hurts to think of her. When will that pain ever go away?"

Mamu took a break from the fish stew simmering on the old gas stove and joined Miranda on the ratty, lumpy sofa. She gazed at Miranda with knowing in her dark brown eyes. "You ask the wrong questions. It isn't when will the pain go away…it is when will you accept that it wasn't your fault."

"I know," she said but *Mamu* shook her head. There was no bullshitting the woman. Miranda didn't even know why she tried. "Logically I tell myself it wasn't my fault. Bad things happen, but I can't help but wonder how things might've been different if I hadn't been such a jerk about a stupid sweater that I can't even remember any longer. Simone is gone because of that one decision."

"No. Simone is gone because a bad man took her. When you finally take that to heart, you will no longer suffer as you do."

Yeah, probably but not likely. More's the pity. It might be nice to live without a constant reminder of her guilt. "I have a new boss," she said abruptly. Maybe she thought she needed to confess her sins because the words were tripping from her mouth as if shoved. "He seems decent enough." *Mamu*'s eyes were wise and she smiled, waiting for Miranda to come clean. "I, sort of, met him informally before the rest of the team."

Mamu chuckled, reading between the lines, but all she said was, "A warm body on a cold night is a good thing."

"Not when that warm body turns out to be your boss," she muttered, and *Mamu* sighed, her eyes twinkling. "You're incorrigible. I could get fired for something like this."

"Bah. It's no one's business. More people should spend less time with their nose in other people's business and more time tending to their own. Is he nice?"

"Nice? In what way?" Miranda asked cautiously. "I mean, he's very professional, very buttoned-down, which is obviously what the administration was looking for since they picked him over me, but I can't say much more because I don't know him."

"Nothing more telling than seeing how a person acts in their birthday suit," *Mamu* said, disagreeing. Miranda's cheeks heated but *Mamu* shrugged. "You're a grown woman and a mother besides. What does your heart tell you about the man?"

Miranda startled. "My heart?" she nearly squeaked. "My heart doesn't say anything. My heart wasn't involved. My heart only has room for one little man and that's my son."

"A son like Talen is a blessing, but someday Talen will go find his own path and will leave his mother behind. What then? This path you're walking will lead to many cold nights and an empty bed."

"Well, that's a long time from now," Miranda said, uncomfortable with *Mamu*'s wisdom. She didn't like the idea of being alone for the rest of her life, but she wasn't interested in finding out what she could do to change that possible future, either. "Even if I was mildly open to the idea of finding someone to share a future with, it certainly wouldn't be with my new boss. That's just an invitation for bad luck." Miranda stifled a yawn, ready to put an end to the day and the current conversation. "I feel run over. Get your stuff, buddy. Mama needs to hit the bed soon."

Mamu shuffled off to ladle some fish stew for Miranda to take home, and then after hugging her tightly she sent her on her way.

Later that night after she'd wolfed down the stew, bathed Talen and read him a story and then put him to bed, she fell into her bed and expected sleep to claim her within minutes. But that didn't happen. Instead, she caught a whiff of Jeremiah's cologne still clinging to her sheets and immediately fell into a sensual memory of everything they'd done in that very bed less than twenty-four hours ago. God help her, she rolled onto her stomach and buried her nose in one of the pillows to inhale deeply. Why'd he have to smell so good?

She pulled the pillow to her and hugged it tight. It was a full minute before she realized how ridiculous she was being and actually tossed the pillow to the floor. She wasn't the kind of woman who did that sort of thing and the fact that she'd just done that made her a little ill. That was it, she grumbled to herself as she kicked the covers free and began ripping the sheets from the bed and tossing them into the laundry hamper. *I'm not going to spend all night assaulted by Jeremiah's lingering scent in my bed.* She made quick, angry work of changing her sheets, and then once she was satisfied nothing remained of Jeremiah, she climbed back into the bed and fell into an exhausted sleep.

Too bad her dreams were hot, steamy—and filled with Jeremiah.

So much for stripping the sheets for peace of mind.

CHAPTER SIX

EARLY NEXT MORNING Jeremiah found Miranda in her office already working. He recognized her drive as a trait he had himself and couldn't help but admire her tenacious spirit, even if he knew that same drive might cause friction between them at some point.

"I read your poaching reports," he stated reluctantly. She looked up and waited for him to continue. "Very thorough," he admitted.

"Thank you. They have to be thorough to catch the bastards. What did you think?"

Jeremiah took a seat opposite her. "Tell me more about the bear carcasses."

"The first carcass showed up two years ago. The hands, feet and gallbladder had been removed and there'd been some kind of grease smeared on the trees, which had served as bait, luring the bear to his death. That summer we found seven bears killed in the same way but we were never able to track the poachers."

"Black-market trade for bear parts is very lucrative. We faced similar issues in Wyoming. As long as there's a market for illegal animal parts, there will always be poachers." Poachers were difficult to find and even harder to prosecute as they were lower-tier criminals in the justice system. Fining a convicted poacher wasn't a stiff enough sentence, in Jeremiah's opinion. He hoped there was a special area of hell reserved just for poachers, rapists and child molesters, but not everyone agreed that poachers represented the same level of threat, which resulted in budget cuts that reduced the number of rangers who kept the poachers in line. "They must know something about erasing the tracks if you couldn't find them." His statement wasn't a dig and he was glad she didn't take it that way, either. "What else do we know about them? Their habits? The territory they target?"

Her eyes lit up with something that looked like respect for his interest and she readily gave up all the information she had. "I think they have a tracker with them. They definitely know how to clear their tracks, how to avoid capture. Only someone who knows this area and knows what they're doing could evade us for this long. I think if we had more resources we could finally catch these bastards."

"Resources in this economy are hard to come

by. As you know, the state is running lean, as most states are these days."

"Someone has to take a stand and send a message."

"I'd love to be that man, but the budget doesn't have much wiggle room. I appreciate and understand your passion but we have to prioritize our resources."

She frowned. "Why'd you even read my reports if you had no intention of helping me with the cases?"

"If it were in my power I'd give you the resources you need but the budget represents a pie that everyone wants a slice of. You're a smart woman—you know how it works."

"I'd hoped that things would be different with some new blood but I can tell you're just as disinterested in rocking the boat as Virgil was."

"Miranda, I'm not saying you can't work to catch these poachers. You've gathered some thorough notes and information. I'm sure what you're doing will help the cause."

"Please don't patronize me. It's not necessary."

"I'm not patronizing you in any way—I'm being honest with you."

Miranda's gaze cut away from his, plainly disappointed in his answers. He didn't want to give her false hope that he'd suddenly find a pot of gold at the end of the rainbow when budget time rolled around. "If it means anything, I support what you're doing. But since I'm the new guy, I can't really go and start adding more personnel, new equipment and additional costs to an already-tight budget. I wanted to read the reports because I'm interested and I wanted to show you that I care about what my team members are working on."

Miranda jerked a short nod but asked, "Have you ever come across the mutilated corpse of an animal knowing full well that animal was butchered illegally for the purpose of greed?"

"Yes, when I was a ranger. It sucks and I understand your anger, but you have to be smart about this."

"Being smart never seems to get the results I need. Maybe it's time to be reckless."

He shot her a warning glance. "You're angry," he stated. "Once you simmer down you'll regret anything you do in a fit of frustration."

A hot and ready disagreement brimmed in her eyes but she held it back. She may well have been choking on the words she wanted to say, but she managed to give him a curt nod, then said, "You're the boss," and effectively ended the conversation by returning to her office.

Jeremiah hated the friction between them so early in their working relationship. Even though he couldn't hire anyone else to help with the poaching problem, maybe he could spare a little of his own time to give the situation a fresh look. He considered the mountain of administrative paperwork he had to shuffle through and resigned himself to more late nights staring blearily at reams of paper. He rejoined Miranda in her office. She looked up warily. "Did you forget something?"

"I agree a fresh pair of eyes could help the case. Why don't you take me out to the site where the bears were found."

Her brow rose. "You want to survey the site? Why?"

"I don't know the area and it would be helpful to get an actual view of the landscape instead of only seeing pictures. Gives me a better mental picture."

"So me and you...tromping around in the wild together?"

"Is there a problem?"

"Not with me. I'm fine. I'm surprised you'd want to do that, is all."

"I didn't always start off behind a desk," he said, deliberately ignoring the other point she was hinting at. He could handle alone time with her without suffering anything inappropriate. "I'd like to get started on this right away. I have this afternoon free. How about you?"

"I suppose I can move some things around."

"Great. Since you know the area, how about you drive?"

"I'm surprised you trust a woman driver," she said.

"Are you a bad driver?" he asked bluntly.

"Of course not."

"And why would I have a problem with you driving? My masculinity is not in question here." At that a faint blush rose to the tips of her cheeks, and he knew what she was thinking of because he was thinking of the same thing. He allowed a faint smile. "I'll see you after lunch."

THE MINUTE JEREMIAH left her office Miranda let out a long breath she hadn't realized she'd been holding. She rubbed at her chest where it ached from the tension and mulled Jeremiah's offer. She'd hoped to convince him to let her hire a part-timer to help her sift through evidence, files and do more survey hikes around the area last affected, but she certainly hadn't expected the man to offer up his own time. Virgil had always been so tightfisted around budget time that it'd been nearly impossible to shake loose enough cash to purchase more than a few extra paper clips for the office. Maybe getting Jeremiah out into the field would be to her advantage. Perhaps some hands-on fieldwork would prompt Jeremiah to look for more creative ways to massage the budget to her favor. Maybe…

Except, she didn't want to work with Jeremiah; she didn't want to be around Jeremiah; she didn't want to do *anything* that would put her in close proximity with Jeremiah.

And that *certainly* included tromping around in the forest with the man.

But, as she'd quipped with a fair amount of snark, he was the boss, so what choice did she have? She'd always loved animals, even as a kid. Maybe it was because her mom was too busy ignoring her, but animals always provided entertainment, and love, so when she found creatures being abused, whether they were wild or tame, it drove her batty. And it also sliced at a raw nerve that she hadn't been able to catch those damn poachers yet. It was as if they were thumbing their noses at her and laughing behind her back that she hadn't been able to nail them to the wall. Preventing and catching poachers was not only her passion, but it was part of her job description, and it made no sense to her that more resources weren't being thrown at this problem.

She'd been planning to stop by her parents' house today but that would have to wait. She wasn't about to drag Jeremiah with her over there and have him see all the dysfunction running wild through her family tree. She'd already broken enough rules when it came to her relationship with her boss. She certainly didn't need to add trying to explain why her mother had a borderline hoarding compulsion and her father was growing marijuana in a greenhouse operation. Miranda pinched the bridge of her nose. No, she definitely didn't want him to know that.

If only her brothers would take more of an interest in helping her deal with their parents. Trace, her second-oldest brother, was an antisocial hermit who avoided people at all costs, including his own family, and Wade, her oldest brother, was too busy in California pretending he didn't have any family at all. So that left Miranda to pick up the pieces, hold it all together and deal with the overall craziness that was thrown her way on an everyday basis.

Even as she allowed herself a minor pity party, her gaze strayed to the small portrait photo of her son on her desk. Talen's wide and unabashed smile as he held up his first fish warmed her heart. If it weren't for Talen she'd have given up a long time ago. He was the reason her life had taken a turn for the better even if her pregnancy had been a shock.

She remembered the day vividly.

She'd been sick all day and Johnny hadn't been the least bit sympathetic.

"Catch a bug or something?" Johnny lit a cigarette. The corners of his mouth tilted up at her misfortune as he blew a smoke ring her way. "Maybe you need to smoke some weed."

She sent him a withering stare. "Last I checked you aren't a doctor, so shut up."

"Don't have to be a bitch about it. Just trying to help." Johnny took a long drag off his cigarette. "You buy any food when you went to the store?"

The thought of food made her stomach rebel. "No, and don't talk about food," she snapped, just as she ran for the toilet yet again to lose the remaining contents of her stomach.

At first she'd thought it was the flu. But then she realized she rarely got that sick. And one thought led to another until she was staring at the realization that her troubles were not caused by a virus. She took a test the next morning. It'd been positive.

"So you're saying I'm going to be a daddy?" Johnny had asked when she told him the news. But the moment she told him she'd wished she could have taken the words back. She didn't want Johnny to have any part in raising her child. Johnny wasn't the kind of man who should've been around children, animals or even plant life.

It was at that moment that she realized she couldn't keep living the way she was living. Not if she was bringing a child into the world. A child deserved more. Certainly more than Johnny could ever offer. She'd considered lying to him and saying she was going to get an abortion. But lying was a temporary fix for a permanent problem. The minute Johnny knew she was still pregnant he'd want to have contact with his kid. The dilemma kept Miranda awake at night. Until one day, her problem resolved itself. Johnny got busted for drugs—and it was his third strike. Miranda knew she shouldn't revel in someone else's misfortune, but the day they took Johnny into custody, she'd experienced a sense of relief. And when she'd received the call that he had died in prison, it was the most that she could do to work up a single tear. The fact was Johnny was a bad person who'd probably done the world a favor by taking a dirt nap.

The only residual regret that Miranda experienced was when she had to explain to her son why his father wasn't around. She wished she could tell him a story about how his father had died some noble death. The kind of death a soldier, a cop or a fireman might have, saving others, perhaps. There just wasn't a way to pretty up the fact that Talen's father had been a selfish, rude and wholly self-centered man who'd done and said bad things nearly every day of his miserable life.

God, she'd been so stupid to hook up with Johnny. At the time she'd been on a self-destructive streak and Johnny had seemed just the right amount of dangerous to satisfy her need for chaos. She met him shortly after Simone had died. She'd been heartsick, guilt ridden and overwhelmed with regret. Johnny must've homed in on those markers because he moved in on her like a bird of prey after a mouse.

The first couple of months had been great. Their sex life had been the stuff of X-rated movies—exciting and dirty—and for a while she really thought she loved him. And even if she wasn't sure about her true feelings for Johnny, she knew for certain that she loved his mother. Likely, it'd been her relationship with *Mamu* that had kept her around longer than she should have stayed, but there was no point in guessing at this point. By the time Miranda had started to pull herself out of the skid and realized that Johnny wasn't a healthy choice for a partner, it'd been a challenge to break ties.

Her pregnancy had allowed for a certain sense of clarity that'd been missing before and enabled her to think clearly for the first time since Simone had died.

Johnny had been proof that anyone could father a child but not every man was cut out to be a dad. And although Talen looked so much like Johnny, Miranda was ensuring that they were nothing alike.

It was hard to look at Talen's face and see anything but the sweetest, most amiable boy ever created. And she couldn't imagine life without him.

Thank God, Johnny had never had a single day of influence on the boy. For that, she was immensely grateful.

Talen was the reason she never brought men home with her when he was home, why she never introduced Talen to any of her boyfriends— though the term *boyfriend* was a stretch, because she rarely allowed them to hang around long enough to require stashing a toothbrush at the house. She didn't want anyone getting the wrong idea. She wasn't looking for a daddy figure for her son, which was a change from the usual single-mama drama that happened in town. Nope. Not looking for daddy material. Just a friend with benefits.

Her thoughts strayed to Jeremiah, and for a moment she allowed her mind to drift over the details from the night before. Jeremiah's *friendship* would've been a wonderful benefit. Just remembering their time together made her shiver with awareness.

Okay, enough of that nonsense.

She shook her head, trying to dislodge the imagery, and scooped up her papers as she stabbed the power button to shut down her computer. Miranda didn't know how she'd manage to forget all she and Jeremiah had done, but she'd have to figure out a way because at the moment it seemed downright impossible to work side by side with the man and not want to stick her tongue down his throat.

And that just made her grouchy.

CHAPTER SEVEN

JEREMIAH CLIMBED INTO Miranda's Range Rover and immediately noted how tidy the interior was. "Not a fan of clutter, I see."

It was true she didn't care for clutter, possibly because her mother was such a pack rat, but the fact that he noticed just how meticulous she was with her vehicle made her shift uncomfortably. It was as if he'd somehow caught a glimpse into her inner psyche and that left her feeling vulnerable and exposed. "And in your experience are most women comfortable with a mess?" Generally, she hated when someone answered a question with another question but she couldn't help herself when it came to Jeremiah. Just being around him put her on the defensive. "It's not so much that I hate clutter—it's that I hate disorganization. I like being able to find whatever I need, when I need it." Why was she explaining herself? She should've just left her answer and moved on. "How about we only talk about work rather than personal details?"

"I make you uncomfortable."

"Of course you do." Why should she lie? "But given our relationship, aren't you uncomfortable, as well?"

"I thought we agreed to act as adults?"

Of course he would point out that she was being the difficult one. She glared for lack of a good defense. He held her stare. Finally, she shrugged and admitted, "We did."

He released a sigh as if disappointed. "What if we hadn't met the way we did? Would that have changed our relationship?"

She shot him a warning glance. "I don't deal in hypotheticals. We can't change the fact that we know each other intimately. I would love to step back in time and redo that decision but we can't. What happened, happened. We just have to deal with it. But the more you bring it up, the more it's in our faces. We need to be able to work together as peers and we won't be able to do that if you keep talking about what we did."

She didn't know if she was angry with him because he kept bringing it up or if she was just angry at the circumstances, but she couldn't prevent the snap in her tone. The fact was, as much as she tried to bury it, the memory of their night together continued to badger her at the worst moments. She wanted to lean in to catch a whiff of his cologne; her gaze was drawn to every muscular line in his body. The fact that she couldn't push him from her mind as readily as any other man from her past irritated her.

"Can we please just get to work?" Focusing on a detail within her scope of expertise was the most efficient way of stopping the inappropriate thoughts and conversation. However, she stopped to ask him a question that had been bugging her. "Whatever brought you to Alaska, anyway? According to your bio you had a pretty good job where you were. Why would you want to start over in a foreign place with people you don't know?"

Jeremiah's expression shuttered and she knew right away there was something painful he was protecting. She knew that look. She knew it deep in her bones. She knew it the same way she knew the discomfort of an old, worn shoe that in spite of the damage it was doing to your foot, you couldn't bring yourself to throw away. Whatever he was protecting, whatever pain he was trying to suppress, it was something that rode him without mercy just as Simone's death rode her every single day of her life. The fact that she could sense the pain inside of Jeremiah caused her to mentally stumble. "I'm sorry. It's none of my business." She didn't want to know his pain. She didn't want to know what caused that look in his eyes. She didn't need reasons to identify with Jeremiah Burke.

Jeremiah accepted her exit from the conversation and simply jerked a nod. "Tell me about the suspects in this case."

JEREMIAH COULDN'T BELIEVE how swiftly one single, innocent question from Miranda managed to tilt him on his ear. He'd known people would ask why he would leave a good job in Wyoming to come to the wilds of Alaska. And he'd had a ready answer. But when she'd asked that single question he couldn't give her the practiced speech he'd prepared. It'd been on the tip of his tongue to admit that his son, Tyler, had been killed and he couldn't fathom staying another minute in the place where there were so many memories. For a heartbeat, he almost envisioned sharing his personal pain with a total stranger.

Okay, she wasn't a total stranger but he really didn't *know* her. He didn't know who she was. And what he did know about her, he wasn't sure he agreed with. He was grateful she had given him an out. But in that moment he'd seen something in her eyes, something that identified with him in a way that shocked him to his toes. There was something in Miranda's past, something she was just as sensitive about as he was about Tyler. Something told him he could probably find out fairly easily where her pain originated. That was the beauty of a small town. But going behind her

back and snooping into her past seemed wrong.
If Miranda wanted him to know what she was
protecting, that information ought to come from
her. Not that there was a snowball's chance in hell
that she'd share.

"JUDGING BY THE evidence, what little there was
left behind, we think there are five men involved. But that's pure speculation because they
cover their tracks so well. Sometimes I wonder
if they're somehow making it look as if there
are more people when there's only two. Who
knows? But it's definitely someone who knows
what they're doing. Which leads me to think that
it's a local. As much as I hate to think that. But
who else would know the area the way they do
and who else would know how to get in and out
of those mountains without dying? It's rough terrain. An inexperienced person could easily slip
and fall to their death in these mountains. But
whoever these people are they have the sure-
footedness of a Billy goat."

"Could it be one of the indigenous people?"

Miranda's expression was grim. "Possibly.
I've asked around but the tribes around here are
pretty tight-lipped when it comes to their own.
Even if they knew one of the tribal members was
committing the crime, they'd never tell the authorities. They don't trust easily, and like many

indigenous tribes, they have reason to distrust those in authority."

Jeremiah seemed to disagree with her comment but he didn't chase after that train of thought and she was glad he'd remained quiet. She was protective of the Yupik and their rights because in her son's blood ran the proud heritage of the local people. *Mamu*'s ancestors had fished the frigid waters and lived in harmony with Alaska before any white man had stepped foot on the shores to show them the "right" way to live. "I can check and see if there's been any poaching crimes that fit the M.O. of the poachers here and see if anything pops up that might help. If they're running a black-market operation, chances are they aren't hunting only in Alaska."

Miranda nodded. "That's true. I made some inquiries but no one seemed all that interested in miring themselves in research for someone else's pet project."

"Poaching doesn't rate on the same level as homicide or even grand theft. Every federal agency is underfunded and understaffed these days it seems. No one wants to take on more work than they have to," he said.

"Don't I know it," she grumbled. "I've had a heck of a time getting anyone in our office to lift much more than a finger to help. No one is interested in fieldwork these days and tracking poachers is time spent away from the comforts of a warm office and their topped-off coffee mug."

"When I was younger I used to spend a lot of time in the field as a ranger. I loved the solitude and the quiet of the mountains. Sometimes I was able to make more sense of what was going on in my life when I was completely surrounded by nature than when I was among other human beings."

"'The clearest way into the universe is through a forest wilderness,'" Miranda said with a faint smile.

"John Muir," Jeremiah murmured with approval. "I'm a huge fan."

"Gotta love an activist with his heart in the right place," Miranda said. "I think my brother Wade fancied himself a modern-day John Muir. Fitting, seeing as he moved to California to become a law-enforcement ranger in Yosemite National Park."

"I did a stint there in my early days. Beautiful country. The valley floor takes your breath away. Have you ever been?"

Miranda shook her head. "Nope. Alaska is enough for me. I don't share my brother's wanderlust. Besides, I have plenty to keep me busy right here."

Miranda allowed silence to fill the cab as she maneuvered the streets out of town and up toward the forest access roads. Jeremiah was unlike any man she'd ever met, particularly for an administrator. Virgil had been content to play by the rules without poking his head up too often to attract attention. His belief had been that if they kept their heads down, when budget cuts came around, Homer's small satellite office would get overlooked for bigger fish. So with that in mind, Virgil never updated anything in the office, which included the furniture, the carpet, the leaky toilet. Perhaps his strategy had worked because Homer had been left alone when the last round of cuts had come around, but then, they'd been operating on such a ridiculously low budget, Miranda wasn't sure where they could've cut expenses unless they'd started forgoing toilet paper and started using newspaper for their bathroom business.

As if keying into her thoughts, Jeremiah asked, "How was your relationship with your former boss? Virgil was his name, right?"

"Yes. Virgil was Virgil. Good, solid guy. A little on the cranky side at times but otherwise harmless. Why?"

"Just making conversation."

"How was your relationship with *your* former boss?" she asked, lobbing the question right back at him.

"My boss was a jackass."

"Why didn't you like him?"

"She," he corrected, "was a power-hungry egomaniac on her best days. However, she didn't want to bother with my department and left me to run it as long as nothing landed on her desk that would make her look bad. Thankfully, I did my job well, and thus, our paths crossed only a few times a year for the obligatory dinners, and we managed to smile civilly for appearances' sake."

"So why do you call her a jackass?"

"Because she was as tough as any man I'd ever known and I figured the term fit."

She chuckled. "Something tells me you're not going to send her a Christmas card this year."

"Crossing her off the list was done with more than a little zeal."

Miranda laughed a little harder, picturing Jeremiah striking a name with a big black marker and an expression of maniacal glee. Jeremiah graced her with a wry but knowing look. "You just imagined me as a crazy person in your mind, didn't you?"

"No, of course not," she lied, her smile remaining. "Nice to know you're human just like the rest of us."

He shot her an assessing glance. "Should I be flattered or concerned that I come off as inhuman?"

She faltered, realizing she may have inadvertently insulted him. "I'm sorry. I don't know where that came from. We really shouldn't talk about personal stuff. It's a slippery slope given our history."

"It's okay," he assured her. "I have a decent sense of humor and I hardly consider polite banter between two people as crossing a line. Our history doesn't have to be the elephant in the room."

"But it *is* the elephant in the room," she disagreed. "Normally, I wouldn't have a problem joking around with my superior if I found that person open to it, but I'm not entirely comfortable doing that with you because of my fear that we're becoming noticeably too familiar. The last thing I need is people talking about my professional relationships." She added, grumbling, "They do enough talking about me as it is."

Jeremiah chose to let her comment slide and she was grateful because she should've kept that complaint to herself. Her mother was fond of saying, "It's your bed, now lie in it," and ordinarily, she wouldn't have given two flips of a sea otter's fin how others felt about her, but for some reason she cared what Jeremiah thought about her. She'd dig into those reasons later. For now, she wanted to ignore them.

"I like to get to know my team," Jeremiah continued. "I feel it helps me to be a better leader if I know the strengths and weaknesses of the people around me. I don't know how to get to know someone without discovering some personal details about them."

"And how did your team back in Wyoming feel about you poking your nose into their personal business?"

"I didn't ask intrusive questions…. I simply showed that I was interested in knowing what they cared about. And you know what, my team appreciated my interest. They said it made them feel as if I was doing more than only being their boss because it was my job." He paused before admitting, "I prided myself on being more than a superior, but I don't know how to do that with you."

"I think you know me well enough," she muttered. "The way I see it, we already know each other too well."

Jeremiah caught her gaze briefly but it was long enough for Miranda to see the heat smoldering behind those beautiful eyes and she knew in an instant that he was thinking of all the ways they'd spent the evening worshipping each other's bodies. Her cheeks flared and her breath hitched in her throat as words escaped her. Jeremiah saved her from further embarrassing herself by speaking first. "I'm trying to operate as I've always done with employees. I'm trying to forget our first encounter."

"How's that working out for you?" she asked, unable to help herself.

"As well as it is for you," he retorted drily. "But I'm going to keep trying and I suggest you do the same. In the meantime, if I don't treat you the same as I treat everyone, it will look odd. So…I will ask you about your family, your pets and your hobbies just as I would for Todd or Mary or anyone else on my team. Got it?"

"Yeah, I got it." She didn't like it, but Jeremiah's statement made sense even if the idea of giving up more personal information, however superficial, made her squirm. But she had to admit, having a boss who actually cared about things wasn't entirely bad. "You're a good guy, Jeremiah Burke," she decided with an irritated sigh. "Things would've been a lot easier if you'd been a total ass. And ugly."

She was pleased when he simply acknowledged her grudging compliment with a slight head nod. If he'd mucked up the sentiment with more words, it would've ruined the good feeling she had about him. And she was glad that he hadn't.

CHAPTER EIGHT

JEREMIAH WAS NO stranger to a beautiful landscape but the Alaskan wilderness took his breath away. Nearly literally.

He shrugged and shifted in his down jacket, shuddering as the cold jarred his bones, reminding him with an icy touch that he wasn't as young as he used to be. An old skiing injury always flared up in the winter, aching and protesting when the temperature dropped, just like it was now. Miranda caught his subtle wince as they climbed the trail winding deeper into the Kenai Mountains and stopped with a frown. "You okay? If you aren't up to this, we can turn around."

"I'm fine," he answered, determined to keep going. He didn't want Miranda to see him as a weak desk monkey, though he knew it shouldn't matter what she thought of his masculinity. He gritted his teeth and ignored the dull pain throbbing in his knee. "Show me the way. I'm right behind you."

"If you say so, but the trail gets pretty rough up ahead," she warned as she turned and kept trudging along the trail that was clogged with deep foliage and ruts caused by snow runoff. The bite in the air smelled sharp and clean even if it cut through his bones. He probably should've picked a warmer clime—like Arizona or Nevada—but if anything said "you're old and can't take it" faster than a move to Arizona, Jeremiah didn't know. Besides, he hated the extreme heat even more than he hated the idea of being thought of as a soft-handed desk monkey.

They came to a ridge overlooking a meadow that bumped up against the edge of a lake, and the beauty filled him with joy. "Pretty as a postcard," he murmured in appreciation. "This is definitely God's country."

"Yeah, nothing is better than Alaskan wilderness to remind us just how small we really are." She drew a deep breath. "I'd match up the glory of Alaska to any place in the United States."

"You love Alaska."

"I do," she admitted softly. "I don't know why—by all rights, I ought to hate this place—but I can't imagine my life anywhere but here. Guess I have Alaskan ice flowing through my veins."

"You couldn't pick a more scenic place to call home," he said. "It's no small tragedy to wake up to this every day." She smiled and agreed. A moment stretched between them and Jeremiah wondered if he ought to ask about her cryptic comment about her past but he sensed she wouldn't share and so banked his curiosity for the time being. "Are we close to the spot where the first bear was found?"

"Yes, just around this bend in the trail and up about a mile into the trees." She sent him a short smile. "Think you can handle it?"

"Of course I can."

"Don't feel bad if you're not accustomed to this much physical activity. Most administrators never leave the comfort of their office."

"Thank you for your concern but I stay pretty active. My stamina is just fine," he said, hoping with an almost-wicked grin that she recalled in vivid detail how he'd propped her against the wall without issue, without once wincing at the strain. Her cheeks colored prettily and he knew his wish had been granted. His grin widened just a tiny bit and she firmed her mouth, eyes flashing, before turning on her heel and quickening her pace. Yeah, she definitely remembered. Was he a bad person for delighting privately in that knowledge? Maybe a little…but it was worth it.

Miranda stopped at a copse of dense trees that spiraled into the frigid sky and pointed unerringly at a spot that otherwise appeared the same as the spot of dirt beside it, but it was as if Miranda could still see the blood splatter from the mutilated bear. "I'm not sure what upsets me more, the cruelty or the disrespect."

"Disrespect?"

"Yes, disrespect. The indigenous people believe that when a bear gave up its life to sustain another, it was the ultimate sacrifice and deserving of gratitude. Poachers don't give a damn about the bear, just the cash it represents. The greed sickens me." Her voice rang with passion and he knew that until these poachers were caught she'd bear the weight of their actions as some kind of punishment.

"You're an intriguing woman," he admitted, earning a sharp look from Miranda, but he shrugged, emboldened by the privacy of the mountains. "Tell me why you're so unlike any woman I've ever met?"

"Not sure how to answer that," she murmured, glancing away but not before he caught the sudden flush in her cheeks. "Are you asking about my passion for my job or my personal life?"

"Maybe a little of both but I suppose we should stick to the job. I'd be a liar, though, if I didn't admit that I'm drawn to the woman behind the uniform. In my experience people don't just spring out of the mud as complex as you unless life has thrown them a few hardballs."

"I'm complex? I never considered myself particularly hard to figure out."

"You want to know what you remind me of?"

She hesitated but curiosity won out. "Sure."

"Nothing bad so wipe that look off your face. You remind me of one of those thousand-piece puzzles."

"A puzzle?"

"Yeah, because most people get halfway into the puzzle and realize there are too many pieces and give up. However, those who don't give up and actually finish the puzzle discover something pretty worthwhile for their effort." The pink in her cheeks deepened and she seemed at a loss for words. Jeremiah had to pull himself back from the ledge he was tottering too close to before he tumbled over. "All I'm saying is, I'm guessing when people don't give up on you, good things happen, but I suspect plenty of people have, which is why you keep people at a distance."

At that Miranda stiffened. Either he'd hit the nail on the head or he'd completely insulted her. "As entertaining as your philosophies about me are, I'd rather we keep our conversation to those appropriate to our jobs. Okay?"

"Right. I'm sorry," he said, biting back a sigh. Way to go. But even as he knew he should've kept his mouth shut, he couldn't let go of the feeling that he'd been correct in his theory about her. Not that being right gave him any leverage—if anything, the knowledge may serve to deepen the chasm between them as Miranda scrambled to keep him at arm's length at any cost.

Miranda placed her hands on her hips, surveying the land, her breath pluming before her. "You say I'm complex? But really, I'm not. I care deeply for the land, my family and the animals. What fries me is that poachers don't care about anything or anyone but themselves. They certainly didn't care if anyone came across the carcass because no attempt was made to bury the evidence. What if a kid had come across the bloody, eviscerated mess they'd left behind? It's not only disgusting but horrifying."

"Were the other carcasses found in the same general area?"

"No, there's a twenty-mile radius. But they were definitely tracking the migration from the higher elevation knowing that the bears were going to follow the food and water source. These poachers are seasoned hunters."

"Have you checked the local hunting tags? Maybe it's someone who's pretending to abide by the law so as to avoid notice."

"I did a check on the tags but it's really difficult to run down every single tag purchase because we have so many out-of-state tourists who purchase big-game tags when they come up here."

"How many big-game outfits are operating in Homer?"

"Just one, but in the state of Alaska? Plenty more. There's no guarantee the poachers are from Homer. I'd like to think that they aren't but I can't ignore the possibility."

"True. Have you talked to the local owners of the big-game outfit?"

"Yes, Rhett Fowler has been running Big Game Trophy for as long as I can remember and he runs a decent operation. I'd be willing to stake my livelihood on the belief that he's not a part of the poaching ring. Besides, he makes plenty of money with his business, so he doesn't need to supplement his income with black-market goods."

"Someone infected with greed doesn't have to be starving—in fact, usually, it's the opposite. Even when people have enough, they still want more."

She nodded, a frown marring her face. "I'll do another round of checking and asking questions." Miranda regarded him with a dubious expression. "Do you want to keep going? It's going to be dark soon, and if you think it's difficult terrain now, wait until you can't see what's in front of you."

"This is sufficient. I just wanted to get a feel for the area so I have a visual in my mind."

They started back down the mountain trail and for a while there was nothing but the sound of their feet hitting the ground as they traversed the uneven terrain. Jeremiah enjoyed the silence and the company and he wasn't above hoping that he and Miranda could build a solid friendship, though at this point he was being realistic about the chances of that happening. As much as he talked a good game about putting the recent events behind them and starting fresh, it was hard as hell not to stare at her backside and remember how it felt to have that pert, rounded flesh gripped in his palms. Sweat popped along his brow that wasn't caused by the exertion, and as he wiped it away, he half growled at himself to keep his thoughts on the straight and narrow before he ended up twisting an ankle and looking like a total fool.

He managed to fill his thoughts with the paperwork he needed to go through when they returned, but about halfway down Miranda asked, "So what's the real reason you came to Alaska?" and he lost control of his thoughts again.

The question hung between them as if it were a living breathing thing, and Jeremiah supposed the truth would come out sooner or later, but he wasn't quite ready to talk about Tyler. "Needed a change of scenery." He flashed her a bright smile. "Alaska seemed like a good place."

She accepted his answer and they kept walking, but her question rang in his mind and dampened his good mood. The urge to tell her about Tyler was an irritant in his mind. It niggled at him and dragged his thoughts into dark places. By the time they reached the car his mood had dipped into melancholy.

MIRANDA SENSED THE energy change between them, and while she desperately wanted to know what had triggered the change, that small voice inside of her warned it wasn't her business. The man was allowed his secrets. He was a virtual stranger; there was probably plenty she didn't know about him, nor did she need to know.

"Have you found a place to stay?" The inquiry was meant to be polite—wasn't that the sort of thing people talked about in superficial circles?—but she really should have thought her question through before asking. She should've asked something more vague, more impersonal. Perhaps, was he enjoying the weather? But the question was out there and she couldn't very well take it back, so she simply waited for his answer.

Jeremiah bit off a short sigh. "No, not yet. Seems there is a shortage of rentals. I'm staying at a small motel that's more of a tourist trap than something suitable for my needs."

"I can ask around for you," she offered. Without connections the man would likely be sleeping in a hotel bed until spring. "Any preferences?"

"Anything fully furnished would be great. When I left Wyoming, I left everything behind."

"You didn't bring anything with you?"

"Just a suitcase full of clothes and shoes. I figured anything I needed I could find here."

Miranda's mind picked at his statement. She appreciated the benefit to packing light, but when you uproot your entire life to move to another state wouldn't you want to bring some mementos of your previous life? Unless whatever he was leaving behind was something he didn't want to remember. *Damn.* She hated that she wanted to know more, almost *needed* to know more. "I'm guessing a one-bedroom studio would work?"

He nodded. "That would be perfect."

Mary's brother, Otter, dabbled in real estate. He fancied himself an investor and had a few rentals. Seeing as Otter had always had a thing for her, Miranda might be able to put in a good word for Jeremiah.

They reached the car and climbed in, made small talk that was nearly excruciating as Miranda hated useless chitchat, and by the time they were returned to the office, it was time to go home. She wasn't surprised when Jeremiah went to his office with the plan to work late. She admired his dedication, his drive. Virgil had been a clock puncher. Not that she'd blamed him entirely. He'd been an older man who enjoyed his recreation more than the time spent at the office. Mary always liked to point out that no one had the same kind of passion that Miranda did. As Miranda shut down her computer and saw the light burning in Jeremiah's office, she realized Jeremiah was probably her work twin.

She chuckled at the irony and headed to the after-school day care to pick up Talen.

Later that night after she'd scrubbed the mud from behind her son's ears, she was grateful for the distraction of his usual bartering for a later bedtime because otherwise Jeremiah's voice remained in her thoughts.

He'd compared her to a difficult puzzle that most people gave up on. How had he managed to find such an apt way to describe her life? Maybe it wasn't that people gave up on her, but rather, the other way around? She kept people at a distance for a reason—no one could hurt her if she didn't stand within their swinging radius.

"Mama, Brandon said he gets to stay up until ten o'clock, even on a school night! How come I can't stay up until at least nine?" Talen's voice cut into her thoughts and she shook her head at her son's argument.

"Well, I'm not Brandon's mother, and I'm not saying that Brandon's mother isn't a good mom, but obviously, his bedtime isn't the only thing she doesn't adhere to a strict schedule. The boy has enough dirt behind his ears to grow corn."

"It's too cold to grow corn," Talen countered grumpily. "It's not fair. I'm not a baby anymore."

"Life's not fair, my sweet boy. That's the honest truth and anyone telling you different is selling you something. And I hate to break it to you but you'll always be my baby no matter how old you get." She smiled and ruffled his hair, but he wasn't having any of her usual ways to cheer him up, which bothered her a bit. "Hey, buddy, is there something aside from your bedtime bothering you?"

"I don't want to talk about it."

Miranda frowned. "Talen, what's wrong? Tell me, son. Whatever it is, I promise not to be mad or anything."

Talen regarded her with his impossibly dark eyes that reminded her so much of Johnny, and she swore sometimes when she looked at her son she felt as if her kid's spirit stared back. *Mamu* always said Talen was an old soul, and while Miranda respected *Mamu*'s ways, there were times when she experienced a full-body shudder, particularly when she spoke of Talen, that made her wonder if *Mamu* was right.

"Sometimes I wonder if things might be different if I had a dad."

Miranda drew back, surprised. "What do you mean?" Oh, God, she wasn't ready to talk to Talen about Johnny. Not yet. She hadn't yet figured out a way to sugarcoat the truth.

"You make all the rules. Maybe a dad would have different rules. That's all."

"Like different bedtime rules?" she said, holding her breath, hoping against hope Talen was still pouting about his bedtime rather than something deeper. To her immense relief Talen nodded. "Well," she said as she tucked Talen into his bed, "I imagine even if there was a dad around, I would still make the rules because everyone knows that the moms are the best at making rules."

"What do dads do, then?" Talen asked, perplexed.

Uh…she didn't know. She pulled a memory from her own childhood. Her father had been the muscle around the house whenever something needed muscling. "They open pickle and jam jars," Miranda answered, hoping her young son didn't see right through her lame answer. "Anyway, sorry…all you have is a mom but a pretty good one, right?"

"Yeah, you're pretty good," Talen agreed with a reluctant smile that warmed her heart. "But I still want to go to bed a little later. I'm not even tired."

"Good night, my son," she said with a knowing smile. For a boy who professed he was still wide-awake, he was already rubbing at his eyes and fighting a yawn. He'd be asleep within five minutes.

Not long after the house had been closed up for the night, Miranda climbed into bed and checked her emails from her laptop. As she scanned the emails, she was disappointed to see that Trace had not responded to her latest email. He hated technology but he grudgingly kept an email address because he didn't actually have a regular mailing address and this was the only way his family could reach him at times. But sometimes he went weeks without checking his email, which defeated the purpose. She sighed and closed her laptop, more than a little irritated at her brothers.

It was unfair that both of those nitwits were happy to let her deal with their parents when they knew full well neither their mother nor father were easy to handle. This latest situation with their mother was a pain in her backside and she could use a little backup.

Miranda leaned over and grabbed her cell phone. It was a long shot, as Trace turned on his cell phone as often as he checked his email, but she was a little desperate.

"Hey, Trace, this is Miranda. I need you to check in as soon as possible. I need to talk to you about Mom. It's important, so please don't blow me off for another few weeks while you roam the countryside like an antisocial wild man. Love you."

She tossed her phone to the bed and yawned. It wasn't late but she was beat. Most days she could handle everything without blinking an eye but it seemed that the weight of all her responsibilities was heavier than usual. She hated nights like this—emotionally exhausted yet too wired to actually sleep—and she knew she would toss and turn all night while her brain refused to shut down for a blessed minute. It was nights like this that she craved a warm body beside her and a shot of whiskey to warm her insides. She swung her legs free from the bed and headed for the kitchen. At least she could manage the whiskey, if not the man.

One generous shot later, she returned to her bed and climbed beneath the covers. Maybe tonight would be different. She wouldn't dream of her sister or anyone in her family.

Maybe she would just drift into nothingness and her brain would stop jabbering long enough for a moment's peace.

Maybe.

Not likely.

CHAPTER NINE

THE LOUD BUZZ of her cell phone rattling on her nightstand jarred her from a restless sleep. Miranda fumbled for the phone and answered in a sleepy mumble to hear her brother's voice on the other line.

"I got your message. What's up?"

Miranda sat up to rub the sleep from her eyes as she answered, "I can't believe you actually called me back so soon. I half expected not to hear from you for another couple weeks."

"You said it was important," Trace reminded her. "So what's going on?"

Miranda yawned as she slowly came awake. "The situation with Mom is getting out of control. I need your input. She won't listen to me, and of course, Dad is no help. I hired an organizer to go out there and help her and she sent the woman away. And then she was mad at me for sending the woman to her home."

"Of course she was mad. I wouldn't want a stranger poking her nose into my business, either."

Trace's irritation rubbed Miranda the wrong

way. He didn't know what it was like to deal with their mother on an everyday basis. He'd conveniently skipped out on the family, same as Wade, the cowards. "Trace, the way she's living is dangerous. She's a hoarder," she maintained with an edge to her voice.

"Come on, Miranda. I think you're exaggerating. Mom likes to collect stuff but she's not a hoarder."

"No, that's where you're wrong. You haven't been down here to see the house lately. It's a nightmare. I don't know how she walks through the house. It's gotten so bad that Dad is practically living in his shop."

"I'd be more concerned about Dad selling pot than I am about Mom liking to collect things."

"If you visited more than once a year you'd know that Mom's *collecting* is the bigger issue. I can't do this by myself. You and Wade have put all the responsibility of our parents on my shoulders and it's not fair. I need you to come home."

"Nobody told you to stay in Homer."

Great defense, Trace. Blame me for choosing to make a life here. "I have a job that I love. It's not just about staying in Homer. This is my son's home, too. I'm not about to tear Talen away from his heritage just because things don't always go smoothly."

"Is this all you want to talk about? I'm on a job

and I only took a few minutes to make the call because you made it sound urgent."

"It *is* urgent, damn it. Our mother is going to *die* in that house because it's unsanitary and unsafe. I can't let Talen visit anymore because I'm afraid he'll be smothered by the towers of crap she has in her house. I'm sorry if you felt that was beneath your notice."

The silence on the other end told Miranda she'd hit a nerve. Good. Trace lived close enough to at least check in on his parents every now and again instead of the annual obligatory visits he made. "Fine. After this job I'll make some time to check things out. Stop getting so worked up about it. You should focus more on your own life than fixing those of other people."

Miranda bristled. "What's that supposed to mean?"

"You know what I'm talking about. Get your shit together, Miranda."

Someone had been flapping their jaws to her brother about her activities. God, she hated that. Living under a microscope was a pain in the ass. It was times like this when she wished she had moved away, too. "You're one to talk," she shot back. "I'm not the one hiding in the mountains because I can't handle being around people."

"Whatever you say, Miranda. I'll be in touch."

There was a pause and then Trace added, "Give the kid a squeeze for me."

The line went dead and Miranda knew that Trace had ended the call. She loved her brother but he drove her crazy with the same argument about her lifestyle. As if he had room to talk. It wasn't as if he were the epitome of normal living. He wasn't some bastion of emotional stability. And yet, even knowing this about her brother, he still managed to get under her skin when he made comments like that. "Damn hypocrite." She tossed the phone to her nightstand and tried to get a few more minutes of sleep before her alarm went off and she had to get Talen ready for school.

JEREMIAH DIDN'T KNOW why he thought leaving Wyoming would mean the end to his insomnia, but he'd had high hopes that the nights of staring at the ceiling with eyes burning from fatigue were over. However, by 4:00 a.m. he knew his hope had been misplaced and that simply lying in bed for another two hours was an exercise in pathetic futility. He quickly showered and dressed, grabbed a coffee and headed to the office, almost grateful to be doing something productive rather than pretending to sleep. By the time 8:00 a.m. rolled around he'd already made a serious dent in the stack of paperwork he had scheduled to study as part of his first week of acclimation and he was in good shape for the rest of the week.

If only he didn't look and feel like crap.

He wasn't surprised when Miranda walked in first, bright and early. From what he could tell, Miranda was also an early riser. She must've been accustomed to walking into an empty office, because when she saw he was already there she briefly startled. There was a moment's hesitation, as if she was contemplating ignoring his presence and walking straight to her office, but he was glad when she walked in with a guarded yet polite expression. "I'm not used to anyone being here before me. Virgil liked to roll in around nine, and Todd and Mary wander in around the same time. So, is this what I can expect of my new boss? How am I supposed to get away with anything if you're just as dedicated as I am?"

He chuckled. "I've never been one to sleep in. Besides, I have plenty of work to keep me busy, and since I'm still living at my hotel, I really don't have anything to do but stare at the walls when I'm not at the office." Add in the fact he didn't know a soul aside from his coworkers, spending extra time at the office was actually preferable to wandering around like a lost tourist. "That's my excuse. What's yours? Consummate workaholic?"

"A lack of dedication has never been my problem," she said, smiling. "But since my son has to be at school at 7:30 a.m., it makes sense to come straight to the office after I drop him off."

Jeremiah's easy smile froze. "You're a mother?" he asked, trying to sound casual when in fact, he was stunned. It shouldn't matter but it did. "I didn't realize."

Her cheeks colored. "Whenever I have guests over, I take Talen to his grandmother's place." She cleared her throat and met his gaze. "Is it so surprising that I'm a mother?" she asked, slightly defensive.

"No, of course n—" He stopped and changed course, admitting, "Actually, yes. I don't usually put much store in stereotypes but I didn't expect you to have a child. I apologize for my assumption. What's his name?" he asked, striving for polite interest when in fact, he could feel himself shutting down inside. Since Tyler's death, Jeremiah did his best to avoid putting himself in situations like these.

"Talen."

"Talon. Like the bird claw?" he asked in spite of himself.

"Yes. His father was Yupik and I wanted a name that would reflect his Native heritage."

Tyler had been named after Jeremiah's paternal great-grandfather, who had fought in World War II. The disagreement between him and Josie over the name had been epic. In the end, Jeremiah had won out only because Josie had been certain she was pregnant with a girl and thus had agreed to allow Jeremiah to name the child if it popped out a boy. The decision to wait to find out the gender until birth had worked out in Jeremiah's favor. He still remembered the feel of his newborn son in his arms, the smell of his sweet skin, and the way Tyler had squalled loud enough to bring the hospital walls down. Unwelcome tears stung his eyes and he cut his gaze away from Miranda abruptly. "Well, I guess I better get used to sharing the coffeepot if there are going to be two early risers around here," he said with a brief smile, signaling the end to the conversation.

"Maybe tomorrow I'll surprise you with doughnuts," she said, smiling, but he saw the questions in her eyes at his demeanor change. He wished he had the guts to explain but he wasn't ready to let anyone know about his past—not yet.

Miranda retreated and headed for her office, leaving Jeremiah to his work.

But Jeremiah's mind was not focused on work any longer. Perhaps it was the sleep deprivation, or maybe it was the stress of the move, but Jeremiah's thoughts were as unruly and undisciplined as a willful puppy that nipped and bit because it didn't know how sharp its teeth were.

Jeremiah tried not to think about Tyler. His pain and lingering grief made the topic of his son off-limits. In the months after his wife had left him, he'd often wondered if his talking about Tyler would have helped his wife deal with her own grief. But his ex-wife was consumed with hatred as well as grief and deep down he knew it wouldn't have made a difference. But somehow blaming himself for the demise of their marriage seemed appropriate. Maybe it was his way of doing penance, even though he knew there was no escaping the guilt he felt for buying Tyler that damn ATV. The logical part of his brain told him Tyler's accident had been simply that—an accident. But logic and emotion rarely lived in the same house. He still remembered the tipping point of his decision to buy the all-terrain vehicle. He'd been working eighty-hour weeks and he'd wanted to make it up to Tyler somehow. He'd known the boy had wanted an ATV, and even though his wife had disapproved, it'd seemed a small price to pay for his son's instant gratitude. Of course, he'd had no way of knowing that the true price would be far more than he could afford to pay.

"Dad, I'll be a good driver. I promise." Tyler's earnest voice rang in Jeremiah's memory. "All my friends already have one. Their dads don't care. Why are you being so protective? I'm not a baby anymore."

"I don't know.... Your mom might skin my

hide if I go against her in this." Truthfully, Jeremiah had been uncertain about the safety. But Tyler had seemed so sure of himself that he'd been swayed by his son's confidence. "Let's think about it for a while," he'd suggested, hoping for a little more time to do some research.

But Tyler wasn't going to be put off. He knew what he wanted and he knew exactly what to say to get it. "Dad, having an ATV isn't just for fun. I could use it to check the property. When you're gone I can use it to check the fence line. You know that last storm blew out the south side fence and we didn't even know about it until a few weeks later."

Tyler made a persuasive point. They'd actually lost two calves who'd somehow wandered out and broken their necks after falling in a small ravine. Not that Jeremiah was a cattleman, per se, but he enjoyed having a few livestock. Made him feel closer to the land. "You'd have to promise me there'd be no hotdogging." A slow smile crept across Tyler's face as he sensed victory. Jeremiah chuckled. "All right, who gets to break it to your mom?"

"You married her. That falls under your jurisdiction."

Jeremiah laughed. "Caught on a technicality. We'll break the news to her tonight. You better not make me regret this, boy."

Famous last words. He'd live to do more than regret it.

But he still remembered Tyler's smile, the joy shining in his eyes. Given the choice he'd take it all back, but all Jeremiah had now were the memories of his son's laughter, his son's smile, and everything else that'd made Tyler an amazing kid. Aww hell, why'd he have to go down this road? He'd left Wyoming for a purpose and yet it seemed the ghost of his past rode shotgun beside him.

Would this ever end? Would he ever find peace? Tears pricked his eyes and he fought to hold them back. Bawling at his desk was not the way he wanted his coworkers to see him and he definitely didn't want Miranda to see him so weak and pathetic. *Put it away, Jeremiah. The past is the past. Leave it there.*

Maybe if he kept working on burying the pain, it would finally work.

A sigh rattled out of his tight chest and he forced himself to focus on anything but the memory of his son.

Thank God for a demanding job.

JENNELLE SINCLAIR WOUND her way through the hall around various piles of magazines, books, newspapers and other assorted paper items and let herself into the spare room that had once belonged to her daughter Simone.

A sense of relief followed as it always did for inexplicable reasons when she closed the door and took a seat on the neat and tidy twin bed. Jennelle was the only one who came into this room, which gave her the opportunity to treat the room as her own personal haven.

The pictures on the walls were entirely of Simone and her various accomplishments—of which there'd been so many!—and each time Jennelle let her gaze rest on a photo, she remembered happy memories.

It was like stepping back in time. Simone, her bright and bubbly little ball of sunshine, had been such a happy child. Always wearing a smile, Simone had never met a person she hadn't wanted to befriend. And people had flocked to her like flowers to sunshine. Who could blame them? Simone had been pretty as a picture with more charisma than a movie star.

And being in this room, surrounded by her daughter's things, gave Jennelle a sense of peace even if it was something no one else could understand. No one was allowed in this room. Not even her husband. Not that he was interested in coming inside. No, Zed avoided even the mention of their daughter's name. It was as if she'd never been born. And that was unconscionable in Jennelle's opinion. To pretend as if the girl had never brightened their lives, never blessed them with her presence, was almost downright evil.

But what did he know about a mother's grief? Men weren't capable of understanding the complexity of a woman's emotion. She'd carried that child in her womb for nine months, nourished and sustained her, only to lose her to some sick bastard.... It was more than a mother's heart could bear on most days. This room...well, it soothed that wild grief, if however briefly—and she wasn't giving it up.

Jennelle smoothed her hand over the thick quilt that she'd made for Simone on her eighth birthday and smiled as she remembered Simone asking in her sweet little voice, "Am I your special girl, Mama?"

"Always and forever," Jennelle murmured to the phantom voice that was never far from her mind. Her eyes welled as they always did when she thought of Simone. "Why did you leave us so soon?"

If only Jennelle could stay in this room forever. This was a special place. A place where she could forget that her lovely Simone was brutally killed and her case was never solved.

She could blank out the fact that Simone had been alive when that person had left her on the mountain to die. And that if Trace and Miranda had been better trackers they would've found her. There were so many things Jennelle had to forget in order to function. When Simone had died, people had told her it would get better, time healed all wounds. They were wrong. It hadn't gotten better, the pain hadn't gone away, and she still missed Simone every single day. So, she made this room, filled with all of Simone's things, a slice in time protected from everything and anyone who might try to take Simone away. In this room she could pretend that Simone was alive and well and about to burst through the front door any moment, chattering about her day, filling their lives with light.

Some days she absolutely needed the illusion to function. And besides, it was none of anyone else's business how she coped with her grief.

Not even Miranda's.

CHAPTER TEN

JEREMIAH WALKED INTO Miranda's office, a contemplative frown on his face as he perused what appeared to be a permit of some sort.

"Educate me on nature immersion as a tourist attraction," he said, handing over the permit.

Miranda didn't need to see the permit; she already knew who and what it was for. "George and Crystal Belkin apply for a salmon permit every year for their nature-immersion excursions that they run through their company, Nature's Bounty. Basically, people pay to learn how to pick native berries, fish for salmon and otherwise *survive* in the Alaskan wilderness."

Jeremiah's brow rose. "You can learn how to survive on the land over a weekend?"

"No. But it sounds good on the pamphlet."

"So this is another tourist trap?"

"I wouldn't call it a trap, per se. The trip is fun at least. And George and Crystal don't actually stress the survivalist angle. It's more of a fun, outdoorsy excursion for those who aren't from around here."

"You've done the trip?"

"Once. George talked me into it. Said it would be good for me to try it out in case anyone ever asked what it was like. They comped my trip in exchange for a few good words when people come to the office looking for things to do in Alaska."

He frowned. "We're a government entity, not tour salespeople."

"Settle down. It's not as if we're pushing one service over another. If anyone asks, I give them an honest answer about my experience. That's all."

"So these Belkin people, you check them out for the poaching angle?" At Miranda's incredulous frown, he said, "Listen, you've already established that whoever is pulling off these bear kills knows the area. Wouldn't a tourist-based naturalist know these areas pretty well?"

She hated to admit it, but yes. "I'm not saying you're off base. I'm just saying that the Belkins are the gentlest bunch of hippies you'll ever meet. I mean, they're all about protecting the environment and doing what's right for the land as well as protecting endangered species. I doubt the Belkins would squash a fly even if it landed on their tofu sandwich. You get where I'm coming from?"

"Are you friends with the Belkins?"

"No." She didn't have an abundance of people she'd call true friends. "But they're harmless. Trust me." She drew a deep breath. Jeremiah seemed off today. As if something were really chewing on his shorts. Why'd she have to notice? "Are you okay?" she asked reluctantly. "I mean, you seem a little grouchy."

"Grouchy? No. I'm trying to offer a fresh perspective. You've been working this case for so long you've ceased to question all leads."

"Excuse me? I beg your pardon but you need to check yourself. I know this case better than anyone. I can assure you I haven't overlooked anything. I just know when I'm barking up the wrong tree and I'm not about to waste my energy on a false lead."

He stiffened. "I disagree. And as your boss I'm telling you to double-check their backgrounds."

"That's a waste of time," she nearly growled, fresh irritation washing over her spark of concern for whatever might've been bothering him. "If you want to poke around in the Belkins' background, be my guest, but I have plenty to keep me busy otherwise."

"You really have no control over your mouth, do you?" he asked. "A bit of a job hazard, don't you think?"

She narrowed her stare. "Did you come in here to pick a fight? Because you're doing a bang-up job."

Curious stares began to swivel their way and

Jeremiah paused to close the door before their conversation became everyone's topic of discussion around the watercooler. He advanced to lean across her desk, his eyes flashing. "Given our history, you might think you can talk to me as if I were not your superior, but that would be a mistake," he warned quietly. Her stomach muscles tightened as adrenaline rushed through her veins, the urge to seal her lips to his warring with the righteous anger burning a hole in her gut. "If I ask you to follow a lead, I expect you to do it without question."

Miranda rose slowly to meet him, staring hard into his eyes so he knew she didn't take this kind of bullshit from anyone—not even her boss. "I don't follow *any* instruction without question. It's not in my nature. And since you've undoubtedly read my personnel file, you've already gathered that I'm hardly the type to meekly accept whatever is thrown my way like some pathetic little underling hoping to catch some favor from the boss."

"Why are you being so damn difficult about this?"

"Because it's in my nature," she quipped with a hard smile. "That's probably in my file, too."

They were standing toe-to-toe, the close distance hardly appropriate and they both knew it, yet neither made a move to pull away. It was a standoff of sorts, and the instant, almost-palpable heat between them was enough to set off the ancient sprinklers poking from the yellowed ceiling. Would he kiss her? For a wild moment, she desperately hoped he would. But as her heart threatened to stutter to a stop with anticipation, Jeremiah remembered himself with a start and abruptly pulled away. His stare cleared of the heat clouding his gaze and his mouth compressed with frustration. "I... Damn," he muttered, looking away. He blew a tight breath and walked to the door, saying, "My directive still stands. I want you to look into the Belkins. No more arguing the merits of my decision. Got it?"

She didn't trust her voice and simply nodded. If her hands hadn't been supporting her weight on the desk, they would've been shaking. It wasn't until he'd left her space that she could breathe again.

What was it about that man? He turned her upside down and backward. If Virgil had made a similar request she would've been annoyed but not to the degree that she was when Jeremiah had asked. She'd just about jeopardized her job by openly defying her boss for no discernible reason aside from the need to be difficult. She cradled her head in her hands and groaned softly at her own idiocy. *Way to be mature, Miranda.*

She sat at her desk, forcing herself to regroup

and find a way to apologize for being a colossal ass for no good reason at all.

On second thought, it might be easier to quit.

JEREMIAH'S HEART THUMPED as if he'd just run a marathon when all he'd done was pick a fight with Miranda because he was out of sorts and scattered.

Was this a nervous breakdown? He wasn't sure, having never suffered from mental-health issues, but he supposed a person actually having those kinds of episodes rarely knew until it was too late. He squeezed his eyeballs with his thumb and forefinger, desperate to get his head on straight for a blessed moment so he could think of a way to apologize for his brusque behavior. Was it a big deal that she was second-guessing his instructions? On one hand, he was her superior; on the other hand, he knew she was probably chafing at his handling of the situation. He'd never been so uncertain in his life about a work relationship or how he should handle himself or his employees. *Well, you've never slept with one before...*

Astute observation.

He released a shaky breath. There had to be a way to get past the elephant in the room without bumping into it every time they were together. It certainly didn't help that, God love him, he'd probably choose to sleep with her all over again.

The memory of their one night together was scorching what little dream time he managed when he closed his eyes.

They'd tried the frank conversation—the adult way—and yet they were still unsure of how to act around one another, and now they were sniping at each other behind closed doors at the office. Not off to a great start.

But wait a minute…he had a valid concern that she was too close to the case to see what clues might be right under her nose. The benefit of his involvement was a fresh pair of eyes and that meant going over every stone that she'd either disregarded or overlooked. He wouldn't apologize for sending her to reexamine the evidence but perhaps he could soften his delivery. He leaned back in his chair and laced his fingers behind his head. He'd thought that coming to Alaska would help ease the tension he'd been living with since his life imploded, but it seemed he'd traded one type of stress for another. He needed a solution and he needed one fast.

Or else he was going to die of a heart attack before his first month was up. And that definitely wasn't on his agenda.

CHAPTER ELEVEN

MIRANDA PULLED UP to her parents' place and took a moment to draw a deep breath before heading to the house. Her parents lived on a sprawling piece of property that backed up to the mountainside. It was gorgeous, although there was an air of melancholy that seemed to shiver with the spirits of those long gone. Miranda had always wondered if perhaps the property had once been tribal land, but when she'd done a short, informal property search, nothing had come up. Still, as beautiful as it was, there was no denying that the mountain breathed and the trees whispered.

From the outside, one would never know the chaos housed by the large log cabin that her father had built himself before Miranda had been born. The cabin had been her father's gift to her mother when they'd been young, starry-eyed newlyweds. It was a little worse for wear as her father had all but given up on maintaining the place, choosing instead to stay in his shop a few hundred yards away, but at least from the outside, it still looked like home.

Miranda eyed the house, chewing her lip in trepidation. She never knew if it was going to be a fight, a tense altercation or just plain uncomfortable when she spent time with her parents, but she could always count on it being unpleasant. She didn't have the kind of relationship most people shared with their parents; there were no joyous homecomings with laughter around the table or merry holidays filled with memories-in-the-making for the Sinclair family. At least not anymore. The Sinclairs had always been a little different, putting the *fun* in *dysfunctional* she'd always liked to say, but after Simone's death the fabric of their family unit shredded under the pressure of their grief.

And as the months turned into years with no answer or closure into Simone's case, a cancer had begun eating away at the Sinclair family that none had been equipped to battle.

Her mother became more emotionally closed off; her father had retreated into his own drugged world; her brothers had split.

But family was family and Miranda couldn't ignore her parents as easily as her brothers did. Heaven help her, she wished she could.

The screen slamming on the back door as her mother went to pull clothes from the line made Miranda want to back up and drive away. Dealing with her mother was emotionally exhausting and Miranda wasn't sure if she was up to sparring with the woman today. Invariably, her mother always managed to make Miranda feel as if she were the worst mother, a terrible provider for her son and an even worse sister because she couldn't get Trace or Wade to come home more often, or at all. Miranda wasn't sure how it happened that she became the scapegoat for their mother's pent-up ire but she was a convenient target.

Her gaze strayed to the shop where her father was likely holed up and contemplated popping in to see her dad first. When she was younger, her father had supported the family with his wood carvings. He had unparalleled skill with a chisel and a piece of wood. Zed's carvings could be found at the best shops all over town. But that wasn't the case any longer.

Not quite ready to face her mother she detoured to the shop. She knocked on the door and then let herself in. "Dad?" She peered into the smoky haze that drifted on the cool air inside the shop and followed the source of the smoke. She found her father in his ratty recliner, a rolled marijuana cigarette between his fingertips. "Hey, Dad," she said, taking a seat as far away from the smoke as possible. At one time, she'd thought her father was the most handsome man in Alaska with his long thick hair that had dusted his shoulders in soft waves. But now his hair had grown lank with long strings of gray threading through the tangled mess. Most times he kept it scraped back in an elastic tie at the base of his neck, like today. She tried not to let her disappointment in his lack of effort permeate her voice because she didn't want to fight. Now and then, she simply missed the man her father had once been. "How's it going?"

Her father, a man who used to be strong as an ox with thick, ropy muscles and a quick laugh, was a shadow of his former self. Sometimes Miranda had to stare really hard to see past the years of grief, anger and general apathy brought on by his marijuana abuse to see the man he used to be. God, it broke her heart. This was the reason her brothers stayed away. It was hard to reconcile the knowledge that their parents were irrevocably broken because then Miranda and her brothers might have to admit that perhaps they were broken, as well.

"I talked to Trace."

At the mention of his son's name, Zed shrugged but there was latent anger behind his disinterest. "Yeah? What's he up to?"

"He's on a job. He said he's going to visit soon."

"We'll see."

Miranda didn't know why she even mentioned Trace's name. Both Trace and Wade had abandoned the family—at least that was how their father saw it.

"Mom said she was worried about poachers on the property?" Miranda tried steering the conversation to safer ground. It was sad that the topic of poachers was considered neutral territory for her family. Her father grunted in response and Miranda took that to mean either he agreed or he didn't care. "Have you seen any tracks?" she asked.

"No." He took a short draw off the cigarette, held the smoke in his lungs for a few moments and let it out slowly. He paused to remove a few bits of stem from his mouth and said, "Your mother just needs something to bitch about. There ain't no poachers."

On most days Miranda wouldn't disagree. Her mother was a nagger but when she heard her father speak like that about her mother she winced. "Well, I'm going to go check around just to be sure. We still haven't caught those bear poachers from the last couple years. I don't want them snooping around this property." She glanced meaningfully at his pot stash and at that he grunted an agreement.

"Fair point."

That was as close as she was going to get to a verbal approval from her father. There was a time when she and her father had been close. He used to take her out squirrel hunting, fishing, and he taught her how to track. Now he seemed a stranger. Struggling to find common ground, she pulled a memory from her mind, one that always managed to make her father chuckle.

"Remember when you tried to teach Simone how to fish?" Simone had been such a princess; she'd squealed and shuddered when the time came to bait the hook.

Her father smiled, nodding. "She never was one for the outdoors. Preferred her fancy clothes and whatnot to trail dirt and bugs. Oh, she hated it." Zed closed his eyes, a faint smile remaining, his smoldering marijuana cigarette momentarily forgotten. "She was a terrible shot but at least I knew she wouldn't shoot her foot off cleaning her gun. Maybe with time she'd have gotten better."

Not likely. Simone hadn't been interested in improving her outdoor skills. She'd been more interested in her social life, boys and the latest fashions—none of which had interested Miranda in the least. For all intents and purposes, Zed had three sons, instead of two sons and two daughters.

Simone had pouted and whined whenever their father had insisted on family camping trips. Sleeping on a cot with a subzero mummy bag hadn't been her idea of a good time. Miranda had loved it. Three whole days of not having to brush her teeth or hair had been absolutely fabulous to Miranda when she'd been young. Simone had treated it as punishment, but the only ones who'd been truly punished were the rest of the family because they'd had to listen to her complain the whole time.

Zed's smile faded and Miranda sensed the end to any reminiscing. Neither of her parents had much tolerance for talk about Simone—no matter if the memories were good or bad—but sometimes it was the only way she knew to feel some kind of connection again. The topic of Simone was fraught with dangerous twists and unpredictable turns that could land a person tipped upside down emotionally within a blink of an eye. But sometimes, Miranda wished they could just remember Simone as she'd been—an imperfect human being—rather than the sainted princess whose life was tragically cut short by some psycho. Zed remembered his cigarette and took a short drag. Miranda could almost see her father retreating from life right before her eyes.

"I didn't get the job," she said, wishing her dad would offer something wise to make her feel as if he still cared. "They went with a guy from Wyoming. He's nice enough. Seems to know what he's doing for the most part."

Zed grunted in response but his eyes didn't open. Frustration and sadness welled in her chest and she wanted to rail at him for checking out and leaving his family to fend for themselves. When was the last time he'd shown an interest in anything aside from his marijuana cultivation? Maybe if she started offering her opinion on better ways to grow pot, her father might be interested in being a part of her life again. "Hey, Dad, do you want to go with me up the mountain and check and see if Mom's concern about poachers is valid? It's been quite a while since we went hunting or tracking together. I wouldn't mind the company," she offered, almost desperately. Zed's eyelids opened half-mast and wild hope sprang in her chest at the flicker of interest, but it died soon enough and took with it her patience.

"Another time," he murmured. "Maybe later…"

"Later when?" she countered beneath her breath. There was never a "later."

"Dad," she said, her disappointment sharpening her voice. "I think Wade and Trace would visit more if you would give up the weed. They don't like seeing you like this all the time." *And neither do I.*

"Those boys don't run my life. They can visit, or they can stay away—makes no difference to me."

Well, it made a difference to her. She was going crazy trying to run interference for all of the different personalities in the family so that no one collided with one another. And frankly, she was sick of it. "I just wish you guys would get along."

"Wish in one hand and spit in the other and see which one fills up faster."

"That's a pearl of wisdom," she muttered, irritated. "Don't you think you're too old for that crap anyway?"

Her father narrowed red-rimmed eyes at her. "You come here to bust my balls, girl? If so, don't let the door hit you on the way out."

Tears burned behind her eyes that had nothing to do with the smoke. She was a grown woman but somehow hearing her father speak to her that way reduced her to a small child again. She struggled to remember she was an adult and willed the tears away. "You can't stay in here and smoke your life away. While you're not paying attention, your wife is slowly trying to kill herself with all the crap she collects in the house. I need your help to get her to change."

"Ain't no one going to change your mother."

Frustration burned beneath her breastbone. Why was everyone in this damn family so difficult? She stood. "What's it going to take, Dad?" He held her stare, but the smoke had already softened the hard edge. He was slipping into apathy; his favorite place. She looked away with disgust. This was why Trace never visited. And why Wade couldn't stand to come home. Why was she the stupid one? "She needs help, Dad. And I don't know what to do. She won't listen to me. Stop burying yourself in this workshop, pretending that what you do isn't anything more than sell and smoke pot, and help me save her."

"You worry too much." A small smile lifted the corners of his mouth. As if she were amusing somehow. "It's good to see you, kid."

And just like that her invitation to stay had been rescinded. She was only too happy to leave.

JEREMIAH OPENED HIS hotel room door to find a long-legged, rangy-looking man staring back at him with a wide smile. "Can I help you?" Jeremiah asked.

"Miranda sent me. I hear you're in the market for a fully furnished studio apartment. I just happen to have one."

Jeremiah stared, trying hard not to judge a book by its cover, but the man did not look the type to own real estate. "It's true," he confirmed warily. "I am looking for a fully furnished apartment. How do you know Miranda?"

"Oh, we go way back. My sister, Mary, works with her at the fish-and-game office with you. But I've known Miranda my whole life. Went all through school together." He stuck his hand out. "The name's David, but everyone calls me Otter." Jeremiah accepted the handshake. Otter smiled. "I'm happy to help out a friend of Miranda's, who also happens to be my sister's boss. I figure it's a win-win."

Jeremiah smiled. The man was friendly, he'd give him that. What the hell, he'd rather live anywhere than in this motel. "I'd love to take a look if you don't mind. That would be really nice of you."

"It's nothing fancy but it'll keep you warm and dry."

Jeremiah's grin widened. "Sounds good to me."

Otter wrote down the address and handed it to him on a slip of paper. "I'll be there today to put in a fresh coat of paint on the walls if you want to come by and take a look. The rent is five hundred a month. Due on the first. There's also a five-hundred-dollar deposit."

Seemed reasonable. "I'll be sure to stop by. Thanks for the offer."

"Thank Miranda. She is the one who made the suggestion. And I was happy to jump on it."

Jeremiah folded the small slip of paper and pushed it into his pocket. Considering Otter knew Miranda so well, it was a struggle not to pry. He wanted to say that he would venture into casual conversation about any of his employees but he knew that wasn't the case. He wanted to know more, simply because he wanted to know more. There was really no way to sugarcoat his reasoning or twist his motivation into something that it wasn't. "I'll be sure to thank her."

Otter smiled and went on his way, leaving Jeremiah to wonder why Miranda cared where he slept at night. She obviously had gone out of her way to find him a place to live, which suggested that she cared about his welfare on some level, right? He shook his head with a chuckle at his own internal blathering. Why was he reading more into this than the situation warranted? He didn't need to guess how Miranda felt about him. He already knew: he was an unfortunate one-night stand that was proving to be a thorn in her side.

Let's not overthink things, he warned himself. Besides, he was totally fine with how Miranda felt because it wasn't as if he were hoping and pining for a relationship with the difficult woman. Even if he weren't her superior and the way was free and clear to bed her every night, the fact remained that she had a personality as soft and cuddly as a hungry bear emerging for the spring.

Heaven help the man who set his sights on Miranda Sinclair for anything more than a few hours of fun. And he was not that man.

Fact was, no matter if she was the sweetest, most caring and kind and amiable sort of woman who could cook as well as his mother and was otherwise the perfect person to be around, Jeremiah couldn't bring himself to take things further with Miranda Sinclair for one reason: her son.

He hated that he was that sort of coward who would backpedal at the mere idea of having a child in his life again but he couldn't run from the truth. He was a coward. The thought of putting himself in an emotionally vulnerable place like that gave him an instant case of the shakes, and as much as he liked to think of himself as a strong person, he just couldn't go there with Miranda, because with a woman like her, he could see himself wanting more than a coworkers-with-benefits deal. He'd want everything she had to offer and then some.

Thankfully, Miranda wasn't the type to make the offer.

Crisis averted.

Sort of.

CHAPTER TWELVE

MIRANDA TOLD HERSELF her interest in Jeremiah's living situation was purely casual, but she hated to admit that she had a hard time knowing that Jeremiah was going to be stuck at the local equivalent of a roadside motel if someone didn't intervene on his behalf. The man looked as if he hadn't had a decent night's sleep since he arrived, and if she seemed concerned, it was simply human nature to care about someone's well-being.

"So I hear our boss took Otter's offer and moved into that studio apartment he has for rent," Miranda said, making casual conversation ostensibly while running a few copies. Mary's desk was located close enough to the copy machine to chitchat while the machine did its job.

Mary turned and smiled. "Yes! He sure did. I'm so glad you mentioned it. Of course, all you'd have to do is say the word and Otter would make it happen because he thinks the sun and stars rise in your eyes," Mary teased, causing Miranda to roll her eyes.

She'd tried to gently tell Otter it was never

going to happen between them but he was a determined sort and simply took her rejections as future opportunity to try again. He was "wearing her down," as he put it.

"Anyway, he took the day to get settled," Mary added. Miranda nodded. So that was why he wasn't in the office, she mused. Suddenly Mary frowned in thought. "Do you ever wonder why a good-looking guy like Jeremiah is still single? Seems to me that either he's gay or there's something terribly wrong with him."

"Maybe he has a wife somewhere," Miranda said.

"Where?" Mary blinked. "You mean back in Montana?"

"Wyoming," Miranda absently corrected, then shrugged. "Or at least that's where I think he's from."

"Wyoming. That sounds right, now that I think about it. Well, if you ask me, long-distance marriages rarely work out. The whole point of getting married is to have someone to cuddle with at night."

"Cuddling is overrated." Miranda deliberately chose to ignore the fact that she had, indeed, cuddled with Jeremiah and found the experience… tolerable. No, better than tolerable, she admitted grudgingly. It'd been amazing. Best night of sleep she'd ever had. "I prefer the bed all to myself."

"Not me. I like to snuggle in real tight," Mary said, giggling. "Plus, when it's cold outside, there's nothing better than a nice warm body to heat you up."

That was what *Mamu* said, too. "Not everyone is cut out for that kind of commitment," she said.

"Oh, pooh to that. You just haven't found the right person to cuddle with. When you do, you'll wonder why you waited so long."

"And what is the color of the sky in Fairy Tale Land?" Miranda asked, batting her eyelashes at Mary before crossing her eyes and sticking her tongue out.

But Mary was undeterred and smiled beatifically. "Someday you'll know, too. Mark my words. Fate has a way of working these things out. You wait and see. Maybe it's even Otter!"

Ugh. Mary was an incurable romantic that no amount of sarcasm could affect. "It's not Otter," she assured Mary with a shudder. "You know I would destroy someone as sweet as your brother. If there's someone out there for me, that person would have to know how to shoot a gun at the very least. Otter isn't what you would call the outdoorsy type."

"True," Mary agreed with a sigh. "Poor Otter. He's more of a city boy than a rugged Alaskan." A coy, delighted smile followed as Mary added,

"Unlike my Jim. He can split a round of wood with one chop."

Mary was newly married to her second husband and Miranda could fairly see stars in her eyes whenever Mary talked about Jim. Their gooey lovefest was cute—if you liked that sort of thing—which Miranda did not, and it certainly didn't make Miranda feel compelled to seek out the same. She scooped up her papers and smiled brightly, saying, "Well, sounds like he's a handy guy to have around when it's time to chop a couple of cords. Did you happen to notice if the permits came through for the Dickens Trail Excursions?" Miranda asked, eager to change the subject before Mary started in on her for still being single in spite of plenty of offers to put a ring on her finger. "They usually come in by now and I haven't seen them."

"No, not yet. That's odd, isn't it?" Mary agreed. "All the expedition outfits usually have their permits in by now."

"Yeah, I'll give them a call and remind them. Maybe it slipped their minds."

"Maybe. Probably," Mary added definitively. "When there's so much going on, things slip through the cracks."

Miranda nodded and returned to her office with her papers. It was moose hunting season but the fish-and-game office always held a Women's

Outdoor Training course and they were gearing up for the promotional push, which included putting flyers into the mail along with a seasonal calendar of events. It was busywork that Miranda hated but it was a job that needed to be done.

Perhaps the reason she hated office busywork was because when she had no choice but to complete a menial task, her brain traveled to places that she'd rather not visit.

Most days she felt completely competent and able to face any challenge—unless it involved Talen. Her boy was her Achilles' heel and she worried that she was screwing him up like her parents had obviously screwed her up somehow.

She had to be mother and father for her son and it was a tougher gig than she'd ever imagined it would be. Sure, the job came with unbelievable sweetness but there were days that she felt lost and confused about everything except the fact that she was doing everything wrong.

She leaned pretty heavily on *Mamu* for advice, seeing as her own mother wasn't a beacon of motherly input, but sometimes she wished she had someone else to help shoulder the weight of all that responsibility.

Ha! Miranda shook herself from the muck of her own melancholy and called herself on that thought. *Like you'd want someone else telling you how to raise your son?* Not likely. Be thankful Johnny wasn't around any longer to put in his two cents about how to raise a child, she reminded herself with a derisive smirk at her own conversation. This was why she didn't spend too much time in her own head—it was too cluttered with junk to navigate safely.

JEREMIAH FINISHED UNLOADING the last of his meager belongings and felt a sense of relief. No more sounds of neighbors' activities—both carnal or otherwise—to rouse him from a fitful sleep and no more choking down terrible instant coffee as he tried to force his eyes to open after a less-than-restful night.

It was a nice enough place, nothing fancy just as Otter warned, but that was fine with Jeremiah. He'd had the fancy house back in Wyoming— a chalet-type monstrosity that he'd gladly given his ex-wife in the divorce settlement—and the simple accommodations appealed to his desire to start fresh.

Here there was nothing remotely connected to his life in Wyoming. Nothing of Tyler, either. He'd brought a few framed photos in the move but they remained tucked away in the boxes. He didn't have the heart to stare at his son's precious face smiling back at him, knowing the boy was gone forever. Jeremiah scrubbed his face with his hands and rubbed the grit from his eyes that seemed a permanent part of his body now. He never felt rested; never felt at peace.

Except once.

His fatigued mind tripped over the boundaries he'd put in place and stumbled into the memory of lying with Miranda—a virtual stranger—sleeping soundly with her in his arms.

How bizarre was that? What weird psychology was at work in his brain that the only sleep he'd managed to catch in the past few months was when he'd been curled up with a total stranger?

Maybe it was delirium setting in but for a split, almost wildly reckless moment, he pictured asking Miranda if she wouldn't mind becoming his sleeping partner.

No sex—just sleep.

He let that notion sink into his brain for a moment and then he barked a laugh at how utterly ridiculous the idea was.

Sleeping partner. He couldn't imagine a more inappropriate partner for such an arrangement. He had a feeling Miranda would rather engage in physical intimacy than something so personal as snuggling up to someone.

A sigh escaped him and he scratched an itch at the back of his neck as he tried to shake the nonsense from his mind. Miranda was his employee. Nothing more. Leave it at that.

Besides, what did he truly know about her?

Not much. She was notoriously private and a bit standoffish with personal details. He knew more about Mary—thanks to Otter's attempts to talk up his sister to her boss—than he knew about Miranda aside from the sexual details, which seemed seared in his brain.

Such as the sweet beauty mark on her left ass cheek. One tiny, bluish dark spot on her perfectly taut and rounded behind that made him want to kiss it right before he drove himself deep inside her, straining against the delicious, enveloping liquid heat that threatened to dissolve his bones from the inside out.

Sweat beaded his forehead and his heart rate quickened. His hands flexed, as if itching to feel Miranda's silky skin beneath his palms, and his jeans tightened as his penis stirred with the memory. Was he a terrible person for wanting to touch her again? For wanting to pull her straight into his arms and plant his tongue into her mouth? He groaned and realized there was no help for it. Something had to be done about this raging, inappropriate desire or else he'd end up doing something stupid and reckless.

With a grim smile, he detoured purposefully to his bedroom and dropped onto the bed as he unzipped his jeans. His hand seemed a poor substitute for the real thing, but as he closed his eyes and pictured Miranda, he knew it was as close as he'd allow himself, so he might as well make the best of it.

Maybe if he wasn't so pent-up with frustration, he could get over this dangerous attraction.

But as he pictured Miranda, flush with desire, moving her body in time with his, he knew with a certainty—Miranda was in his blood.

And he didn't know what to do about it.

"THANKS FOR THE heads-up for the quality renter," Otter said, surprising Miranda at the school when she went to pick up Talen and take him to day care.

Miranda glanced around in confusion until she saw Otter and smiled. "No problem. Otter, what are you doing here at the school? You don't have kids."

"Mary asked me to pick up Hannah," he said, explaining. "Something about delivering flyers to the post office before cutoff, and I'm always happy to spend time with my niece. I love kids," he added. "Can't wait to have a few of my own."

She smiled. "You'll make a great dad, Otter."

Miranda's benign compliment made Otter beam and she could almost see the wheels turning in his head. She withheld a sigh. She wished she could see Otter in any other light aside from a friend because he'd be a great father—and Lord knew, Talen probably needed a male influence at some point—but she just couldn't see herself knocking mukluks with the guy.

"I appreciate you helping out Jeremiah. I'm sure he's glad to be out of the motel."

"Seems like a decent guy. Happy to help out a friend." Miranda let the conversation dwindle but Otter seemed desperate to continue to chat. She waved at Talen and hoped her son booked it over to her so she'd have an excuse to split. "So, Miranda…I was wondering…"

"Oh! I'm sorry, Otter, but I really have to get going. Tight schedule today." Otter nodded, shuttering his disappointment behind an accommodating smile, and Miranda felt guilty but not guilty enough to continue on with a conversation that she knew would end up with an invitation for drinks or dinner. She hated to hurt Otter—he was a good guy but not the right guy for her.

The truth of the matter was…there was no guy who would ever be right for her. She was damaged goods in that department and she didn't have the patience to try to sort out the broken parts just to see if she was capable of holding a decent relationship together. Ugh. Just the thought made her feel all twitchy inside.

"Catch you later, Otter!" She grasped her son's hand and quickly walked away.

Otter, I'm doing you a favor.

Miranda would eat someone like Otter alive

and spit out his bones. And she couldn't bring herself to be that cruel.

She might play fast and loose with moral boundaries but she knew when the stakes were simply too high to ante up.

CHAPTER THIRTEEN

JEREMIAH WAS MORE than glad when his meeting with the department heads came to a close. Administrative meetings were never his favorite part of the job, but it came with the paycheck, so he didn't complain.

Stuart Olly, his immediate superior, came to him with a smile and shook his hand vigorously, almost painfully, and Jeremiah countered with a forceful squeeze of his own. Stuart grinned and nodded, pleased with Jeremiah's understanding of the unspoken code of appropriate handshakes for men. "How's the new office?" he asked. "Settling in all right? No one giving you trouble?"

"New office is great. My team is well seasoned and do their jobs without a lot of hand holding needed. I appreciate that in a team as it frees me to attend to other more pressing details."

"Excellent. Well, not to speak badly of Virgil but he wasn't exactly a go-getter, if you know what I mean. He preferred to keep his head down and simply do his job without anyone bothering him. However, I'd like to see you take the Homer office in new directions. No more running under the radar."

"What did you have in mind?"

"I don't know. Impress me."

"Well, one of my team is tracking poachers who are possibly running a black-market poaching ring to sell bear parts illegally. She's been asking for more resources but with the budget being as tight as it is…you can imagine how quickly her requests have been shot down."

"Poaching…grim business and not particularly what I'd had in mind, but if she managed to catch these poachers, it could make for some good publicity."

"Oh, are we looking for media-friendly stories to pitch to the local news?" Jeremiah asked, half joking, but when Stuart didn't laugh, Jeremiah realized that his boss's request to impress him had come with a specific set of requirements. "If we managed to catch the poachers, it would look good for the Department of Fish and Game," he added cautiously. "But from what I've read in the reports, we're dealing with a highly organized and sophisticated operation. It's going to take more than just a few hours to wrap the case up with a nice pretty bow."

Stuart smiled and rested his hand on Jeremiah's shoulder. "Make it work. I know you will. I look forward to your progress report. Out of curiosity, who's your lead investigator on the case?"

"Miranda Sinclair."

Stuart's easygoing expression faded into a worried scowl and Jeremiah wondered how Miranda had locked horns with the older man. "Is that a problem?" Jeremiah asked.

"She's a loose cannon who doesn't respect authority. It's a wonder she hasn't managed to lose her job yet. Virgil was too lenient on her. I hope you'll get her in line more effectively than he did."

"I don't know her well but she seems a valuable asset. Everyone on my team raves about her tracking skills."

"She's fair in the field—not as good as her brother Trace, which is why she didn't go into Search and Rescue same as him—but she's got absolutely no respect for authority and she's got no problem with cutting her nose to spite her face. Honestly, when she applied for the director position, I had to do a double take. I wasn't sure if her application was meant to be a joke or if she was serious."

"Why wouldn't she be serious?" Jeremiah asked, mildly offended for Miranda's sake. It appeared to Jeremiah that Stuart had a significant prejudice against Miranda and he'd like to know why. "She's smart and capable. I've looked through her file and, yes, she's passionate about certain subjects, but she's a solid employee. She has her bachelor's degree from University of Alaska and she's motivated to see positive changes in her work environment. Forgive me if I seem out of line but…I prefer a passionate employee over one who is apathetic."

Stuart regarded Jeremiah for a long moment, then said, "She's a beautiful woman, no doubt about it. But keep your wits about you when it comes to Miranda Sinclair. She's a man-eater. Don't kid yourself about that."

"I think you misunderstood my intent—"

"You wouldn't be human if you didn't notice what was right beneath your nose, but trust me when I say she's not the kind of woman you take home to Mother. Just some friendly advice from someone who's been burned by a beautiful woman in the past."

Jeremiah couldn't believe his superior was talking so freely about Miranda. Talk about playing fast and loose with the rules of professional conduct. Jeremiah fought to keep his voice calm and bury the agitation twisting his insides in a knot. His ire wasn't solely because the man was talking about Miranda, he told himself. Jeremiah would've been concerned about Stuart talking disparagingly about any of his team, but the fact that it was Miranda did poke him a little harder than he wanted to admit. *Don't put your foot in your mouth over something that's none of your business,* he warned himself. "You don't have anything to worry about. I don't believe in inter-office dating," he said firmly, choking on the hot words that wanted to spill in Miranda's defense. "As long as she continues to be a good employee, I don't care about her personal life."

"Good man. I knew you were the right choice for that office," Stuart said, oblivious to Jeremiah's discomfort. He patted him on the shoulder again and winked. "Keep me posted on any new developments with the poaching angle. I have a reporter I can call who will do the story up right, if you know what I mean. Good press is important these days. Smart to cultivate those relationships."

Jeremiah nodded and couldn't wait to leave. And he'd thought he'd left behind an asshole of a boss in Wyoming. Seemed he'd simply traded one for another.

MIRANDA WAS STUDYING a biologist report on migration patterns of the black bear when Jeremiah returned. She was curious as to how the meeting went, seeing as it was his first official meeting of the brass. Virgil had always returned looking beat-up and worried. Miranda hustled into Jeremiah's office, unable to stop herself. She wanted to know how he'd fared. "How'd it go?"

"Tell me about your relationship with Stuart Olly."

Miranda was taken aback by the question. "What relationship?"

"Just curious. He seemed to have some opinions about you."

Miranda bristled. "There is no relationship between me and Stuart Olly. What'd he say?"

Jeremiah seemed to think better of his line of questioning and dropped it. "Forget it. He gave me a soft go-ahead to pursue the investigation and the poaching as long as it doesn't affect the bottom line. Seeing as I can't hire anyone new to help, looks like you and I are going to be out in the field a bit."

She nodded, still processing Jeremiah's earlier comment. She shifted in discomfort, worrying that Stuart had shared personal biases against her for personal issues. For as big as Alaska was, sometimes the state felt too small for all the tongue wagging that went on about other people's business. "Why the change of heart?" she asked, trying to refocus on the important details. "Virgil always said that Stuart was notoriously tightfisted with the budget."

"Seems there's a good angle to exploit in the media if we manage to catch the poachers."

Ah. Made sense now. "Stuart loves being in front of the camera or quoted in the papers. Pardon my language but Stuart is a media whore."

A short smile lifted the corners of his lips as if he agreed and a moment of camaraderie passed between them that felt good. "Well, maybe Stuart's thirst for glory will play to our advantage. I say we should take whatever leg up we can find."

"Agreed." Miranda turned to head back to her desk.

"Hey, Miranda," Jeremiah said, causing her to pause on her way out. "I'm sorry for mentioning anything about Stuart. And trust me when I say that whatever his opinion is, it doesn't influence mine."

Miranda smiled. "Thank you, Jeremiah. I appreciate that." She could guess what Stuart had said about her as they had an unfortunate history that started way before he'd ever become part of Fish and Game in his current position. Let's just say, it hadn't ended well. She hated that Stuart had said anything at all to Jeremiah when her personal life had nothing to do with her work ethic. She graced Jeremiah with a smile and then returned to her office, troubled and buoyed by the conversation. She didn't like the idea of Jeremiah knowing too much about her.

There were simply some parts of her life that she'd rather forget.

CHAPTER FOURTEEN

"AND FURTHERMORE, MS. SINCLAIR, Talen has been exhibiting some aggressive behavior that we find of concern." Mrs. Higgens, the principal of Little Eagle Elementary School, pursed her lips on a pause as she regarded Miranda with the hard eyes of a raptor in spite of her advanced age. Mrs. Higgens had been around for a while and she had a memory like a steel trap. "You've done an admirable job raising Talen on your own, but considering the stock that Talen comes from—"

"Wait, what?" Miranda interrupted. "What do you mean the stock he comes from?"

"Well, if you recall, I remember what Johnny was like as a student and later as a young man. Sometimes that wildness is inborn."

"With all due respect, Mrs. Higgens, I think you're out of line. Johnny is not the issue, and furthermore, Talen is nothing like his father. I'm offended that you would even imply such a thing when Talen has never once had a behavioral problem before today. And furthermore, what's being done about the other kids who were involved?"

"I cannot discuss the disciplinary details of another student with you as that's confidential. However, I can say they are being disciplined as is appropriate."

"I'm glad to hear that. I'd hate to think that my son is being singled out simply because of who his father was."

"Of course," Mrs. Higgens said with a mild sniff. "Now, the fact remains that Talen hit another child, and thus in accordance with our zero-tolerance policy, I must suspend him for three days. These will be unexcused absences and he will not be able to make up any lost homework." Mrs. Higgens pushed a piece of paper across her desk toward Miranda. "Please sign here that you understand the punishment and the repercussions."

Yeah, she understood. And she doubted either of the two boys involved were being as harshly dealt with but that was a fight for another day. "I appreciate your fair and equitable handling of the situation," Miranda said with a false smile as she signed the paperwork. "Where is Talen now?"

"He's waiting for you in the nurse's office. You may sign him out as you go."

Miranda dropped her smile and went to sign out her son. When she saw Talen, his face was tear-streaked and he looked miserable. Her heart broke at the sight of him and she wanted to rail at whoever had managed to get under her son's skin enough to cause him to lash out in such an uncharacteristic manner. Her son wasn't a troublemaker. He was sweet and easygoing, traits he hadn't exactly gotten from her or Johnny but she'd been grateful just the same. She graced her son with a genuine smile and held out her hand. "Come on, buddy. Let's get out of here. I think there's a cheeseburger with your name on it. What do you say?"

Talen wiped at his nose and nodded. "I'm sorry, Mama."

"No worries, buddy. We'll talk about it over lunch."

They climbed into the Range Rover, and as Miranda headed for their favorite diner, she broached the subject of the fight. "So what happened? Clue me in because I'm a little bewildered over this whole thing. Talen, you're not a fighter as far as I know…did something change?" she asked, half joking. "Do I need to worry about you becoming the school-yard tough guy?"

"No, Mama." Talen's voice wavered but there was an edge to it that worried her. "I don't want to talk about it, okay?"

"Okay," she agreed against her better judgment as she maneuvered the Rover into a slushy parking spot. But she could only hold her tongue long enough to give their order to the waitress before she was touching on the subject again. "Here's the thing, Talen.... I have to know why you got into a fight today. That's so unlike you that I'm more than a little worried. Help me out, buddy. Tell me what happened. Please."

Talen sighed and looked away with a shrug. "It's boy stuff. You wouldn't understand."

Ouch. She pulled back, smarting from that one tiny statement. She'd known that phrase would likely come out of her son's mouth at some point in his life but she'd figured it wouldn't happen until at least the teenage years. Still, she wasn't ready to concede just yet. "Are you sure about that? I grew up with two older brothers. I know quite a lot about boy stuff. Give me a try."

Talen's lips tightened into a thin line as if he were holding back a hot comment, or worse, tears. Then he stared her straight in the eye and said, "Garrett Pollard said that my daddy was a no-good criminal who died in prison from a disease you get from sex. And you were the one who gave him the disease, 'cause you're a loose woman."

Miranda pulled back in shock. What a vile thing for a child to say. She stared, unable to believe something so horrid was being said to her young son by another child, which only meant that the other kid had heard it from an adult. "So you punched Garrett for saying that stuff?" she asked. Talen nodded sullenly. Miranda was mad as hell but she managed a smile for her son. "Well, I guess Garrett should be careful about when and where he runs his mouth. I'd say you taught him a valuable life lesson."

"You mean I'm not in trouble?"

"All right, I'm going to say this once, so pay attention, little man. I would never get mad at you for defending someone you love in a righteous battle. However, that's not a get-out-of-jail-free card for every altercation because violence isn't the answer in most cases. It takes a smarter man to use his words rather than his fists to get his point across. Understand?"

"I think so." Talen paused, then asked, "Was my daddy a bad man?"

What a loaded question. She cringed inside, wishing she didn't have to talk about Johnny at all, but her son deserved honesty for defending her honor in the only way his eight-year-old heart knew to do—by punching the lights out of a classmate. "Your dad was…troubled. He died in prison because he was serving time for drugs when another inmate attacked him with a home-made weapon. He did not have a disease of any sort. He got caught up with the wrong crowd and made some really bad choices. That's all, buddy." She reached across the table and grasped her son's hands in her own. "Listen, however troubled your dad was, that has nothing to do with who you are as a person. You are good and kind and sweet and I'm proud to call you my son. Okay?"

Talen broke into a shy grin and her heart contracted with pure love for the boy. "Thanks, Mama."

"Anytime." She smiled and allowed him to pull his hands free because their food arrived, but as they enjoyed their lunch, Miranda's enjoyment at spending time with her son was dampened by a small voice at the back of her head that worried her past actions were finally catching up to her, but not in the way she'd expected. She could defend herself without caring how others felt about her, but she couldn't fathom her son bearing the brunt of others' censure because of something she'd done.

In the past she'd slept with a lot of people and hadn't thought how her actions might affect her loved ones because she'd figured it was her business and no one else's.

It killed her to think that Talen had had to defend her against such a nasty rumor. What else were people saying about her? Trace's last admonishment came back to her as she slowly chewed her French fry. People were certainly talking about her. She'd never cared before, but now the knowledge gave her a hard pinch. If she were of a mind to change public perception, how would she even begin?

She supposed she could start by settling down.

Otter came to mind, and even as she felt zero interest in him sexually, she knew he was a decent man with a solid reputation around town as a good guy. He'd make a great father. But how fair was that to Otter that she would consider settling for a passionless relationship in exchange for stability and a veneer of respectability?

She hated herself for even considering such a thing but she'd do anything to protect her son—even if it meant reinventing herself in the eyes of an entire town.

JENNELLE WATCHED FROM the window as Zed traversed the yard, heading back to his shop, where he'd taken up permanent residence. She swallowed a sudden wash of bitter tears at the unfairness of it all and allowed the drape to fall softly back into place. My, how things had changed. She remembered a time when Zed couldn't take his eyes from her, followed her like a puppy and gave her gifts of freshly picked wildflowers that were the same wild blue of her eyes.

She squeezed her eyes shut and plucked an old memory free from her locked box.

"I could teach you how to shoot a gun," Zed offered, his boyish charm melting her heart even as she prepared to play coy. He was eighteen and everything she'd ever imagined wanting in a boy, but her girlfriend Stella told her she should never let a boy know right away that she liked him. And oh, goodness, gracious me, she liked him.

"And why would I need to know how to shoot a gun?" she asked, seemingly disinterested, but she flashed him a flirty look from beneath her lashes as she leaned against the base of a large tree. Everywhere around her was blooming with life after the harsh Alaskan winter had lost its grip and allowed summer to thaw the earth. It was nearly warm enough for shorts. *Nearly.*

Zed grinned and slowly advanced until he was close enough to grab and pull her in for a kiss but she simply waited and watched. "Every girl ought to know how to defend herself in case she gets into some trouble."

"And what kind of trouble could I get into?" she asked softly, gazing up at him, falling for this green-eyed boy that much harder.

"This kind," he said, dipping his head to capture her mouth in a soft but firm kiss. Trouble never tasted so sweet. She'd never kissed a boy before but she took her cue from Zed, and within a few minutes of experimentation Jennelle knew she'd want to do it again and again with him. When the kiss ended, Zed pulled away, his eyes at half-mast with a haze of burning desire, and she knew she probably looked the same. Her veins ran with liquid fire, and even though it was hardly warm enough, she wanted to strip her clothes and give herself to him completely. But he surprised her when his gaze cleared and he regarded her with a solemn expression that seemed to pierce her soul as he vowed quietly, "Jennelle Thoreau, I'm gonna marry you—that's a promise."

And she believed him. She gazed at him with adoration. In his eyes, she saw her future. Even though she was only fifteen, she knew they were destined for each other. "You promise?"

"I promise."

"What if I get fat or ugly?"

"You'll always be the prettiest girl to me."

"That's easy to say but hard to mean," she murmured. Her daddy could barely stand to be in the same room as her mama. She supposed at one time they'd been sweet on each other but not any longer. "You promise to always love me, Zedediah Sinclair? Promise me on your life?"

"On my life and then some."

She grinned and pulled him back to her. "Then I accept. I will marry you someday. And I will have your babies and keep your house as long as you keep your promise."

"Always."

Jennelle opened her eyes and found them wet with tears. Apparently, *always* had an expiration date.

Heart heavy and nearing a total breakdown,

Jennelle wound her way past towering mounds of who knew what, ignored the fact that she had to climb over piles that had since toppled from their original location and escaped into the sanctity of Simone's room—to hide from the memories, both good and bad, of her life.

CHAPTER FIFTEEN

MARY POPPED HER head into Miranda's office, agitated and worried. "It's happening again. I just received a call on the hotline reporting a bear found on Woodstock's Trail. The kill is fresh."

Miranda's adrenaline spiked. She'd known it was simply a matter of time before the kills started again but she'd thought they might have another month before the carcasses started showing up. Maybe the poachers were getting greedy—and sloppy. She could only hope. "Thanks, Mary." She dashed around her coworker and ran into Jeremiah's office. "We just got a call on the hotline. A bear kill. You said you wanted to help. You coming with me?"

"Right now?" He appeared stymied. She could appreciate that it wasn't as easy for him to drop everything and go bounding after a lead, but at the moment she didn't care about the logistics. He regarded her critically. "How far away?"

"You don't have to go." She started to leave and he called out to her. She stopped but her impatience showed. "Time is a luxury we don't have.

We've never had a kill this fresh, which means they're still in the area."

He nodded, giving in to her logic. "Let me get my coat." While he shut down his office and grabbed his coat and gloves, Miranda quickly made arrangements for Talen just in case she was gone longer than the day hours. *Mamu* would keep her grandson without complaint, something she'd never been able to count upon with her own mother. Not that she'd let Talen stay with her mother at this point even if Jennelle had offered.

Jeremiah met Miranda at her Range Rover. Neither wasted time and simply climbed in without conversation until they were rumbling out of the parking lot. "How fresh is the information?" he asked.

"Mary just got off the phone with the caller. I don't have a lot of details. But I know they've got to be close. They probably didn't expect the bear carcass to be found so soon. This might be our chance to actually catch the bastards."

"Let's do this, then."

Miranda hit the highway and started up the mountain. Woodstock's Trail was about a mile away from one of the sites where previous bear carcasses had been found. The poachers seemed to like to remain within a certain territory, although it certainly hadn't helped narrow the investigation as the area spanned miles. Dark ominous clouds boiled on the horizon as an unusually frigid storm promised the first serious snowstorm of the late fall season. Experience cautioned her to let this one go due to the storm but she couldn't. Nothing was going to stop her from catching the poachers this time. Jeremiah realized the weather was turning, as well. "Those clouds look pretty dark. How much time before they dump snow?" he asked.

"Not long," she admitted. "Let's hope we have some luck on our side."

"We might need more than luck," Jeremiah muttered. "We might need divine intervention so we don't get stuck in that storm."

"Don't be such a pessimist." She grinned. "This is probably the most excitement you've had in years. Enjoy it."

He barked a short laugh but didn't deny it. "Let's arrive alive," he advised, looking purposefully at her speedometer as she sped down the slick road. "Let's just say we catch them. What's your plan? Are you going to load them into the Range Rover and expect them to behave?"

"I have a gun and I know how to use it."

"Yes, I'm sure you do. However, you can't shoot the poachers. The perpetrators must be brought to justice and tried in the court of law with due process. Promise me you won't do anything stupid."

"Your definition of *stupid* and my definition of

stupid might not be the same," she warned. She wasn't about to make promises that she didn't know she could keep. She'd been tracking these poachers for two years. It was time to bring them down. And if they wouldn't come peacefully, they would come howling from a bullet lodged in their legs. "Listen, I know what I can and can't do within the parameters of the law. Why don't you radio it in? That way we have reinforcements."

"I can do that." Jeremiah grabbed the radio handset and called the ranger station. "This is Fish and Game director Jeremiah Burke. We're on the trail of possible poachers and we may need backup if things get dicey. Will radio our location when we assess the situation. Heading toward Woodstock's Trail."

"Copy that." The dispatcher's voice cracked a long line. "We've got a ranger on his way to haul the bear back to station."

"Copy."

Miranda smiled. "See, that wasn't so hard, was it?"

Jeremiah laughed at her cheeky comment. "Just drive."

They left the highway and started up the service trail. The road became muddy and ugly, necessitating four-wheel drive. Fifteen minutes later they came upon the base of Woodstock's Trail and parked the vehicle. They'd have to walk from there. Miranda shouldered her pack and grabbed her gun as they struck out toward the location of the bear carcass.

Miranda became laser-focused, looking for any clue, any sign of the poachers. She looked for broken branches, disturbed soil, anything that might lead them to the bear killers. Unfortunately, it was a fairly popular trail and there were plenty of old and new footprints that traversed the ground. It was like looking for a particular blade of grass in dense underbrush but she refused to let the odds get her down.

They found the bear, mutilated for its parts, and Miranda felt a familiar rage for the desecration. "They ought to be drawn and quartered themselves," she muttered, examining the evidence. Blowflies buzzed around the spilled entrails, doing their natural job within the circle of life, but the low buzz always reminded her of something else. Dead things, animal or human, emitted a certain scent signature that flies responded to. Flies had already begun to land on Simone's battered face as her sightless eyes stared into the slate-gray skies when Trace had found her. Miranda had come upon the clearing with Trace waving away the flies from their baby sister's face and silently crying. It was the first—and last—time she'd ever seen Trace cry.

Miranda rocked back on her heels, needing a

moment. Jeremiah noticed the sudden change and looked at her with concern. "Are you okay?"

She offered a shaky laugh and waved him away. "I'm fine. Just lost my focus for a minute." She took a step away from the carcass, careful not to disturb the area, and began looking for any clues left behind. As with the previous bear mutilations, the perpetrators had either been very brazen or they didn't care if someone came along to find their kill. And once again, they'd left behind little to track. "Damn it." Miranda scanned further up the trail. "Let's tag the bear with a marker and then head up the trail a bit farther. They can't be that far. The body is still warm."

"You think that's wise?" Jeremiah looked up at the sky. "The storm is coming fast."

"You can head back if you want. But I'm not leaving—not when we're this close."

Jeremiah met her gaze. "You're not going up in those mountains alone. That's foolish. You promised me you wouldn't do anything reckless or stupid."

"And I told you that your definition of *stupid* and my definition of *stupid* might not be the same. This is the first time that we've had such a fresh kill. They could be just up around the bend, maybe a mile out. I'm not walking away."

Maybe it was reckless; she wouldn't know as she was running on pure adrenaline. All she knew was those poachers were out there, laughing at her expense. This was her chance to be the one with the last laugh.

"Are you with me or not?"

Jeremiah shouldered his own pack and shook his head grimly when he realized she was deadly serious. "All right. Give me a minute to call it in. Can you do that?"

She was anxious to get moving but she could give him that. "Make it fast." She felt squeezed by time; every ticking second was one second gained by the poachers. She was going to nail those bastards to the wall.

That was a promise.

JEREMIAH STRUCK OUT behind Miranda, careful to walk where she walked. Her gaze scanned the ground, the trees, looking for anything that might give away the direction the poachers had gone. Jeremiah silently marveled at her skill. What appeared as nothing more than dirt and forest cover appeared as a faint trail to her trained eye. There were times when she would stop and study the ground as if the trees were speaking to her before pushing on with renewed vigor. He envied her boundless energy and he was grateful he'd spent time in the gym as part of his routine when he'd transitioned from fieldwork to administration otherwise she would've left him in the dust.

They passed a small hunter's cabin and he remarked on it. Miranda answered without stopping, "It belongs to Search and Rescue. It's fully stocked with canned goods and firewood. If tourists get themselves turned around, they can wait it out until help arrives. It's also a restocking station for Search and Rescue if they're up here on a rescue and far from resources. Come on. We have to keep moving."

As the day progressed and their feet ate up the miles, the horizon began to swallow the sun and bite by bite the air took a sharp turn into bitter cold as the storm became a certainty. It'd been a long time since Jeremiah had done any fieldwork. His bones protested but he never slowed. Like Miranda, he was riding on adrenaline. He wanted to catch the poachers, too. Not because his boss wanted the good publicity, but because it was the right thing to do. Miranda had been working hard, putting her life and career in stasis so she could chase down these perpetrators, and he wanted to catch them for her sake. Miranda was like a woman possessed. She didn't seem to feel the cold or recognize that they had traveled too far on the trail to make it back to the vehicle before dark. When the first snowflake floated down from the sky Jeremiah knew they were in trouble.

He stopped, breathing hard. "Miranda, we have to turn around."

Miranda stopped and turned to face him, her nose reddened from the cold, her breath pluming before her. "We have to keep going. We're close."

"It's beginning to snow. We'll lose the trail once it starts coming down hard. We have to turn around before we get buried in snow."

Miranda glanced away, scanning the forest until her eyes burned with the strain. She knew he was right. Already the snow was coming down with bigger, fatter flakes. "We are so close, I can feel it. What if they're just around the corner? I haven't lost the trail yet. They didn't cover their tracks as well this time. But if we stop, the snow will cover whatever trail they've left behind."

"Yes, but if we keep going we'll get stuck in the storm and die of exposure. Be smart about this, Miranda."

Already they were pretty far from the vehicle. They wouldn't make it back before nightfall. Walking in the dark while it was snowing was dangerous in and of itself. "We will catch them. Just not today," he said, trying to soften the blow of disappointment.

"No." Miranda's cry of frustration pierced his heart. But he couldn't let her go on. It was simply too dangerous. "Let's go."

Miranda's gaze cut away but not before he

caught the glitter of moisture. "Fine," she agreed with one final look down the mountain. She surprised him when she suddenly flipped the bird, presumably at the poachers, and muttered, "This is for you, assholes. I hope you slip and break your necks." She exhaled a sharp breath and readjusted her pack, moving past Jeremiah without further comment. He let her have her space, sensing she needed silence to process her disappointment.

But before they'd even hit a mile back, the skies unleashed a fury of white retribution for an unknown offense and the two found themselves in a bad spot. The snow came down harder and faster, quickly covering the ground and slowing their return. After an hour of struggling through the rapidly gathering snowdrifts, Miranda yelled to Jeremiah above the wind, "We'll need to make camp at the search-and-rescue station!"

He nodded and they pushed on, knowing they still had to make it to the station and it was probably another mile out. Jeremiah hadn't kept track of how far they'd gone. He cursed himself for not staying aware of his surroundings—which was something that had been drilled into him back when he'd been a young ranger. Guess he'd been behind a desk for too long to remember the basics. If they managed to survive this night, he made a vow to brush up on his survival skills even if he never planned to embark on such a foolhardy venture again. He knew they shouldn't have left without following proper procedure, without backup. He'd foolishly allowed Miranda's passion to overrule his good sense and now they both might pay the ultimate price. He couldn't feel his toes inside his boots nor his fingers in his gloves and he suspected Miranda was suffering the same but she wasn't about to admit it.

It was near whiteout conditions and they were nearly on top of the station when they finally saw it emerge from the blizzard curtain. "Thank God," he said, his teeth chattering hard. Miranda's hands were shaking as she pushed open the door, and they both stumbled inside, slamming the door behind them. Miranda found her way in the darkened cabin to a rudimentary shelf and lit the kerosene lamp while Jeremiah worked as quickly as his frozen bones would allow to build a fire in the cold grate. The kindling sparked and caught the dry oak, and within moments, a cheery fire blazed in the hearth, providing further light in the tiny shack. Jeremiah and Miranda stood before the flames warming themselves for quite a while, too cold to speak. The shack was well insulated, and before long, the heat from the fire had chased away the freezer-locker chill.

Jeremiah took stock of the small station. It was as simple as they came but, then, it wasn't made for luxury. It was made to save lives. A double bed was tucked in the corner and canned goods lined the wood shelves. He took a final look out the window and knew with a certainty that they weren't going anywhere tonight. Particularly when the radio was in the car and both their cell phones were dead.

Miranda sat on the bed, pulling her sodden socks from her wet boots and laying them to dry near the fire. She quietly watched the flames, disappointment and something else reflecting in her stare.

He knew she was beating herself up and he wasn't about to let her take all the blame. He went to her and placed a hand gently on her shoulder. She reluctantly met his gaze. "It's going to be all right. Neither of us knew the magnitude of this storm or how quickly it was going to strike. Let's just ride it out and start fresh. Okay?"

She accepted his attempt at comfort but then she pulled away. "It wouldn't have mattered. I would've gone either way. I guess that's the reckless streak everyone likes to point out. I'm sorry I got you wrapped up in this, too."

He wasn't sorry. Strangely, he was relieved that he'd chosen to tag along. If he hadn't, Miranda might've died on the mountain. "I wasn't a helpless victim. I chose, remember? Now, enough of this talk. Let's pick out dinner. I'm just hungry enough to think that canned sardines sound pretty good."

She chuckled in spite of herself and got up from the bed. "You're something else, Jeremiah Burke. Thanks for saving my ass."

He refrained from quipping, "It's the finest ass I've ever had the pleasure of saving" and accepted her gratitude with a smile as he held up the choice of two cans. "Canned corn and potted meat on crackers or peaches and canned halibut on crackers? Hell, I'm feeling adventurous…how about both?"

"Sounds good to me. Go wild, boss man, while I find the plastic forks."

Jeremiah opened the cans and grimaced at the slightly smoky scent of the canned halibut, and as he worked with Miranda to prepare a dinner of sorts for the two of them he realized with a start there was only one bed in the room. As his heart rate accelerated, he made a second realization that jolted him to his bones—he couldn't wait to sleep beside her one more time.

And that was bad. Very bad.

But he also knew neither had a choice in the matter.

Miranda caught his gaze and she realized his thoughts. "We can handle this, right? We're adults caught in a life-or-death situation. Nothing is going to happen between us."

He wanted to reassure her, but as her tongue snaked nervously along her sensually plump lower lip, his groin tightened and he knew it was going to be rough to deny each other. Still, he would do his damnedest. "We're adults. We can handle simply sleeping beside each other," he agreed gruffly. He gestured to their makeshift dinner. "Let's eat."

She nodded and they ate in silence—both knowing with a certainty that something likely might happen but they were going to fight it until they simply couldn't deny the attraction any longer.

Jeremiah exhaled as he chewed tersely. "It's going to be a long night."

"Tell me about it," Miranda agreed on a sigh. "A very long, *frustrating* night."

Amen to that.

CHAPTER SIXTEEN

MIRANDA FINISHED HER makeshift dinner and swished her mouth with a gulp of water before eyeing the bed as if it were the enemy. She started talking just to alleviate the tension in the room as she checked the blankets to ensure nothing creepy crawly was also sleeping in the bed. "I don't know why we're so freaked out about this. We're both adults and, besides, we're going to be wearing all our clothes, so it's not as if we're going to be rubbing up against each other naked." She forced a laugh at the idea. "I mean, it's just like camping, right? We're going to bunk up for necessity and be completely mature about the situation so that no one can say anything about it."

"Of course," he agreed. "But I think it's best to keep this to ourselves to avoid becoming the gossip of the week."

"Right. I mean, we don't need to explain to anyone what happened. We can just tell people that we went our separate ways after tagging the bear. No one needs to know."

Miranda ignored the improbability of her suggestion and clung to the possibility that it might work. She finished fluffing the thick insulated blankets and stood beside Jeremiah, staring at the bed, waiting.

"I'd prefer to sleep on the outside, if you wouldn't mind," Jeremiah said.

"I suppose for one night that'll be fine." Miranda took a deep breath and climbed into the bed, scooting over to the far side nearest the wall. She pulled the blankets to her chin and stared at the ceiling while Jeremiah climbed in beside her. Good God, she felt like a nervous teenage girl. She stiffened when Jeremiah's body pressed against hers. "We need to share the space," she reminded him with irritation.

"It's a very small space," he countered, equally irritated. "I don't think we'll be able to sleep on our backs. We'll have to spoon."

"Are you kidding me?" she asked. "I am not spooning you."

"It will simply save space and allow both of us to share body heat," he said. "I promise my suggestion is nothing more than being logical given the situation. Trust me, I'd rather be anywhere but lying beside you right now."

Ouch. "Is that so?" she said, grudgingly flipping on her side and allowing her backside to settle into the cove of his big body. "Well, hopefully you'll be able to suffer through one night."

There was a long pause and then Jeremiah said, "Don't take it the wrong way. I like the feel of you against me. That's the problem, Miranda. I like it too much. Before you get all screechy about not being interested in a relationship, I'm not looking for a girlfriend. But I am attracted to you and it'd make my life a lot easier if I weren't. And even though we are adults, it's not so easy to remind my libido of that fact when you're pressed up against me. That's all I'm saying."

Her face safely hidden from view, Miranda allowed a tiny smile. She knew how he felt because she felt the same. Why'd he have to be so handsome? She remembered in fresh detail how it felt to be touched by him, to feel him moving inside her, filling her to the point of near-delicious pain.

"And there's something else," he added softly, and she stilled to listen. "I haven't had a decent night's sleep since that night together and I'm exhausted."

"Me, too," she admitted on a whisper. "What does that mean?"

"I don't know. Let's get a good night's rest and think about it in the morning."

"Okay." She smiled and relaxed, her body toasty and warm and feeling wonderfully sheltered by Jeremiah. She almost wished they didn't have so many clothes between them. She wanted to feel his skin against hers but as she yawned she accepted that this was probably as close as they were going to get to a repeat of their time together. As she tumbled into sleep, Miranda thought this was something she could get used to…if things were different.

JEREMIAH'S ARM WAS wrapped firmly around Miranda's midsection and it felt completely natural to have her against him. His body settled into the lethargy of sleep, and within moments, he was oblivious, but his extreme exhaustion wreaked havoc with his mind and soon his REM sleep was filled with vivid dreams.

The Wyoming skyline filled his vision. He stood on a precipice overlooking a great prairie, the Big Horn Mountains rising like craggy giants from the grassy plains, sentinels from a time long forgotten. As far as Jeremiah's eye could see was a vast wild landscape, untouched by man, uncontaminated by electronic waste.

A sense of beginning filled him as he stared with wonder at what could only be described as a pristine, virgin land. This was the stuff of country and western music, ballads and cowboys.

A spire of smoke caught his attention. Within seconds, the smoke gathered and caught until the shrubs and grasses curled and disintegrated beneath the onslaught of the flames licking the mountains and threatening to destroy everything in the fire's path. Frightened animals charged and bleated, running for their lives as certain death rained down with orange fury. He watched in helpless horror as everything beautiful and free succumbed to the ravaging fire, leaving nothing but blackened destruction in its wake.

Jeremiah sank to his knees and found himself off the precipice and down in the destroyed valley. His hands dug into the charred earth, and charcoal stained his fingers. Tears wet his cheeks and he began to clear away the dead grass to the soil beneath. He continued to dig until his fingers sank into fresh, clean dirt that was cool and moist to the touch. He stilled as a butterfly alighted on his shoulder, seemingly incongruous with the bleak landscape. When he looked again, his fingers were clutching green shoots of grass that had poked their way through the hard crust of devastation.

And as quickly as things changed in a dream with no rhyme or reason, Jeremiah was kneeling before Tyler in a deep conversation, yet Jeremiah couldn't understand a word his son was actually saying. Tyler grinned as he chattered gibberish and Jeremiah fought the frustration of not being able to comprehend his son and simply went to pull the boy into his arms for a tight, desperate squeeze but his son was gone like mist dissolving in the harsh ray of sun.

"No!" Jeremiah fought the panic and the growing sense that he was slowly awakening. He didn't want to wake up if it meant his son wasn't there waiting for him. Tyler was alive in his dreams. Jeremiah wanted to stay. But sleep was losing its grip and the cobwebs of dreams were already dissolving, leaving behind a general sense of grief and sadness.

He awoke slowly to Miranda staring at him with concern. "You were yelling in your sleep," she said softly.

It was still dark; he must've dropped straight into REM as soon as his eyes closed with exhaustion. "I'm sorry," he said, pulling her close. He was grateful when she didn't resist or try to remind him that it was inappropriate. She rested her head on his chest and he held her tightly. He didn't care about the why or how but Miranda calmed the wild panic fluttering in his chest and he desperately needed something to cling to. The dream had left him on the edge of sobbing wildly when he hadn't felt that overwhelming tidal wave of grief in a long time. It scared him that he could tumble so easily into the abyss when he'd thought he'd left that far behind.

"Are you okay?"

"I'm fine," he lied. "I'm fine."

If she didn't believe him, at least she didn't call him on his falsehood.

And he was grateful because if she'd pressed just a little, he wasn't sure what might've been unleashed. All he knew was it wouldn't have been pretty.

CHAPTER SEVENTEEN

MIRANDA AWOKE SLOWLY. Disorientation caused her to panic until she felt Jeremiah beside her. She settled against the comforting bulk of his body and allowed herself to enjoy something that had never before given her joy. Snuggling, cuddling, *spooning*...simply weren't part of her repertoire. But with Jeremiah, such intimacy felt normal.

She wanted to ask him about his dream. Something had caused him to cry out in his sleep. She knew it wasn't her business but she couldn't bring herself to forget.

"How long have you been awake?"

Jeremiah's sleep-roughened voice gave her a silent thrill. She smiled. "Long enough to know that you snore."

"Everyone snores in their sleep."

"I wouldn't know. I never let people sleep over, so no one has ever complained."

"That makes two of us."

She arched an eyebrow as she rose up to meet his gaze. "Is that so? So back home in Wyoming were you a love-'em-and-leave-'em sort of guy?"

Jeremiah chuckled. "There was no loving being done. Before coming to Alaska and meeting you I'd been on a self-imposed dry spell, remember?"

Ah, yes. He had mentioned that he'd been purposefully celibate. Seemed a waste given how glorious his body was beneath those sensible desk-monkey clothes. "Why?" She shouldn't have asked but she wanted to know just the same. "You seem like a man with a healthy appetite. Were you punishing yourself for something?"

Jeremiah's easy smile faded and she sensed that she'd hit a nerve. He glanced away. "Not exactly. Life seems less complicated without entanglements, sexual or otherwise."

She did understand that. "Life is complicated enough, right?"

"Yeah."

"But sometimes the body needs a little release, though. Nothing personal, just biology."

"I guess I just learned to shut it down," he said. "Besides, I had plenty of work to keep me occupied. Made it difficult to date and I don't troll for one-night stands. Not my style."

"What was I, then?"

"You were different."

"How?"

"You just were."

As she gazed down at him, propped on her elbow while he remained on his back, she caught something vulnerable about him. There was something hidden deep, something that he protected from prying eyes. The mystery drove her crazy.

HE REGARDED HER with solemn eyes, pushing a lock of hair away from her gaze. "You have beautiful eyes," he murmured.

"You have a beautiful mouth," she countered softly.

She felt a pull toward him and she slowly lowered her mouth to his. Seconds before their lips met, a voice in her head reminded her why she shouldn't. She had good reasons to pull away, to stop. But none of her solid, logical reasons were stronger than her desire to touch and feel Jeremiah again. He was like a drug in her system and she was aching for a fix.

Miranda allowed Jeremiah to roll her to her back, never breaking the kiss as their tongues danced and tangled between them. She allowed herself to sink into the sensation of being protected and cherished as Jeremiah's touch ignited a firestorm of need and desire she hadn't known was smoldering beneath the surface.

Within moments they were tearing off their clothes, eager to feel skin on skin, heedless of how reckless they were both being. Jeremiah nuzzled her bare breasts, taking his time as he slipped a nipple into his hot and greedy mouth. She gasped and arched against him, clutching his head to her breast, desperate for more. Their bodies created their own heat as snow fell outside the tiny window, blanketing the world in blinding white. As the storm continued to rage, Jeremiah and Miranda allowed their pent-up need to overrun their good sense, openly delighting in the ways their bodies complemented one another.

"So perfect," Jeremiah groaned, sweat beading his brow as he moved above her, sliding inside her tight heat with one fluid push. He shuddered as he buried himself, taking a full fifteen seconds to enjoy the friction of that first thrust before flexing his hips as she met him, clasping her legs around him, driving him deeper. He gasped her name and she thrilled at the sound of it. She didn't remember the last time she'd lost herself with such abandon. Jeremiah brought out an animal in her that would not be tamed and she left scratch marks on his back, which he bore without complaint.

They rode the edge together until both arrived, crashing into oblivion and taking no prisoners as they fell back to earth. Miranda could barely speak, could hardly breathe, she was too buffeted by the pleasurable contractions squeezing every last moment of pure happiness from her body. When she finally dropped back into awareness of her surroundings and the man breathing heavily beside her, she knew with a certainty that so much more had changed between them this time.

And he knew it, too.

She swallowed, her throat dry from crying out, and he responded by reaching down on the floor to retrieve a water bottle she'd placed there before they'd gone to bed. She sat up and accepted the bottle without comment and simply drank deeply. She needed time to think. Time to process. She checked the storm outside and she could see that the snow hadn't let up, which meant they weren't leaving anytime soon. She'd give anything for a rescue.

A rescue from the pending moment.

Jeremiah looked fairly adorable with his mussed hair and his arm across his eyes as he tried to recover. The chill in the room pebbled his nipples and she was tempted to bend down and tease the hardened tips with her teeth just as he had done to her earlier. She shook her head to clear her thoughts but she was seduced by the scent and sight of the man lying beside her who was likely freaking out inside his head.

"We won't tell anyone."

"That might've worked the first time, not a second."

"It will if we make it work."

He dropped his arm and regarded her intently.

"I want you, Miranda. There's no getting around that fact." He swiveled his head straight to stare at the ceiling. His mouth curved in a fatalistic smile. "I'm not going to delude myself into thinking anything different."

"You make it sound like a death sentence," she groused, taking another swig of her water. "And maybe I don't want you, so your angst is unwarranted." His sigh told her he didn't believe her for a second and he was right; she wanted him like a little kid wanted cake. What a mess. "Let me save you the trouble. I'm not the right girl for you."

"I already know that, but for the sake of argument, what are your reasons?"

She grabbed her discarded clothing and began dressing. "Because I'm an emotional mess. My ability to screw up my own life is directly proportional to how quickly I could screw up yours if we were to try and make something real out of this."

"What makes you think you cornered the market on screwed up?" he asked with a sad but wry grin. "I know it won't work out between us. Doesn't mean I'll stop wanting you. That's where I'm at right now. I'm trying to find a way to deal with what I know to be true and what I know to be the worst decision I could possibly make for my career and my life."

She nodded. "Me, too." Well, not so much the

career part but definitely her life. "Maybe we could see each other on the side?"

"Meet in clandestine hotels out of town and hope and pray no one recognizes us?" His dark chuckle was answer enough to his own hypothetical. "That's not my style."

"Me neither."

"This is rich. The solution is staring us right in the face but neither wants to admit it." He met her stare and waited but she wanted him to say it first. He exhaled loudly. "We simply can't see each other. This has to be it. We'll have to chalk this up to an extreme situation and forget it ever happened as well as vow it will never happen again. I'm crazy attracted to you, Miranda, but I'm not going to jeopardize both our careers over something that neither of us is ready to entertain."

She nodded in agreement but felt hollow inside. Everything he said made perfect sense. So why did it feel wrong? It was official: she had a backward way of thinking. When she ought to feel solid about making the right decision, she felt cheated; when she ought to feel guilty, she felt a sense of freedom. She'd make some psychiatrist rich trying to unravel the yarns of thread in her head. "Okay." She supposed he was right. No sense in making bigger messes by trying to make something work that neither of them understood.

She watched as he dressed, silently mourning the loss of all that smooth, muscular skin on display.

After dressing, they put together a makeshift breakfast on the shelves and rekindled the fire in the grate. They ate in silence, both processing their own thoughts until Miranda broke the quiet with a question she couldn't quite stop wondering about.

"You were crying in your sleep. Before you deny it, I have to say I've figured out long before this moment that you're probably running from something. Why else would you uproot yourself and bring nothing from your previous life with you aside from a few clothes and shoes?"

Jeremiah stared, something flickering in his gaze that alternately frightened and drove her to know more, but he slammed the door on the conversation before she could press. "There are some things I'm not going to talk about. I left it behind in Wyoming and that's where it will stay. Please leave it there."

Miranda nodded. "Okay," she murmured, but she knew in her heart she couldn't let it go. Not now. She had to know.

THE CABIN WALLS were closing in on Jeremiah. He didn't blame Miranda for her curiosity but he couldn't bring himself to share that deep, dark pain lurking inside him. He could make love to her every day and night, sharing the utmost intimacy, but he couldn't share his grief over losing his son. He knew she wouldn't judge him—hell, no one's judgment weighed heavier than his own—he just couldn't allow himself to break down, because if he did, he didn't know if he'd be able to put himself back together again.

"We need a game plan. If we don't show up at the office today people are going to worry."

"The storm isn't letting up, but maybe if we could get to the vehicle, we could use the radio to call the station to come and get us."

"People are going to talk," she said, shaking her head as if there were no help for the questions they were going to face. She swore under her breath. "Damn freak storm."

"We can handle the gossip as long as we don't give it power. Don't act guilty."

"I'm not guilty. I don't regret anything," she said with a shrug, and he envied her attitude. She might not care what others said, but he had to care. If Stuart found out...his job could be on the line. His concerns must've become apparent in his expression for she softened and said, "I'll play it cool. Don't worry. I understand what's on the line. For what it's worth..." She hesitated as if unsure whether she wanted to share or not, and as he waited, she smiled, then said, "If there were a whole lot of different situations at play instead of the reality…you and I might make a decent couple. I mean, we're obviously compatible in bed and we share the same work ethic."

He agreed with a cutaway glance. "If only those were the only factors to consider."

"Yeah." She seemed disappointed in his answer. Had she been expecting something more romantic…more declarative? Before he could clarify, she'd moved quickly to the window, exclaiming with excitement, "The snow is slowing down. I think if we strike out now, we could make the car and radio for a pickup."

"Let's do it, then," he said, quickly donning his coat, gloves and gear. "The sooner we return to base, the better."

Miranda nodded and headed for the door but suddenly stopped and turned to face him so fast, he nearly bumped into her. "What's wrong?" he asked.

"Loaded question. Kiss me."

He stared into her eyes, questioning the smarts of such a move, but as her lips parted, ready and waiting, he didn't hesitate. He pulled her to him and swept his tongue inside her mouth, loving the tiny gasp she made that seemed so incongruous with her tough exterior. His touch gentled her wildness and he took pride in that it was *his* touch and no one else's that she craved. When he released her, they were both breathing heavy and heated from the inside out, tempted to touch each other intimately just one last time, but they both knew it wasn't wise and withdrew.

She opened her eyes and smiled warmly before turning on her heel and pushing out into the snowy landscape without looking back.

Jeremiah couldn't help the smile that followed even though he suffered a great sense of loss. He'd get over it just as he got over every great tragedy in his life—by burying himself in work. Getting over Miranda would be no different.

CHAPTER EIGHTEEN

MIRANDA AND JEREMIAH reached Miranda's vehicle and both groaned when they saw they had their work cut out for them. The road wasn't ordinarily maintained as a major thoroughfare and the freak snowstorm had done its best to bury the Range Rover. They started digging the car out using their gloved hands, working as quickly as possible so they could reach the radio. "This will teach me to run off half-cocked without checking to make sure my phone is well charged," she said, her teeth chattering.

"You and me both," he agreed, clearing away enough snow to crack the door open and slip inside. Miranda followed, and as soon as she could get her keys in the ignition, she revved the engine and turned up the heat while Jeremiah worked the radio. "This is Jeremiah Burke. We're at the base of Woodstock's Trail and we're snowed in. We're going to need a plow out here to free the vehicle. Over?"

"10-4. Everything okay? Rangers hauled the

bear carcass away but there was no sign of you or Miranda."

"We're all right. Just cold and ready to go home."

"Copy that. We'll send a plow ASAP."

Jeremiah sighed and returned the radio handset. "Now we just have to sit tight. It shouldn't be too long."

"Yeah. Maybe an hour, tops, assuming the grade isn't too iced over. Commence with the awkward silence while we wait."

At that Jeremiah laughed and she grinned, too. "So…what do you think of Alaska so far?" she asked with mock politeness and a sweet, fake smile.

"Aside from the occasional wiseass in the form of a beautiful woman, it's been great." The mood light, Jeremiah countered, "My one complaint…there seems to be a whole lot of yoga studios around here. Everywhere I look, there's some kind of überflexible person looking zen and mocking my stress level. It's a bit rude, if you ask me."

"What do you have against flexible people?"

"Nothing. Pure jealousy," he admitted. "And I hold true to the belief that nothing good comes from being able to fold in half. It's just not natural. Same rule of thumb applies to men and the splits. Just shouldn't be done."

Miranda laughed. "True. I've always wondered

how male dancers manage it without losing something valuable down there."

"Just not natural," he repeated with a shake of his head and a grin. "Now, a woman who can do the splits…"

"Hey now," she warned, and when he laughed his handsome face changed into boyishly cute, something she'd never noticed before. "You should show your sense of humor more often. It's a good look on you," she said.

"I have to give my employees something to complain about," he joked, then turned it around on her. "The same goes for you. You could show your lighter side now and then. You have a stellar smile."

Even though the compliment was benign, she blushed. She caught herself and rubbed at her cheeks as if she could rub away the evidence that his comment had flustered her. "I'm sure you say that about all the girls," she said.

"No. Not really." And just like that the conversation turned serious. It was as if there were two threads running parallel to one another—one was surface playfulness; the other was the deeper meaning behind the words they couldn't say. "You're hard on yourself. In the short time I've known you, you haven't given yourself an inch of slack. You work long hours—you prob-

ably work on your own time, too, so as not to
burden the OT budget—and you're passionate
about the things most people simply don't have
the energy to tackle, which shows that you're
driven by something. Who is Miranda when she's
not a federal employee?"

Miranda paused, a pithy answer on her tongue.
Who was she? Good question. "When I figure
that out, I'll let you know," she answered.

"I know you don't go home to anyone," he said,
pressing a little harder. "What are your hobbies?
What do you do for fun?"

"I do go home to someone," she contradicted
him. "My son."

"Right, of course," he said, forcing a smile.
Miranda sensed his immediate withdrawal even
before she saw his gaze shutter and slam shut.
"It's hard for me to switch gears and see you as
a mother," he said quietly.

"Why?"

"Selfish reasons," he admitted, looking away.

"Do you have something against kids?"

"No." But he seemed to choke on the words.
"Kids are a blessing."

Miranda suffered the distinct impression Jeremiah was only feigning interest but she didn't
want to insult him by stating as such on the off
chance that she was wrong. "I never would've be-

lieved that until Talen came into my life. I know I've done a lot of screwed up things in my life, but when I look at my son, I know he's the one thing I did perfectly right."

"How old is he?"

"Eight. And the love of my life. He's the biggest reason I don't allow anyone to get too close. He doesn't deserve a parade of different men in and out of his life as I try and get my life together."

"Admirable." He forced a smile. "If only all single mothers were so accommodating of their children's feelings and well-being."

What was wrong with Jeremiah? He was suddenly colder than a polar bear's paw. In fact, it might be warmer outside than sitting beside the glacial chill coming off Jeremiah. "You don't like kids," she said flatly, unable to hold back her disappointment.

He looked at her sharply, yet his gaze was distant. "I like kids just fine," he said, glancing at his watch. "What's taking that plow so long?"

"It should be here soon. Wow. Talk about running hot and cold," she groused. "You're worse than a PMS-ing woman. One minute you're all laughter and jokes, and the next, you're just a jerk."

"Our conversation was probably getting too familiar as it was. It's good to remember that we're colleagues, not friends."

"Well, we're sure as hell not friends with benefits, because it'll be a cold day in hell before I let you into my private life again." She crossed her arms, angry. No, not angry—insulted. And strangely hurt for Talen's sake. He didn't even know her son and yet he was acting as if she'd just told him that she'd caught a disease and it might be contagious. "What is your problem?"

"Nothing. Drop it."

"No. I'm not going to drop it. You're being rude."

"So be it. I'm rude and I'm also your boss, so drop it."

"You're my boss, but not the boss of me, so stick it up your keister." If she didn't think he might freeze to death, she'd kick him out of her car to wait for the plow. The idea of staying another minute in a confined space with the man seemed a fate worse than death. Or at the very least plain annoying. "Just when I was beginning to think you were different…"

Jeremiah closed his eyes, patently ignoring her dig, which only further incensed her, but she chose to swallow the rest of the tirade she felt brewing. Good, she told herself. This simplified matters by half. She'd been worried how she was going to deny herself his company when they'd plainly been so good together between the sheets, but now he'd taken care of that problem quite nicely. Thank you very much.

She certainly agreed with Jeremiah on one point—that stupid plow couldn't get here soon enough!

How COULD HE let his libido get in the way of the facts? They weren't two consenting adults without obligations and responsibilities and she wasn't available to him in any way possible. He should've been stronger than his desire and put a kibosh on the heat level between them the minute he felt it spark to life.

Miranda had a son. He couldn't imagine a bigger obstacle between them, and yet, in the moment, he'd completely blitzed past the fact because he'd been crazed with lust for the woman. He didn't want her to have a son and, therefore, his brain had conveniently shelved that information in the far back recesses of his mind.

He'd seriously screwed up this time. The rules had been tipped upside down and backward. Sleeping together the first time had been an innocent mistake, and the knowledge that she had a son hadn't come into play because they'd both agreed it couldn't happen again. Now he couldn't deny the attraction burning between them, which was a bigger problem than dealing with an unfortunate error in judgment.

He bracketed his forehead with his fingers, squeezing. Talen was younger than Tyler but close enough in age to have commonalities. He couldn't handle being around kids right now. Just couldn't face them knowing his was gone.

It was why he'd left his last job. A fresh start was a bonus and a really good excuse. The fact of the matter was, Jeremiah had been charged with overseeing the Junior Ranger program that his old boss had engineered knowing full well about his tragedy. He'd hated himself but he'd practically begged to be let off that assignment, to hand it off to someone else, but she'd been adamant. A part of him wondered if she'd hoped that he would quit, because immediately after he'd accepted the position in Alaska, the man she'd been seeing had been selected as his replacement. Jeremiah hadn't cared, though. He'd been ready to escape and he was glad to put Wyoming behind him. Besides, he figured the evil hag would realize soon enough that she'd been used to get the job and that would be punishment enough.

But now the woman he was insanely attracted to—that he'd harbored secret thoughts about pursuing in a legitimate fashion—posed a bigger issue in his life than he was ready to admit.

And she thought his attitude was because he hated kids.... If it were that simple, he'd just admit it, but he couldn't actually share the true reason. Literally. His mouth simply wouldn't open and allow the words to spill. His grief over Tyler had taken a toxic turn and he knew it was festering inside of him but he was helpless to stop the spread of infection. And he really didn't want to drag Miranda into his quagmire. It wasn't fair to her.

Yeah, try and act as if you're being altruistic in your cold rejection.

Disgust at his own pathetic weakness choked him until he was blinking away panic. She was peppering him with short, angry comments, but even as he sensed the hurt, he couldn't bring himself to explain.

It was better this way. They shouldn't be tempting fate anyway. From this moment forward, no more inappropriate mental walkabouts where Miranda was concerned. No more thoughts or actions that weren't completely grounded in professionalism.

Miranda, realizing he wasn't going to take the bait, quieted and the silence cut deeper than her anger, but he withstood it with stoic resolve. In time, they'd both see how he was doing them a favor.

By the time the plow arrived and cleared the road so Miranda could pull free, Jeremiah escaped the confines of the Range Rover with a flimsy excuse that he would ride with the plow driver. Miranda cut him a short glance and didn't say a word.

She didn't have to. He could read her feelings in the windows of her eyes and it wasn't pretty.

He deserved this.

He'd been beyond reckless and foolish.

He might've just screwed himself all over again. Was Miranda so hurt and offended that she'd go to Stuart and rat them both out? She'd get a reprimand—but he'd get the pack-your-desk letter. And if by some chance she did rat them out, Stuart wouldn't turn a blind eye. No, he'd be furious. And rightly so. If the shoe were on the other foot, Jeremiah would deem it a firing offense, as well. Ah, hell.

He'd know by tomorrow.

Bad news traveled extraordinarily fast.

CHAPTER NINETEEN

MIRANDA WALKED INTO *Mamu*'s house and within two seconds the anger she'd been carrying on her shoulders dissolved into bewildered hurt. Why would Jeremiah react so negatively the minute she mentioned her son? Even as Talen leaped into her arms and she twirled him around, happy to see him, her mind was still working overtime to solve a puzzle without all the necessary pieces.

"What happened to you, Mama? You didn't come home last night and I had to stay with *Mamu*."

"I got stuck in a snowstorm and had to wait it out until it was safe to leave. Besides, I thought you liked staying with *Mamu*?"

"I do," Talen said, nodding his head, but he pursed his lips and said in a grumpy voice, "She made me take a bath and brush my teeth."

"Good. Because you probably stank," Miranda said, scrunching her nose playfully at her son. He laughed and she put him down. She stretched and realized her days of picking up her boy were growing short. Talen ran off to get his stuff in the spare bedroom and it gave Miranda a few minutes alone with *Mamu.* "Thanks for keeping him. I couldn't get to a phone or a radio until after the storm had passed. It was a rough night but at least I didn't worry about Talen because I knew he was with you."

"You look as if you have the weight of the world on your shoulders, child. What happened?"

Where to start? "Long story. Not fit for young ears."

"He's not in here. Give me the shortened version of events."

Miranda didn't want to share that she'd slept with her boss but she did want some advice, so she sanitized the details. "There's a guy that I think I really like and I thought he felt the same— or at least I know he did—until I started talking about Talen. Then he turned into a cold fish. He hasn't even met Talen. Who is he to judge me or my son?" *Mamu*'s brown weathered face crinkled into a smile and Miranda stared at the older woman, bewildered. "*Mamu,* how can you find this funny?" she asked. "I'm really upset about this."

"Young folk always think the world revolves around them. Chances are his issues are his own just as yours belong to you. If it's meant to be, things will work out."

"Oh, forget that. This is why I've stayed away

from any kind of relationship. Too much work and aggravation for too little reward. I have a roaring headache from clenching my teeth so hard after one conversation that went sour."

"Life isn't always about the sweetness but the sour, too. Without the dark, there is no light."

Miranda stared in mild exasperation at the older woman. Perhaps if *Mamu* had taken less of a passive role in Johnny's life, the direction wouldn't have taken a nosedive into the toilet. Oh, that wasn't fair, she immediately chastised the uncharitable voice that had cropped up in her head. *Mamu* wasn't responsible for the choices that Johnny had made.

Miranda exhaled slowly and closed her eyes for a brief moment before opening them again to say, "I know, *Mamu*. But you didn't see the way he looked at me. It was as if I'd suddenly shared something completely distasteful and, frankly, it was a huge turnoff. Me and Talen are a package deal. He can't have me if he doesn't want Talen, too. It really solidified my decision to remain single, that's for sure."

Mamu chuckled, and before she could offer another opinion, Talen came running back into the room with his backpack and coat on. "Ready, Mama," he announced with a gap-toothed grin. Miranda smoothed her son's pitch-black hair and smiled. This boy was where her heart resided and that was all that mattered. Jeremiah could wallow in his own misery alone. She wasn't about to become a part of whatever issues he was carrying with him.

SEVERAL DAYS HAD passed and Jeremiah had successfully avoided all contact with Miranda. After his less-than-gallant behavior, he didn't blame her for the cold shoulder but he wished she wasn't being quite so open about her disdain for him. He supposed he shouldn't complain—she hadn't run to Stuart to blab about their indiscretion, so he owed her for that one—but he knew if they didn't start thawing around each other, the staff were going to start talking.

"Jeremiah…can I talk to you for a minute?" Mary asked, venturing into his office and interrupting his thoughts.

"Of course," he said, gesturing for her to come in. "What can I do for you?"

Mary glanced around and then surreptitiously shut the door. Her need for privacy made Jeremiah sit a little straighter. Was he paranoid for worrying that Mary was suspicious of his involvement with Miranda? He kept his expression impassive and waited for her to continue. "Forgive me if I'm talking out of turn, but I just feel compelled to put in a word for Miranda."

Jeremiah did a double take. "Come again?"

Mary twisted her fingers and fidgeted, plainly feeling as if she was treading on dangerous ground, but she continued anyway. "She is my friend and I know her pretty well. She's got the best heart, and whatever she said or did to create the tension between you, please know that she's probably kicking herself right now because she's better at hindsight than being in the moment."

It took Jeremiah a full minute to realize that Mary thought Miranda had done or said something reckless to him as her superior and Mary was worried for Miranda's job. If it weren't such a chaotic situation, Jeremiah might've laughed at the irony. He smiled at Mary to put her at ease, but in truth he was simply relieved that Mary was clueless as to the true reason for the tension. "Everything is fine between me and Miranda. She's a valuable member of this team and I'm sorry if you got the impression that there was tension between us."

"She called you some names under her breath," Mary admitted, appearing guilty for sharing. "But she's always had a hot temper and sometimes she just can't seem to control what comes out of her mouth. But she's a very good person. The best. And that family has been through so much it just doesn't seem right to come down so hard on her for something she can't truly control."

"I admire your faith in your friend and coworker but you're worried for no reason. I'm curious, though…. What did you mean about Miranda's family?"

Mary looked as if she'd shared something she shouldn't have but then said, "Well, it's not as if it's a secret. A big murder case is hardly commonplace around here, and it was on all the national news outlets, so you're bound to hear about it sooner or later. Although you should probably hear it from Miranda…." Mary paused, perplexed, but when the prospect of sharing the juiciest gossip she knew was on the table, she simply couldn't pass it up. "Eight years ago, Miranda's younger sister, Simone—prettiest girl you ever seen, I'll tell you that—she went missing only to turn up dead two days later. She was battered and bloody but she didn't actually die from her wounds. No, the bastard who took her left the poor girl in the mountains and she died of exposure. But that's not the worst part—" Mary paused for a breath. "Trace—that's Miranda's brother—and Miranda tried to find her but didn't in time. By the time they found Simone, she'd been dead for at least two hours. And no one was ever able to solve the case. Whoever killed Simone Sinclair is still walking around, free as you please."

Jeremiah stared, shocked. "How awful."

"Yes," Mary nodded sadly. "Not the kind of

thing that our little township wants to be remembered for, but God must've needed his angel back because they couldn't save her in time. And Miranda, bless her soul, has never really gotten over it. Well, come to think of it, none of the Sinclairs have really come back from that one event. Such a tragic mess. So now you know why I'm concerned. We're all a little protective of Miranda, even though she'd hate to hear us say something like that. She's a stubborn thing."

Jeremiah mulled the information. This certainly put recent events in a different light and he felt like a shit for weirding out on her because of his own tragedy. The least he could do was explain. "Thank you for sharing, Mary. I appreciate the insight."

Mary smiled and said, "Please keep this between us. Miranda is a very proud woman and it would kill her to know I've spoken so freely about her personal business."

"Your secret is safe with me," he assured her, and Mary let herself out.

Jeremiah leaned back in his chair and reflected on everything that had happened in the past week. The poachers had disappeared; whatever tracks they'd left behind had been erased by the storm and they had no choice but to wait and see if they left another carcass behind. The necropsy had confirmed that the gallbladder had been removed, which supported the theory that they were poaching for the Asian black market, but Jeremiah wasn't sure how to catch them in the act in order to make the charges stick. He understood Miranda's frustration and, in a way, thanks to Mary, he understood her passion. She needed to make a difference, to catch the bad guys because her sister's murder was still hanging over her family's head. God, he couldn't imagine the heartache. Tyler was gone but at least Jeremiah had answers. How did the Sinclair family mourn when all they had were questions? He needed to apologize and explain himself. It'd be a miracle if she'd listen.

Since that day on the mountain, he'd replayed every word he'd said—and hadn't said—and he winced in shame. He may appear put together but inside he was a mess. But whatever his own issues, it wasn't fair to Miranda to dump them on her.

He clapped his hands over his face and rubbed slowly. Once again, he wasn't sleeping. The overall fatigue was beginning to make him delirious. He slept soundly with Miranda at his side and the unbelievable bonus was the phenomenal sex before and after the shut-eye. But even realizing that fact, it wasn't very useful. He and Miranda had no future together. He owed her an explanation about his behavior but he knew in his heart that he couldn't slip into any sort of parenting role with Miranda's son. The memories of being a father would kill him.

Here's the plan: apologize and start fresh.

Seemed he was doing an awful lot of apologizing lately when it came to Miranda. Was that their lot in life? God, he hoped not. He didn't want her to think he was unhinged—or worse, realize that he was too fundamentally damaged by crushing grief to be of use to anyone.

But that was the thing, though; he *was* damaged. And he probably needed Miranda to know that, even as much as it hurt his male pride. Men were supposed to be able to shoulder the heavy weight, no matter what it was. He'd failed his ex-wife and his son. There was no help for it; he had to admit that shame if he was ever going to get past it.

Good luck with that.

Yeah. Thanks.

CHAPTER TWENTY

JEREMIAH REALIZED BELATEDLY that a bottle of wine might not have been the best choice but he thought flowers would've been even worse and he hadn't wanted to show up empty-handed when he groveled.

Miranda opened her front door and gasped when she saw him standing there. She edged the door closed and stood on the stoop, glaring at him warily. "Are you lost?"

"Can we go inside?" he asked, but when she didn't budge he tried a half grin as he said, "I know I deserve some kind of retribution for my behavior but making me stand in the cold until I freeze seems a little harsh."

The tension in her jaw lessened incrementally but she didn't seem inclined to invite him in and it dawned on him…her son was home. Her gaze narrowed when his understanding became clear. "Yes. My son is here and I don't expose my child to strange men. And you're the strangest I've ever met," she tacked on.

He winced. "I deserved that. Fine. We'll talk

right here and I'll make it fast. But first, here, I brought a peace offering." He handed her the bottle of wine, which she accepted with a frown. "Frankly, I don't know if there's an appropriate offering for whatever we have going on. I hope you like merlot."

She smiled briefly and tucked the bottle under her arm. "Make it quick. I have to help my son with his homework."

Homework. He remembered helping Tyler with his math because the boy had struggled so much with fractions and Josie hadn't been able to make heads or tails of the math problems. He'd give anything to be able to sit down at the table and work equations with his son again even though at the time Jeremiah had wanted to tear his hair out. "I was wrong to act the way I did," he said abruptly, getting straight to the point. "I'm sorry."

"Is that it?" she asked.

Her disdain threw him. "What do you mean?"

"Aren't you going to tell me why you acted the way you did? You went pretty nuts on me. For a second I thought maybe you had a split personality because you went from zero to weirded out in sixty seconds and people don't do that unless they have some deep psychological damage. Trust me, I know a thing or two about inner demons."

"Because of your sister…"

She looked at him sharply. "How do you know about my sister?"

"Small town." He didn't want to rat Mary out but he wanted Miranda to know that he knew. "I'm sorry."

"I don't want your pity or your sad eyes. Don't you think I get enough of that around here? She's gone. End of story. I'm trying to live my life but everyone around here doesn't seem okay with that and keeps throwing it in my face about my sister. Let her rest in peace, for God's sake."

"I know a thing or two about guilt," he shared quietly. "If you want to talk about it, I'm here for you."

"Are you deaf? No, I don't want to talk about it. I'm tired of talking about it. I wish everyone else would tire of it and move on to someone else's tragedy." Sudden tears glittered in Miranda's eyes and she wiped at them with a groan. "Is that all? The apology wasn't necessary and thanks for the wine. Now go away before people have yet another reason to talk about my personal business."

Before Jeremiah could lodge a defense, she'd disappeared behind her front door and the lock had slid into place. His breath plumed in frosty curls before him and his toes had begun to tingle inside his shoes. He wanted to bang on the front door and make her talk to him but he wasn't about to make a scene in front of her son, and he couldn't very well continue to stand there on her front stoop, hoping she returned.

So much for the grand gesture.

He sighed and reluctantly returned to his car so he could drive home. What had he expected? That she'd welcome him with open arms, listen patiently to his explanation and then wrap him in a sweet embrace so they could cuddle together? Ugh. What an idiot he'd been to spring an apology on her while she was on her own turf. From what he knew of Miranda, her son and their home were sanctuary and she didn't let anyone sully that haven. Why he thought she'd let him, he had no clue. Temporary insanity.

Maybe this was a sign from the universe—move on. He had no business having any sort of relationship aside from a professional one with Miranda Sinclair. He had a clear and obvious opportunity to allow the severed ties to remain shredded.

But even as he justified all the reasons he and Miranda were a terrible idea, he couldn't deny that he still wanted her. It was something he couldn't quite fathom but it was there, pulsing like a raw wound just beneath the surface.

Damn it.

He'd have to try again. Miranda deserved that much.

But he'd give her a few days to cool off, he decided.

Already he was wishing he could simply take her into his arms and show her with his actions how sorry he was, but he knew that sort of gesture would backfire. She might even bite his lip for his attempt. In spite of his failure, a smile edged across his mouth. He'd never met a woman so filled with spirit. Her passion was unlike anything he'd ever experienced. He couldn't expect that sort of passion to have a limited application. Miranda loved, played and fought as hard as she did anything. He had to admire that kind of thirst for life, even if it promised to complicate his life in so many different ways.

He just wanted to make things right between them. Even if it meant they weren't together. That was all he wanted.

Sure. Keep telling yourself that.

He ignored the cynical voice of reason and put his mind to work thinking of another way to make it up to Miranda.

MIRANDA CLOSED THE door and briefly shut her eyes, unnerved by Jeremiah's sudden appearance at her doorstep. Did he really think that by showing up with a bottle of wine all was forgiven? She glanced at the wine and noted the quality. Well, at least he had good taste. She considered pouring herself a glass but decided against it and put the bottle into the pantry instead.

"Who was at the door, Mama?" Talen asked, looking up from his homework just as she slid into her seat beside him with a smile.

"No one. Now…let's see, where were we?" She redirected Talen back to his word problems and they spent the next half hour solving the fish dilemmas of Fisherman Frank as they added and subtracted their way to the final answers.

Finally they were finished, and as Talen was putting away his papers and books, he stopped and looked pensively at her after he'd pulled a crumpled piece of paper from his pack.

"What's up, buddy?" she asked, frowning when she saw the paper. "What's that? Is it for me?"

"It's a permission slip," he said but he didn't hand it over.

"For what?"

"A field trip."

Miranda frowned when Talen seemed reluctant to hand it over. "Buddy, don't you want to go? Let me see…"

Talen handed her the crumpled paper and she scanned it. Talen's class was scheduled to visit the Petersen Bay Field Station. "Oh, this sounds fun. I remember doing the same trip when I was your age. What's wrong?"

"All the boys are going with their dads."

Miranda's stomach twisted but she forced a

smile. "I'll go. Sounds like a good time. I need a day off anyway."

"No. It's okay," Talen said, refusing her offer.

She stared in hurt shock. Her son had never rejected her offer of volunteering at the school before, much less attending a field trip with him. She tried not to let her hurt show. "Okay, that's fine. I don't have to go. But, just out of curiosity, why don't you want me to go?"

"Mama...all the boys are bringing their dads. I don't want to be the only boy who brings their mom. I'd rather go alone."

"Oh." Miranda couldn't believe how much her son's admission hurt. Everything was changing much too quickly for her to absorb. "I bet I can do anything those dads can do," she promised her son. "Your mama is pretty cool."

Talen gazed at her with a small smile but his eyes were sad as he said, "You can't be a dad."

"No, I can't," she admitted. "I'm sorry, buddy."

"It's okay," he said and shouldered his pack to go to his room. He paused at the hallway and turned around, his face scrunched in thought. "Mama, isn't there someone out there for us? I know I'd have to share you but Kenny said the best part about having a dad is being able to do 'guy stuff' together, like fishing and hunting and farting because that's what guys do."

"I can do all those things. Even...fart." She

couldn't believe she'd just said that. But she was desperate. She felt her son slipping away from her and it was happening faster than she could imagine it ever would. "I'm a really good hunter and fisher."

Talen nodded but she could tell by his expression he didn't feel she understood his point. Oh, she understood. But it hurt like hell. All this time she'd been shielding her son from temporary father figures only to find that he was hoping she'd find him one eventually. She didn't know how to make him understand that she wasn't interested in finding a man to fulfill the role of daddy. She'd become a little too set in her ways to allow another person's input, particularly when it came to her son. "If you change your mind, I'd be more than happy to go with you," she said. "Just say the word and I'm there."

Talen's disappointment cut at her heart as he turned and said, "Thanks, Mom," before disappearing into his room.

Mom? Talen always called her Mama.

Oh, that hurt even worse.

Miranda dropped her head into her hands. Maybe it was time to figure things out in her head. If only she knew where to start...

CHAPTER TWENTY-ONE

MIRANDA CHICKENED OUT twice before actually reaching her parents' house, but when she finally pulled into the driveway she knew there was no turning around. She needed to find a way to reach her mother before it was too late for them both. The problem? Miranda had no idea how to speak to her mother—she never had.

Miranda knocked and pushed open the front door, grunting a little as it hit resistance. She put her shoulder against the door and finally pushed aside whatever had been blocking it. She stepped into the mudroom—or what used to be the mudroom—and tried not to cry out in dismay and horror. Piles of papers and books, magazines, clothes, boxes and bags littered the tiny room so that the door barely had clearance. She checked behind the door to see what had been placed there and found another box filled to the top with more stuff. "Who's there?" her mother's voice called with an edge of panic from the other room. "Zed, is that you?"

"No, Mom, it's me, Miranda. Where are you?"

"In the kitchen."

Miranda eyed the tiny path winding its way through the mess and she swallowed her aversion to going deeper into this hell so she could try to talk some sense into her mother.

"What are you doing here?" her mother asked, a deep frown creasing her forehead.

Miranda ignored the annoyance in her mother's voice and tried to find a chair to sit on, but there simply wasn't a place that wasn't covered with a towering pile. Even worse was the smell. Miranda covered her nose, grimacing. "Mom… what is that smell? Something is rotten in here." *Somewhere.*

Jennelle stiffened. "I don't smell anything."

"Then your nose must be broken. Something is plainly rotting to death in this mess." She cringed at the word *mess,* knowing it would likely set her mother off. And she wasn't wrong.

"As much as I love these visits where you insult me, was there anything else you needed, Miranda? Perhaps you're planning to sic the official authority on house tidiness on me again? That was an unexpected and unwarranted shock."

"A shock?" Miranda gestured wildly at the clutter. "Really?" She supposed all semblance of tact was out the window now. "Mother, this is getting ridiculous. I couldn't even get through the front door!"

"Seems you made it in just fine," her mother said in a wintry tone, adding under her breath, "More's the pity."

"Oh, come on, Mother. Can't we have a decent conversation for once? I'm worried about you."

"You worry about things that aren't your concern. I am not in any danger. I like my things and I don't want anyone poking their nose into my business."

"Your business is about to bury you," Miranda shot back.

"Nonsense."

"Mom, when was the last time Dad even stepped foot into this house?"

Jennelle's mouth quivered for a moment but her jaw firmed a second later as she shrugged. "Your father comes and goes as he pleases. Miranda, I hate to shatter your illusions about marriage, but sometimes after a certain number of years, it's more about being pleasant neighbors than lovers."

Miranda stared at her mother, not buying Jennelle's answer. "There's no room for him!"

"Now you're being melodramatic," Jennelle scoffed, but there was something—guilt perhaps?—in her mother's eyes. "I'm not going to argue with you. I don't traipse into your house and start criticizing the way you keep it."

Miranda's frustration threatened to bubble over in an explosion of angry words but she choked them down and took a breather. She didn't come to fight. "Mom...I need to talk to you."

"About what?"

"Simone."

"No." Jennelle pushed past her, not purposefully, only because there wasn't enough room for two people to pass. "There's no sense in bringing up the past."

"Mom, please don't run away from me when I'm trying to talk to you," Miranda pleaded, following her mother into the crowded living room. "You know this family is falling apart and no one seems to notice or care." Jennelle scoffed at that but Miranda wasn't going to stop. "Wade never comes home, Trace is in denial and Dad never comes out of his shop. We used to be a family who did things together and now we never even speak."

"I can't control how others behave. Your brothers know where to find us. Your father is busy with his carving—"

"Stop! You and I both know that he hasn't carved in years. He's selling marijuana out of that shop. Stop trying to sugarcoat what's really going on."

Her mother's lip trembled. "You're always so quick to find fault with others, aren't you? How in the world did I raise such a critical child? No one is perfect, Miranda. Perhaps you ought to remember that before you start picking people apart."

"I'm not picking anyone apart, Mother. I'm stating a fact that you refuse to recognize. We used to be a family! Don't you see how everything has gone to hell?"

"Circumstances that we couldn't control…" Jennelle started but couldn't finish, fighting back tears. She wiped at her eyes in agitation. "See what you've done? Why does every conversation with you have to be so confrontational?"

In the face of her mother's pain, Miranda's anger lost some of its heat and she softened her tone as she said, "I don't want every conversation to be so difficult between us, Mother. I'm trying to say that I'm worried about you and our family. We're falling apart and we have been for a long time. Simone's been gone a long time. Isn't it time we let her go?"

At that Jennelle's head snapped up and raw panic rimmed her eyes. "Let her go? She was your sister. How can you suggest such a thing? You cannot expect a mother to forget about her child—ever. To even ask such a thing is unconscionable. Shame on you for suggesting it."

Miranda blinked back tears. "I'm not asking you to forget about Simone. I'm asking you to remember that you have three other children as well as a grandson who need you." Miranda cast a despairing glance around the claustrophobic mess crowding every nook and cranny. "I can't bring Talen into this house. It's too dangerous. Don't you want to spend more time with your only grandson?"

"Of course I do," Jennelle answered. "You're the one who keeps him from me. You'd rather Talen spend time with that Indian woman than me."

"Please stop saying 'that Indian woman' with such disdain. She's Talen's blood kin and he loves her very much. Hearing something like that would hurt his feelings and confuse him."

"I would never say such a thing around Talen," her mother said, looking away. "He can't help who he's related to."

That sentiment goes both ways, Miranda thought privately but took a moment to settle the immediate snap on her tongue. "Is it possible for us to talk to one another without devolving into a sniping fight? I'd like to repair our relationship somehow but you have to meet me halfway."

Jennelle softened but remained wary, saying, "You're certainly welcome to visit more often if you promise not to be so critical of how I live my life."

"I wouldn't be so critical if I wasn't worried about your safety."

"I told you—I'm in no danger."

"Mom." Miranda tried to stay on topic. "I disagree. Can't you tell that normal people don't live this way? Don't you care that you're not a part of Talen's life? He barely knows you because you never spend any time together."

Her mother looked wounded. "It's not my fault that you won't bring my grandson to see me. It's not as if I've moved away or something. We all make choices, Miranda, and I can't control how you choose to parent your child. Just as I can't control that you prefer that woman over your own mother."

"She listens to me. She doesn't try to push me away like you do." Miranda couldn't help the sharp retort. Her feelings were much too raw at this point and she was losing patience.

"I don't try to push you away. You create distance between us by constantly criticizing me."

"Me? Criticize you?" Her mother was delusional. "You've made it very clear that I've never measured up to Simone. And when Simone died, your disdain for everything that I cared about only got worse. How am I supposed to feel about that?"

"I refuse to stand here and listen to you reaping all of your problems on my head. Your problems are your own. You're an adult, Miranda. Deal with the choices you've made instead of trying to blame everyone else."

"I'm not blaming anyone. I'm trying to figure out why I am the way I am. Why won't you help me?" Miranda wiped at the tears dribbling down her cheeks. "I can't help but think that if it were Simone coming to you, you'd bend over backward to help. I guess I'll just never measure up to her. Lord knows, you've been blaming me for her death since the day she disappeared."

"That's ridiculous."

"No, it's not." Miranda wished it were. "I'm not blind to the way you feel. Contrary to what you believe, you're not a very good actress. Your thoughts and feelings are always displayed right on your face."

"Children don't come with a manual. And you can't parent one child the same way as the other. I did the best that I could. I refuse to be blamed for whatever you feel went wrong simply because you don't like the way your life turned out."

"I love my life," Miranda nearly shouted. "But I'm beginning to realize that certain choices I've made haven't been the best and I'm trying to make amends. I want to mend our relationship, Mom. But you're making it nearly impossible to do that. You have to take responsibility for *your* part in all of this and that starts with admitting you have a hoarding problem."

"I don't have a hoarding problem! I have a selfish-family problem!" Her mother threw her hands up and stalked away. "I've had enough of this visit. Feel free to make yourself scarce." Jennelle threw a hard stare at Miranda before disappearing behind the one door in the house that wasn't blocked by junk. Miranda had half a mind to go bang on the door but figured, what was the point? Her mother was stubborn as a mule and nearly as mean.

"Thanks for that open and sharing conversation, Mom," Miranda muttered and let herself out.

Hands shaking, Miranda fished her cell phone out of her pocket and dialed Trace's number. When the call went straight to voice mail she left a near-hysterical message. "You have to come home. I can't take this anymore. I'm going crazy. If you don't help me deal with Mom I don't know what else to do. She won't listen, but she needs help. And she likes you way more than she's ever liked me, so please come home!"

Miranda climbed into her car and threw her cell onto the passenger seat. Before she knew it her shoulders were shaking as racking sobs took over her body. She cried into her hands, unable to stop. Everything was falling apart in her life. She didn't have anyone she could talk to; she didn't have anyone who cared. Including her own family. She desperately wanted to talk to Jeremiah but she refused to go to him in a sobbing mess, like some poor pathetic female who couldn't handle her own problems. But just once, she'd like to be able to lay her head on someone else's shoulder and know that they were going to take care of things. That they were going to take care of her.

She spent her whole life taking care of everyone else but no one seemed to notice when she was the one struggling. Her mother blamed Miranda for Simone's death. But wasn't a mother supposed to be there for her other daughter? When Simone died, no one was more overcome with guilt than Miranda. The fact that she couldn't turn to her mother for comfort was an additional slice to her heart.

She sobbed harder, almost unable to stop. Was she losing her mind? Was this what it felt like to have a nervous breakdown? She didn't know but she was nearly paralyzed with fear that there was no fixing what was broken inside of her. What kind of mother could she possibly be to her own son if she was so terribly broken inside? How many decent guys had she disregarded because of her inability to commit? Why couldn't she love Otter? Why wasn't she normal?

After a long moment Miranda managed to catch her breath and slow her tears. When she could focus again she started the car and pulled onto the highway. She felt wrung out and empty from her conversation with her mother. She needed help. Miranda could only hope that Trace would respond.

Frankly, Miranda didn't know what she was going to do next.

JEREMIAH WAS SURPRISED by the sound of an urgent pounding on his door, but he was even more surprised to see Miranda standing there, wearing an oddly fragile smile. "I'm sorry.... I should've called.... I just..."

Jeremiah sensed Miranda was on the verge of crumbling and holding it together by a string. He knew that look; he'd seen it in the mirror too many times after Tyler had died. "Is everything okay? Is your son...?"

"He's fine. He's with his grandmother for a few hours. I just needed to talk to you. Do you have a minute?"

"Of course. Sure." He led her into his tiny living room, which also served as a kitchen, and gestured for her to take a seat on the love seat beside him. "I know it's close quarters but..."

"It's okay. I don't care," she said. "I just needed to talk to you and I don't know why exactly because we shouldn't be this familiar with each other but you're the only person I feel can listen to my problems without judging me because of my past. When my sister died, suddenly I was the sister of that girl who died, instead of being simply Miranda Sinclair. The whispers, the sad looks, the pity…it drove me crazy and that's not even counting what I was going through on the inside of myself. Do you know it's my fault she's dead?"

"I'm sure it's not," he murmured. "I know it can feel that way but deep down you have to know that it's not."

Miranda shook her head hysterically. "No. It's my fault. We fought over a sweater. A damn sweater. Simone had taken it without permission and she had a tendency to ruin anything she touched and I'd just bought it. I hadn't even had a chance to wear it yet. In fact, I think the tags were still on it when she took it. I was so mad." Miranda paced as she shared, unable to sit still, and Jeremiah gave her the space she needed, though he desperately wanted to pull her into his arms and chase away the demons. "I was supposed to be her ride after work but I told her to find her own way home. She was staying with me while she was on Christmas break from college and I thought it would be fun to be roommates for a short while but she was a terrible pain in the ass! She always took my clothes without asking, she was a slob, and she never took anything seriously! So, yeah, I was really mad when she took that sweater, but in hindsight, it wasn't really about the sweater at all. It was all that pent-up frustration and anger over her thoughtlessness and the fact that everyone always made allowances for Simone but I was never cut any slack!" She paused to draw a deep breath. "But because I let my anger get the best of me, my baby sister was killed," she finished with a sad cry that nearly broke his heart.

She squeezed her eyes shut and then covered her face with her hands, embarrassed even as she continued to cry. Unable to resist, he pulled her into his arms. She needed someone to comfort her and he wanted to be the one to do it. She went willingly and clung to him almost desperately. "I loved my sister. I didn't want her to die. And I hate that sweater. I hate it!"

"Shh," he crooned, pressing a small kiss against the top of her head. "It wasn't your fault and it wasn't because of a sweater."

She pulled away, her eyes red. "Then why'd it happen? Why'd she have to die?" she asked almost angrily, but he knew her anger wasn't directed at him. How many times had he railed at the injustice of his son dying?

"I don't know. I wish I had the answers but none of us do. Sometimes bad things happen—" his voice caught and he had to look away and take a breath before he could continue again "—to good people and there's no rhyme or reason to it."

"My mom blames me. She doesn't come out and say it directly but I can see it in her eyes."

"I'd like to reassure you that she doesn't blame you but the fact is she might, but that's not your fault. You can't control how others feel. My ex-wife blames me for something terrible that happened and some days it's hard to remember that it wasn't truly my fault. Trust me, sometimes the weight of that one single situation is enough to cripple."

Miranda held his gaze, not bothering to wipe away her tears. "What happened?"

Here it was. The moment of truth. He wanted to tell her but his throat closed up when he tried. He didn't think he could get the words out. "Wait here," he said and rose from his seat to go into the small closet where one single box was stacked against the wall. He opened the box and pulled out the last school photo ever taken of Tyler, bordered by a dark wooden frame. His hands shook as he held the picture. For a wild, irrational moment he thought better of sharing the pain of his loss, but Miranda deserved to know, no matter how much it hurt him to share.

Her eyes went to the frame he held to his chest and she frowned as she wiped at her eyes. "What is that?" she asked.

"This," he said, "is my son. Tyler." He turned

the frame to her, and before she could ask, he added in a choked voice, "He's dead."

Miranda's mouth fell open and she appeared speechless. "What happened?" she asked, recovering.

"An ATV accident. Tyler was riding on our property and being reckless. He took a turn too sharply and flipped the ATV. It rolled over him, killing him instantly."

Miranda covered her mouth, pain in her eyes. "I'm so sorry," she breathed, shaking her head in horror. "Oh, my God. I'm sorry."

Jeremiah jerked a short nod and hugged the frame back to his chest. "I know a thing or two about blame and guilt. I don't have it all figured out—not by a long shot—but I do know that if you don't put it in its place, it will eat you from the inside out. Your sister, my son...they were taken from us, but we didn't cause their deaths."

"Why do you blame yourself? It was an accident."

"My ex didn't think Tyler was old enough to handle the responsibility of an ATV. I didn't agree. I bought the ATV against her express wishes," he admitted, feeling the weight of that decision settle on his chest. He couldn't possibly convey in words the regret he suffered every day for that one decision. "She blames me for Tyler's death and a part of me agreed. If I hadn't allowed my guilt for being a workaholic to override my good sense, my son might still be alive." He shrugged but there was too much pain in that single motion to come off as nonchalant or flippant. "But there's no way of knowing. Maybe it was just his time."

"I hate that saying."

He smiled. "Me, too. The last well-meaning person who said that to me nearly got my foot in their ass. But sometimes the only way to cope with something we can't understand is to cling to well-meaning but ultimately useless clichés. Most people don't know how to navigate a person's grief. I tried to remember that they meant well but it didn't stop me from wanting to rip their heads off."

"That's why you left Wyoming."

"Yes."

"And why you freaked out when you found out that I have a son."

"Yes." He placed Tyler's picture on the coffee table facedown and returned to his seat. "Miranda...I would find a million different ways to make a relationship with you work if it weren't for the fact that I can't face the idea of fulfilling a father-figure role again. I've tried really hard to get past it, but ultimately, it hurts too much."

Miranda's mouth curved in a pained smile. "You assume too much, Jeremiah. I'm not interested or looking for a daddy for my son. If I were, I'd be smart about it and accept Otter's offer of a date."

"My landlord?"

"Yes. He's had a crush on me since high school and he's a really great guy who would treat my son like his own. But I don't feel anything for him."

Why did that give him a sense of relief? What a selfish bastard he was. He forced the words out. "Miranda, you deserve a good man. Your son deserves to have someone in his life he can relate to. Eventually, he's going to have needs you can't fulfill."

"Such as?"

"How are you going to teach him to shave?"

"How hard can it be?"

"Boys need a father. You're probably a great mother, and I would never say that you're not capable of wearing both hats, but you have to know that you can't be everything at once without sacrificing somewhere."

"I can handle it," Miranda said. "Besides, I've been doing it by myself for so long, I don't think I'd know how to allow someone else in."

"With the right person, co-parenting is a great give-and-take. My ex-wife and I used to have it right until things unraveled." He'd like to say it was Tyler's death that had unraveled their partnership, but the truth was, he and his ex-wife had been falling further and further apart for years. He'd used work to patch the holes punched in his marriage, which had only served to make things worse. Hindsight was twenty-twenty, right? "I wish I could be that man for you," he said.

His quiet admission caught her breath and her eyes welled. "I wish I could let you."

He smiled and knuckled her cheek softly. "We're a pair to draw to, aren't we?"

She nodded and he dipped down to capture her mouth with his. He knew it was wrong. The right thing to do was to help dry her tears, suggest a few days off to collect herself and then get back to his day. That was how her supervisor would handle the situation. But what about the man who craved the touch of her skin beneath his fingertips, the sound of her breathy moans in his ear or the simple pleasure of holding her quietly as they drifted off to sleep? Everything was blurred in his head but it didn't seem to matter because his heart was in control at the moment. Their tongues danced and slid along each other in a sweet tango that nearly broke his heart at the sadness he tasted in her tears. He wanted to shelter her, protect her and chase her pain away, but how could he possibly do that when he'd likely end up causing more pain in the end?

He couldn't offer her what she needed. So why wasn't he letting her go?

Simple—she made him feel alive again.

And he wanted more.

CHAPTER TWENTY-TWO

THEY WALKED SLOWLY to his bedroom and tumbled to the bed. Their kisses became urgent as need eclipsed good sense. Miranda knew it was a bad idea to keep falling into bed with Jeremiah, but she desperately needed to feel something aside from this gaping hole of sadness and loss anchored in her chest. Logic and reason had nothing to do with her decision to sleep with Jeremiah again after staunchly telling herself it would never happen again, and she wasn't going to pretend that there was a future in what she was doing.

They both knew where they stood.

And they didn't care at the moment.

Jeremiah pressed urgent kisses down the center of her quivering belly, pausing to plunge his hot tongue into the bowl of her navel, teasing the sensitive spot in a simulation of what he wanted to do to her. She closed her eyes and threaded her fingers through his thick hair as he dipped lower to nuzzle the apex of her thighs, teasing the sensitive area without actually descending to that hot, aching spot that pulsed with need.

When Jeremiah's tongue finally delved between her damp folds, she was nearly breathless and shaking. She thrilled at the feeling of his strong, firm hands gripping her hips and holding her to him, nursing and teasing her secret pleasure nub as he slipped a finger inside her while his tongue worked dark magic on her clitoris. Within minutes Miranda was writhing, losing herself to the explosive pleasure that radiated pure happiness throughout her body as waves upon waves of sensation zoomed down her nerve endings, leaving her weak and gasping.

Jeremiah kissed her inner thigh and then climbed her body to stare into her eyes. "I can never seem to get enough of you." She didn't need to answer; he already knew she felt the same.

Miranda rose up and framed his face with her hands, pulling him to her. She tasted her own musk on his lips and it thrilled her to have something so primal between them. He responded by eagerly slipping his tongue between her teeth and coaxing her to dance with him again. She didn't need much persuading and they rolled until he was on his back and she straddled his straining member. The heat of her core teased him into delirium and his grip on her hips became urgent. She didn't tease him long and slid onto his hard penis, groaning as he stretched her with his thick length. She shuddered as she moved sensually, riding him slowly as to milk every last moment with him until its inevitable conclusion. "Jeremiah," she moaned, loving the sound of his name on her lips. He tensed beneath her as he thrust against her heat, and as she reached her second climax, Jeremiah quickly followed. She collapsed against him, both of them breathing hard as they recovered, until she could climb off and roll to her back beside him. As the sweat dried on their bodies, awareness of their situation returned.

After a long moment, Miranda regarded Jeremiah. "What now?" she asked as her heart rate slowly returned to normal and the sweat dried on her skin. She tried not to sink into sadness but reality was fast stomping on the euphoria of their reckless abandon and there was no stopping its intrusion on the moment.

"I don't know."

"Me, either," she murmured, sighing. "We can keep saying we're not going to do this again but somehow we always end up right where we started."

"You're irresistible," he said with a short grin that she found adorable. She appreciated the compliment but it didn't solve their problem. She rose up on her elbow and he tweaked her nipple with a half smile. "Any solution that pops into my head sounds unrealistic. I'm open to suggestions."

"I was afraid you were going to say that. I don't

have the answers, either. All I know is I could spend a lifetime in your arms and I don't have a lifetime to spare. I'm not going to suddenly stop being a mother and you're not going to suddenly stop being traumatized by your son's death."

His expression dimmed and he agreed. "Stuart Olly would have a fit if he knew about us. Even if we didn't suffer from the tragedies in our past, we work together and that's against the rules. I would never jeopardize our jobs for something that we don't even understand."

She nodded and settled against him. "So... we're back to square one."

"Yeah."

Great. "So are we going to sneak around? Clandestine meetings in hourly-rate motels like two dirty cheaters trying to hide their extracurricular activities?"

"They wouldn't have to be dirty motels," he said mildly. "I'd spring for a nice place to have my way with you."

She gasped, then realized he was joking and laughed. "Such a gentleman..."

He shrugged. "At times."

The laughter subsided and they simply held each other, naked and sated, until it was time for Miranda to pick up Talen. They shared one last lingering kiss inside the safety of his apartment, and then Miranda left with more questions in her head, a troubled heart, but a body that felt deliciously loose and satisfied.

She supposed two out of three wasn't bad, right?

Yeah...right.

OTTER'S HEART TOOK an uncomfortable lurch as he saw Miranda leaving the studio apartment he rented to Jeremiah Burke. It could be work-related, he thought, but even as he wanted to justify why Miranda would legitimately be seen leaving her boss's place on a Saturday he couldn't deny that she had the look of a woman who was doing the walk of shame. Her glorious dark hair was tousled and her movements were swift and furtive as she ducked into her Range Rover and drove away.

Immediate and visceral rage bubbled from an unknown place and he wanted to shove his fist into Jeremiah's face for being so lucky as to have garnered Miranda's interest but he held it back by the thinnest margin. What a jerk, coming into town and setting his sights on Miranda. What made Jeremiah so special? And he'd been the idiot who'd offered Jeremiah a place to live. The irony was sickening.

Otter stared until Miranda's Range Rover disappeared down the street. Disappointment mixed with sharp pain welled in his chest. He'd hoped maybe with time Miranda might see him as more than a friend. More than that goofy kid who had tried to impress her with his fancy car or his business sense. It was bad enough he'd had to suffer through her brief relationship with that criminal Johnny but now he was supposed to patiently wait for this new terrible idea to run its course? When was it going to be his turn with Miranda? If she'd just give him a chance, he'd show her that he was the best man for her.

"You're a great friend, Otter," Miranda had always said to him whenever he'd tried to broach the subject of a date. In other words: *you're not good enough for me, so stop dreaming.*

Well, if Miranda was too busy screwing up her life with her boss, maybe he had to help the situation.

Maybe if he wasn't always playing the good guy then Miranda might respect him. It was apparent she liked a little edge, a little danger in her relationships. He could give her danger. He could be a bad boy.

He could be very bad.

But first, he had to remove the distraction. Miranda couldn't possibly see what was right in front of her face with Jeremiah constantly in her sights.

Why did it have to go this way? He'd actually liked the guy—he'd seemed like a decent fellow, someone who might be fun to spend some time with tipping back a beer at The Rusty Anchor.

Otter sure as hell wasn't going to share a beer with the man now.

Hell no.

A man had his pride. It was bad enough he'd had Miranda. Otter scrubbed at his eyes as if he could rub away the images that his imagination kept throwing at him with masochistic zeal.

It simply wasn't fair.

He was the better man for Miranda.

He'd show her. Somehow she'd see that he was the man who would make her happy. Not Jeremiah. That guy was a one-way street to disappointment.

He'd make sure of it.

CHAPTER TWENTY-THREE

MIRANDA SAT IN her office, her thoughts in a jumbled mess as she went through the motions of doing her work. This was new territory for her. She'd never had to consider another person in her life or how they might fit into it, not that she was trying to figure out a way to fit Jeremiah into her life, but it did pose interesting questions about where she wanted the direction of her life to go.

Normally, she wasn't an introspective type of person but it seemed as of late she had plenty of reason to question every decision that she made. The revelation that Talen was sad that he didn't have a father had really caused Miranda to take a step back and reevaluate a lot of things in her life. She'd always felt she was doing the best for her son by shielding him from her romantic life but the fact that she'd made no attempts to be committed to any one person apparently hadn't been the right choice after all. In a way, it smarted to know that she wasn't enough for Talen. Intellectually, she knew Talen had the right to his feelings, but the knowledge that he wanted more stung just the same.

Mary walked into her office with a smile, holding a piece of paper in her hand. "Did you see this?" she asked, handing over the printout. "I think it's perfect for you. You should apply."

Miranda glanced at the job listing printed from the federal wire and read over the requirements for the job of Special Services Enforcement Officer. The flicker of excitement at the possibilities made Miranda's heart race. It was her dream job. Higher pay grade, more focused attention on poaching and the opportunity to make a difference at the legislative level. But just as Miranda allowed her imagination to run away with her, reality came crashing down, a rude and unwelcome visitor. There was no way she'd get the job.

"Mary, you know Stuart Olly would never consider me for this job." She handed the paper back. "But thanks for letting me know."

Mary frowned. "You're just as qualified as anyone else for that job. Stuart should put aside his personal feelings and consider your professional merits because that's all that matters."

Miranda loved Mary's naive outlook. "You and I both know that that's not how the world works. Frankly, if Stuart had been able to find a way to fire me before now he would've done it. He and

I are never going to be friends. He's already put in a few choice words to Jeremiah about me."

Mary gasped, appalled. "Is that legal? That doesn't seem legal. Aren't there rules, laws protecting employees? Like some kind of confidentiality clause?"

Miranda shrugged. "Probably. But sometimes people feel okay bending the rules. Particularly when they're at the top."

In hindsight, Miranda never should've slept with Stuart's son. But in all fairness, it was so long ago that she barely remembered the encounter and Stuart's son, Isaac, had long since moved away and married a flight attendant. Why Stuart chose to hold the past against Miranda for this long, she had no idea. But the fact remained, Stuart did not like her and never would. Which meant if he had anything to say about her getting a better position within the department, it just wasn't going to happen. Miranda tried to make the best of it. "I love my job here. Why would I want to leave?" she asked with a quick shrug.

But Mary saw through her false cheer. "Miranda, as much as I love having you around, you've outgrown this office and position. Making copies for mailers and doing permits for recreational hunters is frankly a waste of your talents. You need to be out there making a difference because not everyone shares your passion and we need people out there who are passionate about the things that matter."

Miranda stared at Mary, surprised at her friend's statement. She had always considered Mary as a little flighty, with a stereotypical blond personality. Miranda loved her but never really took her seriously. But clearly, she hadn't given Mary enough credit. "Thank you, Mary," she said with a smile. "I appreciate your confidence in me. I really do. And I would love to apply for this job…but to be honest, I'm afraid of getting my hopes up and being completely smashed by the rejection. There's been a lot happening in my life in the last few weeks that have really knocked the wind out of my sails. I'm not sure I can take another beating."

Mary looked concerned and took the seat opposite Miranda. "What's going on?" she asked.

Miranda sighed, not sure she wanted to share, or which part she should share and which part she should keep to herself. She knew for certain she couldn't talk about Jeremiah, so she decided to talk about Talen. "It seems Talen is feeling out of sorts. He's been making comments about not having a father. It's kind of thrown me for a loop."

"Oh, honey, I'm surprised it hasn't come up before now," Mary said. "Kids are a lot smarter than we give them credit. And Talen is a *very* smart boy. Hannah has quite the crush on him from what I hear." The women shared a smile and a chuckle, and then Mary said, "Miranda, I would never overstep my bounds and tell you how to live your life, but sooner or later Talen was going to realize that you play by your own rules. There's nothing wrong with that but it does make for a harder road to travel especially when everybody wants the people around them to be the same."

"People gossip about my family because of Simone, but they love to gossip about me because I'm still around to remind them what happened. I'm tired of people putting their noses in my business. I can handle it, the censure, but I never wanted it to come back on Talen. Maybe I made a mistake in staying in Homer. I should've moved away like Wade."

"Who's being naive now? How could you possibly think that your actions wouldn't affect Talen? Not to be rude, Miranda, but I would imagine by now you've run out of men to sleep with for your little no-commitment, one-night-stand marathons."

Miranda stared, her mouth dropping open a little.

Mary shrugged and said, "Everybody knows. But the ones who love you, love you for your flaws and your strengths. Besides I can't imagine what it's like to live your life, having people talk about you and your personal tragedy over the dinner table as if it were their right to do so. You're a strong person because you've had to be, but also because you were made to be. But I think it's time to figure out what you really want, Miranda. Time for you to stop hiding behind that reckless, rash persona that you throw up when things get tough or emotionally complicated. It's just time to grow up."

Miranda swallowed, unable to believe what Mary was telling her, but there was no denying the logic and reason in her advice. It was true— it was time to grow up. The only problem? She had no experience in being mature and she was scared of herself.

"I don't think I know how to be different, even if I wanted to be."

Mary smiled. "No one knows how to be different, you goose. You have to take a leap of faith to be different. Make that choice and just go for it. Before I met Jim, I was an emotional, insecure wreck. I didn't think I could go into another relationship after my first marriage had failed so miserably. How could I have not known that Peter was cheating on me with nearly everyone in town aside from you? I felt stupid and ugly and worthless and I was certain everyone was talking about me behind my back. But I knew I had to get myself together for Hannah's sake. I didn't want Hannah to see me as this weak, sniveling woman who didn't know how to be without a man. And even though it was hard, and I was scared, I pulled myself up by my bootstraps and put one foot in front of the other until I found that I could walk on my own. And then at the best possible moment, I met Jim." She paused for a brief moment, as if unable to stop the warm smile that always followed when Mary talked about her new husband.

Miranda had to admit, it must be nice to feel that way about someone.

Mary continued with bright eyes. "And he is the man I've been waiting for. But I wouldn't have met him if I hadn't gone through what I did with Peter. There is someone out there for you, Miranda. I know it. I feel it in my bones. But you'll never get to meet him if you don't take that leap of faith. Open yourself up to the possibility of meeting someone, instead of being so ready to toss him on his ear the minute you're through with him. You might be surprised what you find."

Miranda stared in wonder at her friend, unable to believe the poignancy of Mary's advice. "When did you get so smart?" she asked, half joking, but only to hide the fact that Mary had poked at a very raw nerve. "I don't know what to say. You've given me a lot to think about."

Mary smiled, relieved. "I've wanted to talk to you about this for a while, but you know, that's just not something you can jump into without some kind of invitation because it could be offensive if taken the wrong way and I would never jeopardize our friendship even though our relationship is mostly a work friendship."

"I'm hard to get to know outside of the office," Miranda acknowledged, realizing she had a true friend in Mary and not only a nine-to-five buddy as she'd thought. "And all this time I've been drinking alone," Miranda teased, needing some levity before the conversation made her cry.

But Mary saw through her attempt and said, "You have a lot of people who care about you, probably more than you know. You are a very cool person, just a little troubled from everything that's happened in your life. But you're also the strongest person I know. Honestly, when I was going through my divorce and I thought I couldn't handle one more thing being thrown at me, I thought of you."

"Me?" Miranda repeated, bewildered. "Why?"

"Because you're so strong," Mary answered. "I thought of everything you've been through, from your sister's death, the job, your family and you being a single mother, and I knew that if you could do it, I could do it. You gave me hope and you inspired me to be stronger, not only for my sake but for my daughter's sake. And so I feel I owe you a debt, and if there's any way that I can help you find happiness in your life, I want to do that." Mary smiled and added, "And I'm not just saying this because I know my brother has a terrible crush on you. I'm saying it because I mean it."

Miranda's eyes watered, and she felt overwhelmed. "I don't know what to say."

Mary smiled brightly. "That's easy. Say that you'll apply for this job."

Miranda wiped at her tears and laughed. "Okay. I will. But you'd better be on hand with tequila poppers when I get denied because Stuart hates me."

"If that happens, and I say *if* in a big way, I will pay for all your drinks at The Rusty Anchor. But I have a feeling that even Stuart won't be able to say no because you're perfect for the job and he knows it."

Miranda laughed. Wouldn't that be crazy? Mary's belief in her buoyed her optimism. For the first time in a long time she dreamed of something bigger than the satellite office could provide. The opportunity to make a difference in something she was truly passionate about was enough to give her goose bumps. Mary was right; she'd been allowing fear of failure to keep her pigeonholed in one spot. She didn't know what she was going to do about Jeremiah but she could do something about her career. And perhaps her first step should be to pay a visit to Stuart and clear the air. If she didn't at least do everything in her power to create a path to success, she wouldn't be able to sleep at night, because she would always wonder. Her mouth curved in a tremulous smile. "When does the application period start?"

Mary's smile lit up her eyes. "This Friday."

Perfect. She had time to brush up her résumé and put together a plan. It also gave her time to figure things out with Jeremiah. "Thank you, Mary. I never realized the swift kick in the ass that I needed would come from you."

Mary grinned, openly delighted. "Happy to help. Now, when would you like to start processing the permits for moose season? I have three stacks that just came in this morning."

Miranda moaned and grimaced at the idea of sifting through hundreds of permits, then sighed. "Give me a minute to come off of cloud nine and we can start in thirty."

"Sounds good."

Mary left the office and Miranda couldn't help the smile that kept creeping up on her. The idea of actually having some kind of power to make a difference was enough to keep her grinning for days and temporarily blotted out the other stuff in her life that was tumbling down around her ears.

And for the moment, she was happy to focus

on something positive for once instead of dwelling on all the things that were going wrong. Mary was right; time for change.

CHAPTER TWENTY-FOUR

STUART OLLY FLEXED his fingers and struggled to control his temper. He'd warned Jeremiah about Miranda but the vixen had somehow gotten her claws into him. This was trouble. Oh, this was bad. Not only for Jeremiah's career but for the whole agency. He couldn't have a blemish like this staining their reputation in the media. He wanted to fire Miranda but he couldn't. Technically, if anyone was going to be fired it had to be Jeremiah because he was in a position of power over Miranda. Ostensibly, Miranda might've been coerced. *Yeah, right.* Miranda was a piranha, and if anyone had been coerced it was probably Jeremiah, the poor man.

He still remembered his son Isaac's crestfallen expression after Miranda had discarded him like yesterday's trash. The woman was a moral scourge and had been a pain in his side since the day they met. She was all the things he couldn't stand in a woman: outspoken, brash, with balls big enough to rival a man's. He wouldn't go so far as to say women belonged in the kitchen but he certainly believed that when the gender roles were all twisted up and confused, it complicated relations. Yes, he was all about gender equality in public but privately...he wished things were just a little bit more clearly defined.

And what was he supposed to do with this information? If he fired Jeremiah, the press might catch wind of it and start poking around. It wouldn't take much, a slip of the tongue by someone who didn't know any better, and the story would come tumbling out. *The scandal.* A supervisor dallying with an employee. Lands sakes alive, the idea gave him heartburn. He steepled his fingers in thought. Maybe he could transfer Miranda to another office? Of course, the thought of foisting Miranda on someone else seemed like a bad idea. He sighed, irritated at the sudden turn of events.

Why couldn't Jeremiah have listened to him? It was a simple directive: stay away from Miranda Sinclair. But he should have known—a young red-blooded American man would eagerly fall into the clutches of that green-eyed woman.

Either way, the situation had to be handled. And of course, the dirty work fell to him. He picked up the phone and dialed Jeremiah's number. Jeremiah picked up on the second ring.

"Jeremiah, we need to talk," he said, getting right to the point.

Jeremiah's voice, on the other hand, was congenial yet cautious. "No problem. What about?"

"I think you know and, frankly, I'm disappointed."

There was a long pause and Jeremiah said, "When would you like to meet?"

"I will see you tomorrow, 3:30 p.m. sharp. Do not be late." Stuart ended the call without so much as a goodbye.

He couldn't believe how disappointed he was in Jeremiah's judgment. Perhaps there was something in Jeremiah that reminded him of Isaac, or perhaps of himself when he'd been younger, and knowing that Jeremiah had blatantly disregarded his solid advice really pinched his backside.

Well, he supposed the old adage was true: youth was wasted on the young because when the body was young and able, the brain was brash and stupid.

JEREMIAH PUT THE phone down and tried to quell the queasy feeling in his gut. He didn't bother trying to deny Stuart's suspicions; he'd rather face the situation head-on. Someone must have tipped off Stuart to Miranda and Jeremiah's relationship—if you could call their wild, untamable attraction to one another a relationship. The question was, *who?* Then it hit him. Someone must've seen Miranda leaving his apartment on

Saturday. It would have had to have been some-one who knew them both, and someone who ei-ther didn't like Miranda or didn't like him. Seeing as he hadn't been around for very long, he was willing to put his money on Miranda.

He squeezed the bridge of his nose, feeling a tension headache coming on. He knew this would happen. He'd known it would be a bad idea to pursue anything with Miranda, and although logic dictated that they keep their distance, he really disliked the idea of someone else telling him whom he could or couldn't see. He was will-ing to admit his feelings were childish and im-mature but it didn't stop him from bristling at the thought.

Still, now was not the time to make waves. He called Miranda into his office. "What's up?" she asked. "Not that I'm complaining. I'd welcome anything that would give me a break from moose permits."

Jeremiah smiled briefly and motioned for her to close the door. At his direction her open smile faded. "This seems serious."

"It is." Jeremiah didn't see the value in soft-ening the blow, so he laid everything out there. "Someone knows about us. I don't know who, but it was someone who knows us both and re-ported our relationship to Stuart. I have a meet-ing scheduled tomorrow afternoon to discuss the situation. I wanted to let you know so you have a heads-up."

Miranda sank into the chair, stunned. "I don't understand. We don't even have a *relationship*. And as far as I know no one was in the room with us when we were in that cabin and certainly no one was with us on Saturday. How could anyone have known?"

"The best that I can figure is that someone spotted you leaving my apartment on Saturday."

"Yeah? So? You're my boss. Maybe I was delivering paperwork. Maybe I was doing something work-related."

"Whoever made the report must've seen something to make them believe that your visit was anything but professional."

Miranda searched her memory and then grimaced. "Maybe my clothes were disheveled or maybe I had a look about me…. I don't know…. Damn, I knew I should've gone out the back door."

Jeremiah shook his head. "Listen, there are a million different ways to tear apart our actions but let's not do that. I'm not about to let you pay for this mistake. I will take the heat."

Miranda looked horrified. "You could lose your job."

Jeremiah knew that. "I'm your superior and

I'm in a position of authority. It was wrong. I'm willing to take responsibility."

"No. I'm not about to let you take all the heat. I was a willing participant. Let me talk to Stuart."

"Absolutely not. That's a terrible idea. For some reason he does not like you at all. I think you'll make it worse."

Miranda scowled. "That man is a male chauvinist who tries to pretend that he's anything but."

"Be that as it may, he's our boss. I will talk to him while you lay low and keep your head down."

"I hate this idea. We will have to think of something else. Listen, we don't know for sure that he knows anything specific. We can say it's our word against whoever ratted us out. Besides, what proof is there aside from one person's supposed word? It's practically defamation of character."

"I'm not going to hide behind lies. You start telling one lie and it leads to another until you have a huge mess that you have to try to remember and keep straight. I don't have the energy for that. I'd rather handle the situation and move on."

"Even if it means you could lose your job?"

Jeremiah exhaled and nodded. "Yes. If I have to lie to keep my job, it's not a job worth having."

Miranda's eyes glittered. "That's ridiculous," she fairly snapped. She stood to leave. "If you're intent on trashing your job, so be it. But I want to go on record as saying this is a terrible idea.

And if you would just put your thinking cap on and think outside the box or whatever other cliché you can come up with, you might find a different way out of this."

Jeremiah didn't have a chance to respond before she had slammed out of the office. He was surprised by her vehemence, and oddly, he was touched by her refusal to let him fall on his sword. But all things being considered, he would willingly bear the brunt of Stuart's anger if it protected Miranda. She had enough on her plate; she didn't need that blowhard on her tail, as well.

It was the least he could do. For Miranda, he realized he would be willing to do so much more.

STEAM FAIRLY CURLED from Miranda's ears. She wasn't about to let Jeremiah just throw away his job but she didn't know what to do. Likely Stuart wouldn't want to hear anything she had to say and anything she said might make it worse, but she couldn't stand the idea of sitting on her hands and watching Jeremiah walk to the slaughter. She wished Jeremiah would lie. It was one small tiny white lie.

All they had to do was coordinate their stories and whoever had ratted on them would look like an overzealous tattletale. But damn Jeremiah's sense of nobility. She didn't want Jeremiah to go. Aside from the fact that she liked seeing him every day, he was good for the department. He was good for the office. He cared and he wanted to make change, which was far more than Virgil ever did. Virgil was a good guy but he'd been a terrible boss. For the first time ever they were looking at some positive changes within their office, which went above and beyond new pens and new staplers. It was all because of Jeremiah.

It was easy to say that losing Jeremiah in the work environment would be a huge blow because it was. It was harder to admit that losing Jeremiah on a personal level hurt more than she wanted it to. She didn't want to have deep feelings for Jeremiah—wasn't that the crux of this dilemma? If they hadn't sparked off of that attraction none of this would be happening right now. They tried not to see each other; they tried to stay away from one another. But that attraction—whatever it was—refused to die. She craved his presence, his touch, his camaraderie, and he was part of the reason she enjoyed coming to the office every day. He was a good sounding board for her ideas and her concerns. And the idea of losing him over this made her crazy.

"Damn you, Stuart."

Unable to just sit there and do nothing, Miranda tried to catch up on paperwork but the words blurred as she lost focus and after several attempts simply threw her hands in the air and

274 THAT RECKLESS NIGHT

gave up. She grabbed her coat and gloves and headed out. She needed to move. She needed to do something physical. She supposed now was a good time to do some fieldwork, if only to check some leads on the poaching case.

Jeremiah caught her leaving and hollered for her to wait. "Where are you going?" he asked when he'd caught up.

"Out to do something to keep my mind off your impending career suicide," she whispered in an angry tone so no one else could hear them. "Fieldwork," she added a bit louder for everyone else's benefit.

"Let me get my coat. I'll go with you."

Miranda opened her mouth to point out how that was a terrible idea but she realized her effort was futile. Maybe Jeremiah needed some fresh air, too.

Miranda shook her head, exasperated, and headed for the Range Rover, where Jeremiah soon joined her.

"Are you trying for a record of bad decisions?" she asked as she pulled out of the parking lot. "Because this ranks up there with pretty stupid. You're about to get your ass handed to you for being with me, and yet, here you are...with me again."

"This is different."

"Not to whoever ratted us out."

"We both still have jobs to do and a poaching case that's still unsolved. I directed you to do some follow-up and Stuart directed me to remain involved in the hopes of garnering some positive press if we manage to solve the case. The way I see it, I'm just doing my job. As long as we don't end the day with a kiss and a grope I think we're okay."

She choked back surprised laughter and caught his subtle smile. "You're something else, Burke. All right. Well, today we're going to pay a visit to Rhett Fowler with Big Game Trophy so you can get an idea of some of the bigger names in the area."

"Good. Anything to take my mind off tomorrow works for me."

She smiled. They were birds of a feather.

They pulled up to the expansive, lodgelike home of Rhett Fowler and parked right up front. The home looked like an expensive ski lodge out of Vail, Colorado, with its rock face, thick timbers and extreme size, which fit Rhett well. Rhett was a man with a big barrel chest and a thick, booming voice and an even bigger laugh. A house any smaller just would've felt like a studio apartment.

Rhett met them at the door and immediately gathered Miranda into a bear hug that lifted her from her feet. "Girl, you're not eating enough! I can nearly see right through you. You feeding that boy quality protein? I've got some caribou steaks I can send home with you if you need," Rhett said, then turned his attention to Jeremiah. "And you must be that young cat that everyone's talking about who took Virgil's place. Nice to meet you," he said, pumping Jeremiah's hand with his signature enthusiasm and a wide smile.

Miranda grinned. Maybe she'd forgotten to mention that she'd known Rhett Fowler her entire life and he was crazy about her in a fatherly sort of way.

Jeremiah caught her barely smothered grin and she knew the jig was up, but he smiled at Rhett and allowed him to nearly shake him out of his shoes. "The very same. And you're Rhett Fowler, owner of Big Game Trophy."

"It better be me or else I've been paying someone else's taxes all these years!" Rhett's boom of a laugh bounced off the masculine room filled with the decapitated heads of a variety of animals as he led them into the living room, where rawhide furniture and heated floors awaited.

Rhett gestured to a woman who buzzed by, his third wife, Ambra, and instructed her to get some drinks. "Beer?" he asked Jeremiah. He didn't need to ask Miranda. He already knew she liked dark German imports if she could get them and Rhett always kept a few in his fridge. Jeremiah hesitated the barest moment but then relented and

Rhett approved. "That a boy. I don't trust a man who doesn't enjoy a beer now and then. Makes me wonder, what's his problem? Isn't he a red-blooded American?"

Ambra returned with beers for everyone and then floated from the room, off to do her own thing. Ambra was a snow bunny Rhett had brought back from his last trip to Switzerland two years ago. She was like a Nordic princess with her long, flowing white hair, pale blue eyes and lean, willowy figure. She was also in her late twenties. "The perks of being filthy rich, eh?" he joked with a knowing wink at Jeremiah.

Miranda rolled her eyes. "Shame on you for being a lecherous old man. You'd better be careful—someday you're going to find out that the women only love you for your money."

"Honey, money isn't everything. I keep them happy in other places, too."

"Gahh!" Miranda plugged her ears for emphasis. "I don't want to hear about what a stallion you are in the bedroom. I've known you since I was a kid."

He sobered and asked, "How's your pops?"

Miranda shot him a warning look. She didn't want to talk about her father in front of Jeremiah.

Rhett took the hint and cleared his throat. "As much as I enjoy a visit from my favorite fish-

and-game girl, time is money, love. What can I do for you?"

"The poachers are back," Miranda said. "We're basically examining all the old evidence. Jeremiah wanted to meet a lot of the local game outfits personally. I figured you'd be a good place to start."

"Happy to help. Poachers are bad for business," he said. "When people think they can just take whatever they like, they decimate the game for the legitimate outfits."

"Poaching is big business. We believe the poachers are part of a sophisticated ring that is killing the bears for the Asian black market. A bear gallbladder can go for as much as fifteen thousand a piece. That's big money." Jeremiah leaned forward and stared hard at Rhett. "Pardon me for asking, but what does it take to run an outfit like this? I imagine the economy has managed to take a bite out of your profits. I've checked your permit applications and you've had a twenty percent reduction in applications last year, and this year it seems you're taking a similar hit."

"Ain't it a bitch? Yeah, the economy has taken a bite, for sure." Rhett smiled with a shrug. "But I've got a healthy reserve. I assure you I don't need to start running black-market bear parts."

Miranda didn't realize she'd been holding her breath until Rhett had answered. Her cheeks flushed with anxiety, hating how Jeremiah had put Rhett on the spot with his line of questioning. "I'm sorry…. We had to ask," Miranda said quietly, glancing at Jeremiah in the hopes that they were finished.

"Girl, don't worry. It's your job. I want you to catch those bastards. It's hard enough to run a legitimate operation without people worrying that we're just running around willy-nilly. If the animal activists caught wind of an operation like mine doing something like that on the side, they'd delight in skewering my ass to the wood. I'm not about to give those peckerwoods the power to mess with my livelihood. You ask any question you like. I'm an open book."

"The first kill of the season was discovered last week right before that monster storm blew in. I was tracking them off Woodstock's Trail and then we lost the trail when the snow started to come down in a blizzard."

"Freak storm for so early in the season," Rhett said. "Dangerous."

Miranda nodded but didn't elaborate. She didn't come to chat about the weather and she definitely didn't want to share how she and Jeremiah had holed up in the search-and-rescue cabin. "I don't know how they're getting in and out without being noticed, which makes us wonder if they're operating under the guise of a legitimate business."

"There's a new outfit that just started operating, Vivid Adventures, owned by a gal named Vee Walker. I don't know much about her aside from the fact that she's running the prices so low that it's cutting into business on all sides. My question is, how is she able to operate with such low pricing? I'm not saying she's the one, but I'd poke my nose into her practices if I were you."

"Thanks for the tip, Rhett," Miranda said, looking to Jeremiah.

"We'll pull a few of her permits and take a look at the volume she's doing and where. The kills have been in a concentrated area each time. Thanks for your cooperation and the beer."

They rose and said their goodbyes, but as Jeremiah went ahead of Miranda, Rhett gently held Miranda back to speak to her privately. "Listen, be careful out there. Whenever there's big money at stake, lives tend to have less value...particularly that of a pair of nosy fish-and-game employees. You hear me?"

"I'll be okay," she assured her old friend. "Thanks for allowing Jeremiah to grill you."

"He seems all right," Rhett said, giving her the unofficial nod of approval. "Take it easy, kid."

Miranda smiled and joined Jeremiah in the car.

CHAPTER TWENTY-FIVE

"FOWLER SEEMS LIKE a good guy. Honest."

"He is. One of the best."

"How well do you know him?"

Miranda drew a deep breath. "I've known him my entire life. He and my dad used to be close."

"I sensed there was some history there. What happened?"

"When Simone died, my dad changed. He… stopped caring about the things that used to give him joy and started turning his attention to things that his friends didn't approve of."

She was phrasing her answer cautiously, which made Jeremiah wonder what she wasn't saying. He didn't want to pry but it seemed as if he was missing an important element.

"I shouldn't tell you this," she began sharing in a halting voice, "but I trust you." When she saw that he was listening intently, she continued. "My dad used to carve wooden totems and other types of tourist carvings and he was really good at what he did. At one time his art was everywhere. His carvings were sought after all over Alaska. But then Simone died and it was as if something intrinsic to his art died with her. He started smoking a lot of pot but because he needed an income he started selling it, too. So now he fancies himself a farmer and he's built an elaborate greenhouse system attached to his shop and that's where he spends the majority of his time—either stoned out of his gourd or tending to his crop."

Jeremiah could tell she'd taken a leap of faith sharing that information with him. He had to admit he was a little conflicted. As a federal employee he felt obligated to report such a crime but there was no way in hell he would do that to Miranda. "How does your family feel about your dad's new *profession?*"

Miranda barked a short derisive laugh. "You're being kind. I don't care what people say about marijuana being nonaddictive. My father is plainly hooked. And my family hates it. My oldest brother, Wade, won't even speak to my dad. Trace is so embarrassed he won't admit that it's even happening, and my mother is so locked in her own delusions that she lives in a house filled with junk and won't admit that her own husband has effectively moved out into the shop to avoid her." Miranda wiped the tear falling down her cheek as she laughed again. "I can't believe this. I'm crying. I never cry. But in the last week and a half I've cried more than I have in a lifetime. I don't know what to do for my family. I've called Trace numerous times, trying to get him to come home, but he just won't. I don't know what to say or do to get him here and I've completely given up on Wade. If you thought *I* was a mess, you should see my family."

"Everyone's family has dysfunction in some way or another."

"Yeah, but my family could medal in dysfunction."

Jeremiah chuckled. "I'm sure it feels that way. My family tree has its share of nuts. I'd like to say I'm the normal one but I've come to realize that I have my quirks, too."

"Such as?"

Jeremiah laughed, unsure of how much he should share. He didn't want to come off as weird so early in their relationship. "Well, if you must know, I have an aversion to the sound of people eating popcorn. Like fingernails on chalkboard for me. All I can think of is all that gnashing and spit flying and dirty fingers plunging into the communal popcorn bucket and I want to puke. Makes it hard to go to movies on a first date," he admitted with a rueful grin.

At that Miranda laughed. "So what do you do on a first date?"

"Depends. If she's really set on seeing a movie

I'll suffer through the agony but I'll suggest a matinee so there are fewer people. Or if she doesn't care about going to a movie, I try to throw something unique out there, like skating or skiing or a poetry recital."

Miranda looked aghast. "Poetry recital? Good thing you were on a self-imposed celibacy kick. There is no one who is going to have sex with you after a poetry recital. Talk about boring and very *unsexy*."

Jeremiah agreed. "Well, that was an isolated incident. And the woman I was dating was a New Age type who seemed as if she would enjoy something like that. Personally, it wasn't my cup of tea. But, in all fairness, it wasn't a terrible night. I had a great time even if I didn't particularly enjoy the poetry."

"Aww, what a champion of making lemonade with lemons. But I would never enjoy something like that, just so you know."

Jeremiah's ears perked at that small admission. "Just out of curiosity, what kind of first date *would* you enjoy? Not that I'm looking for information…but you know what I mean."

Miranda shrugged. "I'm not much of a dater. Small talk bores me. I'm a bit of a workaholic and any free time I have I spend with my son. But I used to enjoy snowboarding when I had the time. It's been a long time since I've been able to hit the slopes but if I were looking for an idea to suggest to someone it would definitely be something physical and outdoors."

"I've never snowboarded. But I can ski."

"I won't hold that against you," Miranda teased, then sobered. "Listen, I want to follow up on that tip that Rhett gave us. Honestly, I've never heard of Vivid Adventures and I don't remember a permit with Vee Walker's name on it."

Jeremiah agreed. "I have that meeting with Stuart tomorrow otherwise I'd go with you but I definitely think follow-up is a good idea."

Miranda nodded. "I will. For what it's worth, I don't know if Rhett doesn't like her because she's cutting into his bottom line or because he knows something that we don't, but I know that he would never steer me in the wrong direction."

"Okay. But I want you to take someone with you. How about Mary?"

Miranda grimaced. "Mary hates doing fieldwork. Anything that takes her outside of the comfort of the office is no good for her. I'll be fine. I don't need a chaperone."

"It isn't about needing a chaperone. It's about safety. If this woman is involved with the poaching circles she's not going to like you poking your nose around in her business. I just want to make sure you're safe."

Miranda's mouth curved in a sweet smile that

she couldn't hold back. And for a long moment Jeremiah fought to keep from closing the distance and sealing his mouth to hers. The one saving grace was that she was still driving and he didn't want to distract her but, damn, the urge to touch her was overwhelming. Electricity sparked between them and it seemed the cab of the vehicle had become unbearably hot. He broke the spell when he pulled away and cracked the window. "Just be careful out there."

Miranda didn't protest this time and simply nodded.

"We make a good team," Jeremiah said. "I wish things were different."

"Yeah," she said softly. "Me, too."

At least they were on the same page of a banned book.

THAT NIGHT MIRANDA couldn't sleep. A combination of the information Rhett had shared and the knowledge that Jeremiah was going to admit to Stuart his involvement with an employee had her head in a chaotic tangle. Why did Jeremiah have to be so damn noble? He didn't need to admit to anything. There was no real proof of anything inappropriate. Even as she justified his need to lie to his supervisor, she was a tiny bit proud of his stalwart insistence on telling the truth, no matter the cost.

Johnny had been such a pathological liar that she'd never trusted a word that had come out of his mouth. Jeremiah would never be like that. Not that they were anywhere near similar to one another, but Johnny was the last man she'd shared time with and her relationship with Johnny was the only thing she had to compare to.

How sad was that? Miranda grimaced and flung her arm over her eyes as she lay in the darkness. She missed Jeremiah beside her. When exactly did she become this person who missed cuddling? She shuddered at her own ridiculousness, but even as she derided herself, she longed for Jeremiah's comforting warmth beside her.

She'd slept so soundly next to him, curled into his body like a matching puzzle piece. Miranda groaned and kicked her feet a little in frustration. *Stop. Just stop. Focus on what's real.*

There was no future with Jeremiah. No matter that they were good together, both in bed and in the office. The odds were stacked against them so high that they towered into the sky and touched the clouds.

Miranda squeezed her eyes shut and tried to sleep. Tomorrow was a big day—for her and Jeremiah.

She could only hope he was getting more sleep than she was at the moment; he was going to need his wits about him when he talked with Stuart.

Please let everything work out for once, she said in a silent prayer. *Please. Just this once.*

She'd never put much store in prayer. After Simone had died, praying to a higher power had seemed a useless waste of time.

But here she was, fervently praying for the first time in eight years that a higher power of some sort would take pity on her and turn everything to her advantage. If her mother knew, she'd scold her for being selfish. She'd say, God had bigger priorities than the mundane details of Miranda Sinclair's life. Maybe that was so, but Miranda didn't know what else to do and she had to do something.

When her cell phone trilled to life on her bedside table, she snatched it up, only too eager to do anything aside from try to force sleep. She'd half hoped it was Jeremiah, but when she heard her brother Trace's voice on the line, she was both relieved and irritated.

"Why can't you call at a normal hour?" she groused.

"Were you sleeping?"

"No."

"Then what does it matter what time I call?" It was hard to argue with Trace's logic and he knew it. "You sounded pretty upset with the last message you left. Sorry I was out of range and didn't get your message until I came down from the mountain. What's going on?"

Miranda sighed. "Trace…I visited Mom the other day in the hopes of talking to her and mending some fences but when I went into the house I couldn't believe how much worse it'd gotten in a matter of weeks. I could barely get the front door open there was so much stuff in there but that's not the half of it. The kitchen has something rotten and dying in there—I'm sure of it—and she swears she can't smell anything. I've never experienced anything so disgusting but she won't listen to me. She's going to die in there."

"What does Dad say?" Trace asked.

"Nothing. He's completely in his own world."

"Selfish asshole," Trace muttered, and Miranda winced. At one time they'd all been so close in their own way; their dad had been their hero. Things had changed and not for the better.

"I need you, Trace. I really do. I wouldn't ask if I didn't think it was imperative. I need you to see what I see."

There was a long pause on the other line, and then Trace exhaled with a long and resigned sigh. "I can't come right away. I have another case that just popped up while I was on this last tracking job. It's high profile and I can't walk away from it. I'll come home as soon as I can."

Relief flooded Miranda and she almost cried.

"Thank you, Trace." Her brother didn't make false promises. If he said he was coming—he would. She would just have to tread water until he came. "Be careful out there."

"Always." He paused. "Sis…I'm sorry I haven't been much help lately. I've been dealing with some stuff and work has been crazy busy."

"I know," she said, cutting him some slack. "I can't wait to see you."

"Ditto, kid. Take it easy until I see you, okay?"

She smiled. "Okay."

The line went dead and Miranda held the cell to her chest, so relieved that her brother was finally coming. He might not have any more luck than she'd had but at least he'd see for himself what she'd been up against with their parents. The knowledge that she wouldn't have to face the situation alone any longer made her want to sob with gratitude. She hadn't realized how much the weight of the responsibility had been suffocating her until recently.

She squeezed her eyes shut. "Thank you," she whispered. If this were her one grace…she'd take it.

CHAPTER TWENTY-SIX

MIRANDA FOLLOWED THE directions to Vivid Adventures and surveyed the surroundings. The business was located in an isolated area with a simple sign tacked into the ground advertising the location. She supposed she could look at their sparse presence in two ways: either the business was still too young to have a permanent footprint or they planned to be transient and didn't care to put down roots. She hated to be so quick to judge, but Rhett had planted the seed of suspicion in her mind that was hard to shake.

Against Jeremiah's advice, Miranda had chosen to come alone. Mary or Todd would've been her natural choice, but Mary hated fieldwork, and being as Todd was constantly on the prowl as a single guy, if Vee Walker was anything but a troll Todd wouldn't be much help.

Miranda quickly grabbed her cell and snapped a few photos of the area. Before she had a chance to take too many pictures, an older attractive woman greeted her with a hard smile. "You must be Miranda Sinclair with Fish and Game. What do I owe this pleasure?"

Miranda didn't like that Vee already knew who she was. "You have me at a disadvantage. You know who I am but we've never actually been introduced. Whom do I have the pleasure of speaking with?"

"Vee Walker, owner of Vivid Adventures."

Miranda returned the smile. "Very nice to meet you. I'd like to speak with you about your operation. You're new around here and Fish and Game likes to have an open communication with all the big-game operations."

"Well, how sweet is that. Why don't you come inside so we can chat." Vee didn't wait for Miranda and simply walked into the building, knowing Miranda would follow. Already Miranda didn't like her, but just because she had a terrible personality didn't mean that she was a poacher.

Vee led her into a small sitting room or lobby and gestured for Miranda to take a seat. "Can I get you anything? Coffee, tea?"

Miranda shook her head. "No, thank you," she said, getting right to the point of her visit. "I'm not sure if you're aware but we've had some poaching problems here in the past. I've pulled your permits and you have a fair amount of volume considering how new you are, but I have to wonder how you're able to keep your prices so low and still make a profit?"

Vee laughed. "Would you like a course in business management? Or are you asking if I supplement my income with poaching? I must say where I come from the welcoming committee is less accusatory."

"I apologize if these questions seem a little impertinent. But poaching is a serious issue and there have been some leads that suggest whoever is doing it might be doing it under the guise of legitimate business."

"Imagine that. How clever." Vee shrugged. "I'm afraid I'm a fan of doing things the old-fashioned way. No shortcuts here. You can rest assured I am not engaging in any of that dirty poaching business. Out of curiosity, who tossed my name into the mix? Let me guess—Rhett Fowler?"

Vee's lip curled with scorn and Miranda suffered an unpleasant twinge. "Why do you say that?" she asked, trying to appear nonplussed. "You're new here. Any of the established outfits could've thrown your name in."

Vee chuckled as if she found it amusing that Miranda would assume she was that naive. "When we moved in this area we did a little checking around and we found that Big Game Trophy was one of the biggest, most expensive

operations in Alaska. Naturally, we wanted to
find a way to cash in on some of his success. We
saw how he was overcharging his unsuspecting
clients and we knew we could offer the same experience for less money. Mr. Fowler has not been
pleased with our entrepreneurial spirit. We have
had the pleasure of Mr. Fowler visiting on more
than one occasion."

Rhett hadn't mentioned that small fact. "Be
that as it may, when poaching of this magnitude
crops up we have to explore all leads. I couldn't
help but notice the less-than-permanent footprint
for your business. The seemingly transient nature
of your operation might lead one to believe that
you're not planning to stay."

"I believe in giving my clients the adventure
of a lifetime. If they'd like to stay in some fancy
lodge and drink espresso all day, then they can
hook up with Big Game Trophy. At Vivid Adventures we give them what they pay for—a trophy
to put on their wall."

Miranda nodded, admitting that made a small
amount of sense, but there was something about
the woman that she didn't trust. "I'm going to
need a list of employees so we can run background checks."

"What for?"

"We like to make sure everyone is who they
say they are."

Vee crossed her arms over her chest. "I hate to break it to you, darlin', but you need a warrant for that. I run my business how I see fit. Until you have proof that one of my employees is doing something wrong, you can just go out the same way you came. Unless, of course, you'd like to book an adventure, in which case, Cynthia would be happy to book your reservation."

"Your cooperation would go a long way to creating goodwill."

"Save it. You're on team Fowler, which tells me you're not on team Walker." Vee stood. "I believe I've answered all of your questions...."

Miranda realized she wasn't going to get much further with the interview and rose to leave. "I'll be in touch," she advised Vee with a narrowed gaze.

"I'm sure you will." Vee walked Miranda to the door, and as Miranda approached her car Vee had one final comment. "While you are busy pulling my permits and harassing me, did you ever think to look into Fowler's business practices? We've cut into his business no doubt. And yet he lives like a king. Doesn't that seem odd to you? Instead of harassing the newcomer, why don't you look closer to home?"

Miranda hated that Vee had echoed her own concern—a concern that Rhett had easily swept away with a vague answer about his reserve. As

Miranda pulled away, she couldn't help the over-whelming feeling that one of her most trusted people in the world had lied to her. She didn't want to believe that Rhett was capable of something as heinous as poaching but hard times sometimes blurred moral boundaries for some people.

Now she had to dig a little harder into Rhett's business and the idea gave her a stomachache. As crappy as her day had turned, she could only hope that Jeremiah's day was faring much better.

JEREMIAH WISHED HE could say he had a game plan when he walked into Stuart's office but he'd decided to simply play it by ear so nothing appeared rehearsed. He figured if the day was going to end badly there wasn't much he could do about it.

When Jeremiah entered the office Stuart was standing by the window, gazing at the snow-peaked mountains. Stuart turned slightly to acknowledge Jeremiah's entrance but otherwise did not give up his view. Jeremiah took a seat and waited. Stuart stretched out the moment until Jeremiah nervously shifted in his chair, not quite sure what was happening. He'd expected Stuart to start the conversation with a lot of angry bluster but instead he seemed contemplative and resigned. "Are you having a relationship with

Miranda Sinclair?" Stuart asked point-blank, his voice mildly weary.

Jeremiah answered without hesitation. "No." It was the truth. He was not having a relationship with Miranda but he didn't feel compelled to clarify the exact nature of their acquaintance.

"I received a phone call that someone saw Miranda leaving your house on Saturday. Is this true?"

Jeremiah nodded. "Yes."

Stuart frowned, exasperation in his voice. "And yet you're not having a relationship?"

"No."

"Are you saying this visit was professional?"

"No. Miranda's visit was personal. She and I had shared tense words a few days prior and Miranda came to clear the air. She didn't want to be the subject of office gossip and chose to come to my home and speak privately."

Stuart nodded as if he could relate to losing his cool with Miranda. "Might I ask what this personal business was about?"

"I'd rather not say. It was fairly personal. I'm trying to build a good working relationship with my team and I wouldn't want to betray her trust so early in our relationship."

"Fair point." Stuart sighed. "It seems someone with an ax to grind against Miranda chose to see a situation in an unflattering light. I'm sorry I dragged you into it. I should've known you would have more integrity than that."

Jeremiah winced privately as he knew Stuart's faith in him was misplaced. Stuart thought he'd cleared Jeremiah, but in truth, Stuart simply hadn't asked the right questions. Jeremiah swallowed the words dancing in on his tongue. The urge to admit the truth of his actions pressed down on him but he fought the urge to confess his sins until the moment passed. He didn't want to leave Miranda. And if he told Stuart the truth, Stuart would demand his resignation. Jeremiah simply wasn't ready to do that. "Sir, if I may ask, what is your beef with Miranda? From what I can tell she's a good employee and an asset to the department, yet you're obviously not a fan."

Stuart nodded, accepting the legitimacy of Jeremiah's question without irritation. "I don't care for her personality. I don't like her attitude. And I think a part of me is angry that she doesn't give a damn what I think of her," he admitted.

"She's a strong woman. She's smart and a self-starter. Frankly, the department could use a few more employees like her. Have you taken a look at the research she's compiled on the poaching cases? She may not have law-enforcement training but she's got an eye for finding details that seem out of place. With her tracking skills and some formal training she could be a force to reckon with."

"Yeah, I suppose so." Stuart's chin lifted as his jaw tensed. "I don't much care for women who immediately question every direction you give them. What happened to the good old days when women did what they were told?"

Jeremiah startled at the irritability in Stuart's voice. Somehow Jeremiah didn't think Stuart was only talking about Miranda any longer. "Change is good," Jeremiah ventured cautiously. "Having a woman's perspective on the job is an invaluable asset. Their brains don't work like ours. I've found that having a woman's input on any given dilemma is an immediate bonus. The best part about Miranda is that she works like a man but still thinks like a woman."

"I suppose." Stuart sighed, seeming distracted. "Do you know when I married my wife she wanted to be a homemaker? And she was a damn good one. But then she wanted a career. And suddenly I was fixing my own dinner and ironing my own shirts, and then, if that wasn't bad enough, she wanted me to be sensitive to her needs as if I hadn't already been sensitive to her before. It's damn confusing, if you ask me. Life was simpler when the women kept the house and the men did the work." Stuart's admission shocked Jeremiah. "Times have changed, Jeremiah. And not for the better."

Jeremiah couldn't disagree more. "When a woman has her own career, her own passion, she gains the same amount of pride as a man does when he's done a job well. My father had a saying—'happy wife, happy life.' I believe it's true. My ex-wife was a very unhappy woman and when our son died she had nothing left to sustain her. People need more than just one single thing to fill their day. People need purpose. If keeping house and tending children doesn't fulfill their purpose, if they're smart enough to find something outside of the home to do that, let them. The best bit of advice I can give is, if you want to hold on to your wife, embrace her desire to have a career. Support her. If you don't like ironing your clothes, hire someone to do it, but don't expect her to do it simply because it's convenient for you. Show her that you can change and be the man that she needs you to be."

"Why should I pay good money to do something that she used to do for me for free?"

"You need to change your thinking or you're going to end up alone. I know that much. Do you love your wife, sir?"

"Of course I do."

"Then show her with your actions. Remember, happy wife, happy life. It's a good rule to live by."

Stuart pursed his lips bullishly, and even though he didn't like what Jeremiah had to say there must've been a glimmer of reason that made sense because he jerked a short nod before returning his gaze out the window. "I'm sorry I took you away from more important details. Have you had any leads on the poaching case?"

"A few. Miranda's chasing down a lead right now."

Stuart grunted in approval. "Keep me updated."

Jeremiah nodded and realized Stuart had just dismissed him. As Jeremiah climbed into his car he sat for a long moment and considered everything that had just happened. Somehow by the grace of God, he had saved his own job. In the process he'd caught a small glimpse into the personal life of his superior. He could only hope that Stuart could change his old-fashioned ways in order to keep his wife happy. If not the man was going to end up divorced and bitter during what was supposed to be the golden years of his life.

Jeremiah put the car into Drive and headed back to the office. He couldn't wait to tell Miranda what had happened as well as hear how her trip to Vivid Adventures had fared.

He'd love to solve this poaching case...not only

for the department but to put a much-deserved feather in Miranda's cap.

She needed this resolution and he aimed to help her get it.

CHAPTER TWENTY-SEVEN

MIRANDA NEEDED A GLASS of wine to settle her nerves. Why wouldn't Rhett tell her that he'd already had some altercations with Vee Walker? He could've easily shared that information with her privately before she'd left his place yesterday. It didn't sit well at all that it appeared Rhett had left out some crucial information. At one time Rhett had been her father's best friend. He'd been a staple around their dinner table, teasing her mother about marrying Zed instead of him. It'd been good-natured fun, of course, and Rhett had always treated Zed's kids as if they were his own since he'd never had any children. In fact, when Simone had died, he'd personally put up the reward money for information leading to her killer.

That money remained in an untouched account, waiting for someone to come forward.

Rhett would never lie to her, she thought with an agonized groan when the questions wouldn't stop.

Rhett had assured her that his business was fine—that money wasn't an issue, but Miranda knew that he had notoriously expensive tastes and that kind of lifestyle required a constant influx of cash to maintain. If Rhett's Big Game Trophy income was being cut into, where was Rhett making up the shortfall? She frowned unhappily when her instincts were at war with her heart. Her cell rang and she picked it up anxiously when she saw it was Jeremiah.

"Well?" she asked, nervous. "What happened?"

"Everything is fine. I still have a job," he said.

"You lied?"

"No, I answered Stuart's questions truthfully. It's not my fault Stuart didn't ask the right questions."

Miranda's immediate relief was followed by a gasp of admiration. "Oh, thank God, you crafty man. I was so worried you were going to go down for this for no good reason. Don't get me wrong, I'm all for integrity, but come on—you have to draw the line somewhere, right?"

"Glad to have your approval." Jeremiah chuckled wearily. "I didn't like the feeling that I was trying to hide something, though. It goes against everything I believe in."

"I know. I'm sorry. We have to be more careful."

"We dodged a bullet, but we shouldn't tempt fate. We know all the reasons why a relationship between us wouldn't work. I don't know why we kept ignoring the simple facts."

Miranda's elation deflated. "Yeah, I suppose you're right." What else was he supposed to say? He'd just narrowly missed losing his livelihood over her. She couldn't expect him to invite her to run away for the weekend. She rubbed at her nose unhappily but tried to remember what was important. "I'm glad you were able to keep your job," she said. "I think it would've been a mistake on Stuart's part if he'd let you go."

"Thank you." Jeremiah paused, then added, "Do you know anything about Stuart and his wife?"

"Gloria? She's a teacher, I think. I remember years ago Isaac saying something about his mom going back to school to become a first-grade teacher. Why?"

"Just curious. Stuart shared with me that he was struggling with his wife's newfound desire to have a career."

"Ugh. He's such a male chauvinist. I don't know how Gloria put up with him all those years."

"How do you know so much about Stuart and his wife?"

"I had a brief encounter with their son Isaac and he shared a few details. Plus, I've enjoyed a few conversations with Gloria at department functions. She's a cool lady. Her only lapse in judgment was marrying that fool."

Jeremiah chuckled. "Well, seems he's dealing with a whole lot of change in his household that's hard to handle. Honestly, if he hadn't been distracted by his personal problems I don't think he would've let me off with such a gentle hand. As it was, he seemed eager to put the matter to bed so he could focus on other things."

"His turmoil was our gain," Miranda said, shrugging. "Well, I went out to meet Vee Walker, and let me tell you, she's a tough cookie. On the surface she's gruff, barely civil and plainly not open to cooperating, which under normal circumstances would raise flags, but my gut tells me she's not actually hiding anything. She just hates government authority. And if that were a crime, there'd be plenty in Alaska who were breaking the law."

"So back to square one."

"Not exactly," she admitted, hating what she was about to say. "She told me a few things that have made me realize I need to take a deeper look into Rhett's business."

"Why?"

"Just a hunch that I ignored when we saw him and Vee echoed that hunch."

"Do you want me to chase it down so there's no conflict of interest?" he offered.

"Yeah, that would probably be best. God, I hate this. I don't want to be right."

"Don't stress just yet. Plenty of things can seem suspicious but in the end, be perfectly legitimate."

"Yeah, but I subscribe to the Occam's-razor rule—the simplest explanation is usually accurate."

"Let's wait and see what the evidence says. Okay?"

"Okay," she said. "See you at the office tomorrow."

"Bright and early."

"Oh, and, Jeremiah…sleep well." She didn't know why she'd tacked that on, maybe because deep down she knew he suffered from the same level of insomnia as she did and the one time they'd both slept like babies was with each other. It was silly, but, somehow, hoping that she'd be the last thing on his mind made her smile.

"Ditto," he replied, his voice lowering just enough to sound like a caress. And then he was gone.

RHETT FOWLER BARKED for his wife, Ambra. "Where's that damn beer, darlin'?" What a day. What a damn day! That Walker woman was going to put him out of business. Three more cancellations today. Ambra, his saving grace, came into the room with her usual serene expression and a beer in her hand.

"Darlin', you're the best part about my day," he said, pulling her into his lap. She smiled and allowed him to rest his hand possessively on her pert rump. He sucked down a healthy swig of his beer before asking, "What did you do all day while I watched that woman steal three more reservations?"

"I did as I always do, my love—think of you," she said, bending down to sweep a petal-soft kiss across his lips.

"Is that so?" Rhett asked, his ire slipping away and being replaced by simple need. "Why don't you show me what you were thinking?"

Ambra laughed and slipped away before his hand could reach the full bounty of her ripe breast. "You silly thing, not now. Perhaps later." Ambra walked away, leaving Rhett wishing he could follow her into the bedroom and enjoy the benefits of having a wife who was so much younger than he was, but Ambra was a fickle beauty who doled out her affections sparingly. Usually, he had to loosen the buttons on her blouse with the help of something shiny and expensive. He sighed. And he couldn't afford a shiny new bauble at this rate. He drained his beer and grabbed his expense sheets. There was one saving grace—his new helicopter pilot, Mack, was saving him money. The kid came cheap because he wanted to build his résumé and Rhett had been more than happy to provide the experience for him. If only he'd been able to find ways to cut all of his operational expenses in half.

He was just surfing the Net looking for alternative fuel companies for his fleet of vehicles when a commotion interrupted his research.

Ambra trailed after that horrid woman, Vee Walker, as she barreled into the room and headed straight for him with fire in her eyes.

"You rotten SOB, siccing your fish-and-game honey on me just because you can't handle a little competition? What's the matter? Can't deal with a woman getting the jump on you because you're too damn lazy to start thinking creatively? So we cut a little into your business…tough titty! Fat and lazy, that's what you are, and you're trying to submarine us for simply trying to run a legitimate business."

Rhett struggled to his feet to stand toe-to-toe with the tall woman. "Legitimate business? You can't tell me you're running a clean operation when you cut corners to offer a dirt-cheap price for your clients. How do I know you're not running that poaching ring to supplement your income?"

"I don't need to supplement my income because I don't waste it on frivolous crap." Vee shot a derisive look at Ambra, who shot back a dagger of her own. "I can see where you spend your money and it's not on your clients. Maybe if you stopped being such a little bitch, lapping after whatever crumbs Miss Arctic Snow here is willing to drop you, you'd see what was happening right under your damn nose. Stop poking around in my business and tend to your own. And tell your little fish-and-game honey to back off!"

"Watch yourself. She's like a daughter to me and whatever you're implying is about to get you in a pot of hot water," he warned.

"My apologies for implying that you're a dirty old man who likes women young enough to be his granddaughter," Vee shot back, clearly not the least bit sorry. She threw one last comment over her shoulder as she let herself out. "Tend to your own backyard and stay the hell out of mine, Fowler!"

The door slammed and something breakable crashed to the tile floor. Ambra clenched her little fists and shrieked, "My Waterford!" and ran to determine the damage. Rhett couldn't care less about a piece of crystal, though. He was stewing about Vee bursting into his house and spreading chaos in her wake. How dare she insult his wife? And what was Vee saying about "tending to his own backyard"? What did she know that he didn't?

"She broke the Waterford," Ambra wailed, gingerly holding shards of shattered crystal within a towel. "That bitch!"

"Buy another," he muttered, irritated at Ambra for caring more about a piece of crystal than the fact that something foul was afoot within his business. "I'll be in my study. I need to make a few calls."

He stalked from the room and shut the heavy oak door to his office. Vee was tall for a woman. She'd stared right into his eyes without having to crane her neck like Ambra. There was something strong and vibrant about the older woman that, if she weren't such a ballbuster stealing his clients, he might've respected.

But right about now...he wanted to bury her up to her neck in snow and then leave her to bake in the sun.

Well, maybe that was harsh but he was pretty damn mad.

Probably just as mad as Vee had been when Miranda had shown up asking questions. At that he cracked a smile. He would have loved to be a fly on the wall after that meeting.

Yeah, ol' Vee had probably cursed his name up one side and down the other.

He guffawed. Served her right. Wait until she

found out he'd placed a call to the IRS to have her audited.

Now, *that* was a thought that raised his spirits.

CHAPTER TWENTY-EIGHT

JUST TO COVER all bases Miranda pulled every single permit filed with Fish and Game in the past year for big-game tags. When she started tabulating each of the individual operation permits, she realized the numbers were down for everyone. The economy was bad, and people just didn't have the money for these types of luxuries. It was no wonder Vivid Adventures was doing far better for offering a competitive price.

On one hand, she was relieved that everyone was doing poorly, because then it took the spotlight from Rhett and Big Game Trophy, but she couldn't deny something didn't seem right. It wasn't something she wanted to do, but she'd be cheating herself and the case if she plainly ignored a very big red flag.

Jeremiah walked in adjusting his gloves. "I'll call you when I'm finished." Jeremiah was on his way to interview Rhett again. She just couldn't do it. Besides, if Rhett had something to do with the poaching. it was better that there was some distance between her and the case because of their relationship. Jeremiah had pointed out that a defense attorney would rip apart their case if it was discovered that there was a conflict of interest during the investigation. Jeremiah noted her glum acceptance of the situation and reminded her, "Don't borrow trouble. It could be nothing."

She nodded. "In the meantime, I'm going to place some calls to the other smaller operations to ask them about their volume."

"Good idea."

Miranda watched as Jeremiah left the office and listened as his car hit the highway. A part of her wanted to be there to provide a buffer between Jeremiah and Rhett but she knew that wasn't possible. In fact, it would defeat the whole purpose of Jeremiah doing the questioning. She was terrified that, if in the event that Rhett was linked to the poaching, she'd feel as if she were losing her father all over again. Rhett was the only person she had left in her life who was still seminormal. Rhett had been the only one who hadn't gone bonkers when Simone had died. "Please be innocent," she whispered.

JEREMIAH WAS LET into the house and led into the study, where Rhett awaited him. He'd half expected the man to make him wait a few moments in a show of power, but Rhett seemed ready to put the situation to rest and was there when Jeremiah arrived.

"I'm sure you realize that there is a conflict of interest for Miranda to continue questioning you," Jeremiah began. "She loves you very much and the thought of you being involved in something like poaching is killing her inside. I hope for her sake you had nothing to do with the poaching cases."

"Straight to the point, aren't you?" Rhett leaned back in his big chair, regarding Jeremiah with a strong, steady stare. "What makes you think that I had anything to do with the poaching?"

"Your volume is down, your reported income is down, and yet you continue to live pretty opulently," Jeremiah stated bluntly. "Given the lucrative nature of the black market, it's only natural to wonder where you're getting your cash if not from Big Game Trophy clients."

"I told Miranda I had a healthy reserve. Some years have been better than others."

"That's not good enough of an explanation. I'm going to need to see your financials."

Rhett scoffed. "Going a little far, don't you think? I already told you I don't have anything to do with the poaching."

Jeremiah shook his head. "That might have worked for Miranda. But I don't know you and it doesn't work for me. If you have nothing to hide then getting a look at your financials shouldn't be a problem."

Rhett leaned forward and pinned Jeremiah with his gaze. "How would you like it if I poke my nose around in *your* financials?"

"I wouldn't like it at all. However, if I were being considered as a possible suspect in an open case and I had nothing to hide, I would do everything in my power to clear my name and my *reputation*."

There was a silent standoff between the two men until finally Rhett shrugged and said, "Sorry, son, you're going to need a warrant for that."

"I'd hoped you would have volunteered but I can get a warrant without a problem."

"We'll see about that."

"You know this just makes you look guilty, right? And it's going to kill Miranda. How do you feel about that?"

Rhett looked discomfited but held his ground. "I'm not about to sacrifice my rights as an American citizen without a fight. I told you I had nothing to do with the poaching, and I meant it. However, if my word isn't good enough, then you're going to have to follow due process to get what you need."

"Am I going to need a warrant for your employee list, as well?"

Rhett smiled and pushed a piece of paper across

the desk. "That I can give you. Is there anything else you need?" he asked.

Jeremiah picked up the paper and folded it in half before sticking it in his pocket. "I'll be in touch."

"Tell Miranda not to worry. My hands are clean."

Jeremiah looked long and hard at Rhett and said, "I sure hope so. Because if they're not, I'm going to find out and so will Miranda."

Rhett gave Jeremiah a short dismissive wave. "Good day, Mr. Burke. I will look forward to your apology."

MIRANDA ACCEPTED THE FOLDED slip of paper from Jeremiah when he returned and read it. "Rhett's employee list?" she surmised. Jeremiah nodded and she added, "Tell me how it went. Is he upset?"

"He's irritated but didn't seem overly worried. I think he's mostly pissed at the invasion of what he perceives as his privacy. I've already set in motion the warrant for his financials."

"And I called for the financials for Vivid Adventures. We should have them by tonight if we manage to get Judge Pope—he's a staunch supporter of animal rights and loves to stick it to the big-game operators whenever he can."

"Then let's hope for Judge Pope." Jeremiah

smiled. "Are you doing okay? I know there's been a lot to absorb."

Miranda leaned back in her chair, nodding. "Tell me about it. Yeah, I'm doing okay. I just wish there wasn't so much noise going on in my head. Makes it hard to concentrate. My brother called me last night. He's coming home soon to help me out. That's a huge relief. My parents are a handful." She looked to him, curious. "You never talk about your parents. Are they around still?"

"No. Unfortunately, I lost both parents when I was in my twenties. One to cancer and the other to heart failure about five years apart. The only family I have now is a brother I rarely talk to and an aunt who lives in San Francisco. My family was never what you'd call close-knit. I mean, I was close to my parents, but as far as extended family, we just didn't live near enough to create those bonds."

Miranda felt a pang of sadness for Jeremiah. He had no one to lean on, no one to care about. "As much as my family has a few loose screws, I can't imagine life without them. I think that's what makes the current situation so tough. I have lots of good memories. My dad was like the Alaskan version of Grizzly Adams. He taught us how to shoot, trap, track and basically live off the land if we had to. It was a constant adventure."

"My dad wasn't the outdoors type. He was

probably the only person in Wyoming who didn't own a gun. I had to learn on my own because unlike him, I liked to get out there once in a while. My dad was more of an academic. He enjoyed books and instilled in me a love of knowledge."

"Do you miss your parents?"

"Every day. Some days are harder than others."

That was how she felt about Simone. "Losing a family member...I don't think you ever truly recover from it. I mean, the constant pain dulls but there's always an ache deep inside to remind you of what's gone." Jeremiah nodded and she knew he was thinking of his son. "Did you want more kids?" she asked cautiously, knowing the question was planted in painful memories.

"I did. But Josie had a hard enough time carrying Tyler and we decided one was enough." Jeremiah looked away. "We told ourselves that we'd be able to give our one child everything he needed without having to split our resources between siblings. It'd seemed a solid plan."

"I never expected to be a mother," Miranda shared. "I hardly felt qualified to handle my own life much less be in charge of someone else's. But once I had Talen, my outlook on life changed and I realized he was the best thing I'd ever done. I like to think that kids take the absolute best of each of their parents."

"And Talen's father...?"

"Dead. Thank God." At Jeremiah's quick look, she explained briefly, saying, "He was bad news. I was going through a rough time and he seemed an excellent way to ruin my life and self-destruct at the same time. It was a two-for-one deal."

"Why were you punishing yourself?"

"At the time, I was hurting so badly and I didn't have anyone to turn to. My brothers were going through their own thing and my parents... Well, I already told you how they dealt with Simone's death. It was bad times all around."

"I hate the idea of you in such pain," he said, his gaze soft. She tried not to melt under the warmth of his stare, knowing they had to keep their distance from one another, but it was hard, particularly when they were being so open with one another.

"Well, I'm much better now," she said, forcing a smile to break the connection pulling them together. "Once I had Talen I knew I couldn't chance hooking up with another loser like Johnny, so I kept my distance from commitment of any kind in order to protect Talen."

"Sacrificing yourself for the sake of your child sounds noble, but in the end, it's really you finding a different packaging for your own issues," he said quietly. "Trust me, I know a lot about justifying."

"You're right but I was also right. You see, so

many kids have to deal with a revolving door of people in their lives and it hurts them. I never wanted my son to suffer from my mistakes. And I know I make plenty of them. Yes, I was projecting myself but I was also protecting Talen."

"You're a good mother," Jeremiah said. "Talen is a lucky kid."

She smiled, warming at his compliment. "Thank you. I try really hard. It's not something that came naturally to me but when I look at his face each morning he gives me reason to be better than I was the day before." She laughed a little in embarrassment at her own comment. She cast a quick glance his way. "Sappy, right?"

"Not at all. Never apologize for being a good parent. The world needs more parents who care as much as you do about your boy."

Miranda accepted his advice and a moment stretched between them until she asked, "Where's your ex-wife?"

At the mention of his former wife, Jeremiah's mouth twisted in a sardonic smile that had little to do with anything joyful. "Josie is back in Wyoming, living in our former house with our former dog and her *new* husband."

"Ouch."

Jeremiah shrugged. "It is what it is. Giving her the house seemed the least I could do. Besides,

I didn't want it. Too many memories. I would've gone insane in that house."

"You know it wasn't your fault, right?"

"Yeah," he acknowledged, but his answer rang hollow. He blamed himself as deeply as she blamed herself for her sister's death. He shook himself free from his melancholy and a crooked smile followed. "New rule—no more serious personal stuff at the office. Brings everyone down." He winked and pushed away from the doorframe. "I'll let you know when those warrants come in," he said, and he walked away with an air of sadness clinging to him like smoke.

Miranda watched him go and her heart ached for him. Sometimes life was a coldhearted bitch who didn't play by any rules but her own and it plain sucked to land on the losing end.

When did either one of the players get to reset and start over?

CHAPTER TWENTY-NINE

MIRANDA AND JEREMIAH pulled a late night as they pored over the financial records of both Big Game Trophy and Vivid Adventures. None of the other outfits were big enough to warrant a deeper look, and thus they were stuck focusing on the two rival companies.

"Are you sure you can stay?" Jeremiah asked, as he passed her a slice of pepperoni pizza and a soda. "I could probably do this myself."

"*Mamu* is watching Talen for me so I'm good to stay. Besides, it would take you until tomorrow morning to sift through both financial records and I'd rather just do it together so we can get it done."

Jeremiah nodded, and after shoveling two pieces of pizza down his gullet, he dived into the dizzying number of Excel spreadsheets that detailed every penny spent by either operation.

It was about an hour later that Miranda made a startling realization. "Rhett Fowler is going broke," she said with a catch in her voice. "His reserve is practically gone." She looked to Jeremiah, stricken. "This is why he didn't want us to see his financials…. It wasn't because he was doing anything he shouldn't. He's embarrassed. Here—" she handed him the paperwork "—take a look."

Jeremiah studied the spreadsheet and balances. "It appears he's living way beyond his means. He's got more going out than he has coming in."

"And no big deposits, either. If he's running a poaching operation, he sucks at it because he's drowning in debt."

"This gives him motive," Jeremiah warned. "He could have offshore accounts to hide the money."

"I don't believe that. You can see where his money is going. For ridiculous purchases." Miranda had an idea who was authorizing credit-card purchases for Louis Vuitton handbags and Gucci shoes. "That Swiss miss is sucking up all his cash."

"The price of a young wife," Jeremiah said. "He has to know that he's overextended."

"Oh, Rhett…you dumb ox," Miranda muttered, irritated at Rhett for being so stupid with his money and thinking with a different part of his anatomy. "He's not guilty of anything but being led around by his—"

"That may be true," Jeremiah interjected with

a frown. "But we still need to talk to him about our findings."

"He's going to be mortified."

"They say the lessons that stick with us are the ones that embarrass us or cost us money. Maybe he'll use it as a learning experience."

Miranda cut Jeremiah a short look. "Yeah, that'll happen," she said derisively, then sighed. "All right...I want to take another look at his employee list and make sure no one is siphoning from his accounts."

They spent another hour combing through names and cross-referencing them through the federal database to ensure no one was working under an assumed name, and when Miranda did a double take on one particular name, she had to check again to make sure her eyes weren't simply crossing from fatigue. "Can you hand me the list from Vivid?"

Jeremiah fished out the employee list from Vivid Adventures and Miranda scanned it, looking for one name in particular. "Hmm, that's odd," she said under her breath when she'd found what she was looking for. She looked up and found Jeremiah waiting. "Vivid and Big Game share an employee."

Jeremiah frowned. "Is that normal?"

"Between friendly companies, yes. But between two companies whose owners can barely stand one another? No."

"Who is it?"

"Mack James and James Mack."

Jeremiah scanned the paperwork again and compared. "Someone is using an alias at one of the businesses. Who is he?"

"Helicopter pilot. I remember Rhett saying he needed a new pilot because his former pilot, someone who had worked for him for years, had relocated to Oregon. I guess this guy is the replacement pilot," she added.

Miranda stared at Jeremiah. "We need to schedule a meeting."

"Who should we call first?"

"Both. I want them both in the room when they hear they are employing the same guy. I'm betting there's bound to be some fireworks."

"Sounds good to me." Jeremiah cracked a large yawn. "Thank God. I'm exhausted. Can we go home now?"

Miranda laughed wearily and nodded. "Gladly. Let's get this mess cleaned up and go. I'm about to fall face-first into Excel spreadsheets."

JEREMIAH THOUGHT IT would be best if he had both Vee and Rhett meet at the fish-and-game office to declare it neutral ground. When Rhett and

Vee showed up at the exact same time, the stony glares and stubborn jaws were nearly identical.

Jeremiah took them into his office and shut the door for privacy. Miranda started the meeting by handing them each a copy of their employee list with the man in question circled in red as well as information they'd managed to pull from the other outfits who'd also used his services as a pilot.

"What is this?" Rhett asked gruffly, looking in confusion at the information.

Vee caught on quickly and swore under her breath. "That rotten little pisser. I'll skin him alive."

"What's going on?" Rhett asked, looking for someone to clear up the confusion.

"Someone has been using us," Vee explained impatiently. "James Mack is Mack James."

Understanding hit Rhett and his face colored as his anger blew up. "I'll kill him. When I hired him I told him no freelancing."

"There's a bigger issue at stake here," Jeremiah said. "We believe James Mack, or whoever he is, has been using the legitimate cover as a free-lance helicopter pilot to have a reason to be in the areas where the kills have occurred. He's in and out before anyone is the wiser and no one thinks to question the helicopter pilot. Think about it…

what does your pilot do while your clients are hunting their quarry?" he asked.

"Either they wait at the designated landing or they return to base and return later. It all depends on the job," Rhett said.

"Which means, he has plenty of time to get the job done and split before anyone notices he's gone."

"But what about the blood? I think someone would notice if the helicopter pilot is covered in blood," Vee pointed out, frowning.

"I suspect he's wearing some sort of suit, like a bio-contamination suit that he slips on when everyone is gone, which is why we've found no tracks at the scene, and then after his kill, he only takes specific parts, which he likely stores in a small cooler that no one is going to notice."

Rhett cast Vee an accusatory stare. "Do you know about this?"

Vee glared. "You idiot. He's been using me, too. I thought I was helping the kid out but I should have known he was too good to be true. He was subsidizing his piloting fee by using our legitimate jobs to cover his tracks."

"I knew his rate was too low," Rhett agreed with a growl. "I knew it."

They both looked to Jeremiah and Miranda. "What are we going to do about it?" Rhett asked.

"Unfortunately, at this point our evidence is speculative. We need proof."

"And how are we supposed to get that? I doubt he's going to simply throw his hands up and admit his guilt," Rhett groused. "Maybe I could beat a confession out of him."

"Old man, you'd likely throw your back out before you landed a hit. I'll take care of him," Vee said.

"And how do you plan to do that? Hurl harsh words at the kid and kill him with sarcasm?" Rhett jeered, equally ticked off.

"No one is going to beat or kill anyone." Miranda stood. "We need to catch him in the act. So that means you two need to work together and act as if nothing has changed. So in other words, keep being completely awful to one another."

"That shouldn't be a problem," Vee sniped, shooting a look at Rhett. "I just received word that I'm being audited. My bet is that this oaf had something to do with it."

"If your books are clean, you have nothing to worry about," Rhett countered, not the least bit apologetic.

Miranda snapped her fingers at them both as if they were quarreling children. "Focus, please," she said, ignoring their glares. "If James is tipped off to anything being different it'll spook him and he'll bolt. I've been tracking this guy for two

years and I'm not about to lose him this time. I
need your help, so please put your differences
aside just this once and agree to work together."

Rhett and Vee shared a look and a reluctant
truce followed. Rhett nodded and grudgingly
agreed. "Sounds good to me. I want to nail this
SOB to the ground."

Vee also agreed. "That makes two of us. I'll
play along."

Miranda smiled. "I knew I could count on
you." She handed them both a new set of papers.
"Here's the plan. Please follow it to the letter.
No deviating from the instructions." She looked
purposefully to Rhett and he grunted in acceptance. "The Fish and Game is going to book a
trip at both Vivid Adventures and Big Game Trophy. They will be near the areas where he's been
known to trap bears. We don't know which area
he's going to choose, so that's why we're booking
with both outfits. Whichever gig he takes is the
one where he's already looked and set his traps.
What he doesn't know is every single person on
that expedition will be law enforcement ready to
take him down."

Jeremiah nodded. "There's more. We think he
has someone working on the inside. Possibly at
both of your operations. He's probably paying
them under the table to keep their mouths shut
or help them facilitate his runs. We don't know

who might be on Vee's team but I have my suspicions on who it is on Rhett's team."

"Who is it?" Rhett demanded. "I won't tolerate traitors on my team."

Miranda looked to Rhett with compassion in her eyes. Jeremiah figured the news might come easier if it were delivered by a friend. "Rhett, I don't know how to tell you this but I think your traitor is Ambra."

Rhett stared. "My wife?" He shook his head. "Impossible."

"When we were going through your financials, we found some strange purchases. And they were all made from Ambra's account."

"Strange how?"

"Rope, bear grease and tarp. Unless she's working on a really weird home project, I think James was getting her to make some purchases for him so as not to raise suspicion."

"No." Rhett refused to believe it. "She wouldn't do that to me."

"She's young and James is young. Likely they've been having an affair for quite a while. Because if it was just about money she can get that from you." Miranda winced, hating the hurt she was causing her friend. Jeremiah gave her an encouraging look. Miranda took a deep breath and continued, "I'm not sure how it happened but somehow he convinced Ambra to betray you and the only way that I can think how that would've worked is if there were emotions involved. I'm sorry."

Rhett's bottom lip trembled and it was a hard sight to see. Surprisingly, Vee remained silent. Jeremiah would've half expected her to crow at Rhett's misfortune but she seemed upset for her rival. "Are we finished here?" Rhett asked in a reserved tone.

Jeremiah nodded. "I know it will be hard to go home and pretend as if everything is fine. Don't talk to Ambra. Don't confront James. We need everything to be the same as it was. Understand?"

"Fine." Rhett stood stiffly. "Let's get this show on the road. I want to get it over with."

"We'll set the expeditions for next week. You need to both be ready."

"We will be ready." Vee stood next to Rhett and for a brief moment it seemed a spark of compassion blazed between them. "Let's go, old man. We have work to do until then."

Rhett and Vee left in their respective cars and Miranda said with mild surprise, "Was it just me or did they seem less reluctant to work with one another than before?"

Jeremiah said, "The enemy of my enemy is my friend. They've both been duped and there's a brand of built-in camaraderie when that happens."

"I think she really felt bad for him. Maybe they don't actually hate one another."

"I wouldn't start playing matchmaker just yet," Jeremiah warned. "Rhett is going to be bitter and angry for a while and he'll probably start to take it out on Vee before this is all through."

"Rhett's not like that," Miranda said. "He's actually a real softie beneath that bluster. It's why he never suspected Ambra was two-timing him right beneath his nose." Miranda wrinkled her nose in distaste. "I never liked that woman. I bet her accent isn't even real."

Jeremiah chuckled. "Sheathe your claws. There'll be plenty of time to give her a piece of your mind after we've managed to get the evidence we need."

"I can't wait." Miranda offered a mean smile and then left the room to put the final touches into motion for the raid.

CHAPTER THIRTY

MIRANDA COULDN'T QUELL her excitement. For the first time in two years she had real movement on the poaching case and it felt as if it were finally going to be solved. And she had Jeremiah to thank for that. He pushed her to look at evidence that she had long since discounted. If it weren't for the laser focus required for the operation, she might've been downright giddy.

"Are you in position?" Jeremiah's voice sounded over her walkie-talkie.

"Ready and waiting," Miranda answered in a low voice. "When he touches down I'll have a clear view of all his movements."

"Good. We're all set here in the group. You'll have all the backup you need."

The plan was simple. James had no idea that they'd faked the expedition. Of the two, James had selected Rhett's expedition, which gave Miranda a good idea of where his hunting grounds would be. There was a water source that snaked down from the mountain, which was an excellent place to spring a trap. All she had to do was wait and he would lead her to his spot.

Right on schedule, the low whir of the helicopter filled the air. Miranda looked up from her hiding spot and saw the helicopter touching down in the meadow. She could hear laughter and shouted instructions as Rhett did his part, acting as if the group were part of a true expedition. The law-enforcement agents, an assembled group of federal cops, were outfitted like big-game hunters as they appeared excited to bag their first bear or moose.

Miranda watched from her hiding spot as they headed up the trail, leaving the helicopter pilot behind. She knew he wouldn't leave right away just in case someone double backed. Just as she suspected, he waited a good forty-five minutes before ducking back into the helicopter and emerging in a head-to-toe white Tyvek suit, complete with soft terrain booties to cover his shoes. He checked his watch and then began sprinting down the opposite end of the trail, carrying a blue cooler.

"He's on the move, heading east toward Crandall Creek. I'm heading out," she whispered into her walkie-talkie and began trailing him at a safe distance.

"Copy that. Be careful. We're going to circle around and flank him."

Miranda made her way cautiously, following

James and ensuring she remained downwind. She saw that he was careful where he put his feet, what he touched, his eyes scanning constantly. When he ducked around the bend Miranda was almost afraid she'd lost him. But just as she crested the ridge she saw him hunker down in a hiding spot, a .308 sniper rifle with a custom suppressor in his hand, which had probably cost him a bundle. He must've stashed his gun in the foliage ahead of time, she mused. With her luck no bear would take the bait and they'd have to scrap the operation, but James must've ensured that a bear would be around to sniff out the grease smeared on the tree, because a large brown bear ambled down the creek, his big head swinging side to side as he sniffed out the source of the tantalizing smell. Bears had an excellent sense of smell, and within moments, he was standing on his hindquarters, licking at the grease and pawing at the bark, trying to get more into his mouth. James had his gun drawn and pointed at the bear. One shot to the head and the bear would go tumbling soundlessly to the ground. The gun was high-powered enough to pierce fur, fat and bone without leaving behind too large of a hole. James was fast, efficient and deadly skilled at what he did, and the fact that it'd taken this long for Miranda to figure it out made her see red.

"He's taking a shot! Where are you?" Miranda

whispered into her walkie-talkie. "If we don't move now he's going to kill the bear. We have to stop him."

"Stand down. We are two minutes away. Do not engage." Jeremiah's voice was insistent on the other end but Miranda knew she wouldn't watch another bear die a senseless death if she could stop it.

Miranda reached down and picked up a rock with a good heft. She hauled back and threw the rock with all of her might, beaning the bear right in the noggin. The startled bear scampered off with a bellow. Miranda watched as James cursed at his lost quarry, then scanned the area where Miranda was hiding. "You just cost me thirty thousand dollars, friend. I might have to bill you for that," he said, rising from his spot just as Miranda did.

"Miranda Sinclair, fish-and-game hottie herself. Color me impressed."

His flattery made her stomach turn. "You're going to jail, you rotten son of a bitch."

James smiled. "Really? And who is here to make that happen? You? I don't think so. I am curious how you knew it was me, though."

"It was easy. You cover your tracks well, but in the end you were sloppy. James Mack and Mack James? You really should put a little more effort into your aliases."

"What can I say? I banked on the fact that Vee and Rhett spent so much time caring what the other was doing that they didn't spare a second thought to the cheap helicopter pilot just trying to log some more flying hours for his résumé."

"They're onto you now. I'm pretty sure you've been crossed off their Christmas lists," Miranda said with a narrowed gaze. "Let's go." She gestured at James and he simply laughed.

"Are you forgetting who has the gun? I could put a bullet in your brain right now and walk away. Have fun proving I was even here."

"I don't need a gun. You're going to do exactly as I say and follow me like a good little puppy straight to jail."

"Oh, is that so? And why is that?"

Miranda smiled as the law-enforcement agents emerged from the foliage, their guns drawn, their expressions hard. "Because I have plenty of guns. And they're all pointed straight at your worthless head. James Mack, let me introduce you to the law-enforcement division of the U.S. Fish and Wildlife Department. They're here to escort you off this mountain."

James turned slowly and saw that he was indeed surrounded by the very people he'd believed he was bringing to the mountains for a good time. "What the hell...?" James breathed, unable to believe how soundly he'd been duped. "I'll be damned. Looks like I'm screwed," he said grimly.

"Looks like," Miranda agreed cheerfully. "With any luck, you'll get the maximum sentence. But if by some chance you manage to escape with a slap on the wrist for what you've done, do yourself a favor and don't come back to Alaska."

The officers took James into custody and Vee arrived right on schedule to transport them back off the mountain while Rhett flew the other helicopter back to base. Jeremiah and Miranda rode with Rhett and by the time everything had been processed and finished the sun had long since disappeared from the sky.

"Did you get what you need to put them away?" Rhett asked.

Jeremiah nodded. "I sure hope so. We're practically handing the case to them on a silver platter. He was wearing the suit, carrying the cooler, and Miranda saw him waiting for that bear where he had laid a trap. I'd say this case is pretty solid. But no matter what happens after this, the fact remains that Miranda got her man."

Miranda smiled with open relief, still riding a high. "I didn't do it alone." She spared him a secret smile, unable to stop it until she realized she and Jeremiah were sharing too long of a private look. Miranda pulled her gaze from him and looked to Rhett. "You know, when you're not fighting with Vee, you're actually a good team. You work well together. Have you ever considered combining forces, having a joint operation? It could help both of your bottom lines given the depressed economy. Might be something to consider."

"I have bigger issues than Vee right now."

Miranda knew that Rhett was referencing the business with Ambra. While Rhett had been on the expedition, law-enforcement officers had gone to the Big Game Trophy office to pick up Ambra. She was currently being booked on charges of conspiracy, which would likely earn her a slap on the wrist, but Rhett was already filing the paperwork for a divorce. "I hope you have a pre-nup," Miranda said quietly. "I think she's taken enough of your money in the two years you've been married."

Rhett nodded. "Ironclad. I wasn't so smitten that I lost my head completely."

"I'm glad to hear that. You can rebuild, you know. Maybe downsize a little. Sell off some investments. You don't have to be drowning in debt. Maybe it's time to close Simone's account. No one is ever going to come forward to collect the reward and you need it more than she does."

"No," Rhett said resolutely. "That money will stay there forever if need be. I have other accounts I can tap but not that one—that one is for

Simone." He sighed and for the first time ever looked older than he was. "Ambra made me feel young again. But now I feel worse. I feel like an old fool."

Miranda's heart ached for Rhett. Jeremiah had warned her to put the brakes on any matchmaking but she had sensed a tiny spark between Vee and him, even if they were both too stubborn to acknowledge it. "I think you should consider what I said about you and Vee. She's a lot like you," Miranda said, trying to soften the blow of his wife's betrayal by offering a new perspective. "I really do think you two would make a good team."

Rhett didn't say anything in response to that and Miranda let it go. He needed to grieve and he needed to deal with Ambra's betrayal in his own way. Maybe with time, he'd see the wisdom in her words. Miranda hugged Rhett and she and Jeremiah took to the road.

"I WANT TO CELEBRATE," Miranda announced suddenly, turning to Jeremiah. "I say we hit The Rusty Anchor and throw back a few. Talen is with *Mamu* tonight and I am footloose and fancy-free until tomorrow morning. What do you say?"

Jeremiah should say no. He knew the right thing to do, the responsible thing to do, was to politely decline, but he agreed with Miranda—the closure of this case was worth celebrating.

"One drink couldn't hurt anyone I suppose," Jeremiah said.

"That's the spirit. First round on me," Miranda said, laughing as they climbed into the car and drove straight to the local tavern. "Two beers, Russ," she said to the bartender. Once they each had a beer in hand, they clinked bottlenecks. "We did it, Jeremiah. We caught that son of a bitch." She took a long swallow and said, "I couldn't have done it without you."

"You did most of the work. I just tied up the loose ends."

Her smile lit up her face and in that moment he thought she was the most beautiful woman he'd ever seen. He desperately wanted to kiss her but it wasn't his place. He had to content himself with simply joining in her joy. "You are a sharp investigator. Your skills are completely wasted in this office," he said, "but I'll keep you for as long as you'll stay," he added softly.

Miranda held his stare and for a moment neither was sure if they were talking about the job anymore. Miranda searched his face, her gaze resting on his lips as if she wanted to close the distance as much as he did but she held back. A charming smile followed. "I'm not going anywhere," she said. "Not yet anyway."

"Is there anything else you wanted to do with your career?"

"I'd like to do something that really makes a difference," Miranda said. "I know we do lots of good work in our office, and I'm not saying that what we do isn't important, but I can't help but think that there's something bigger, something better for me out there."

"That's why you applied for my position?" he surmised. "Now that I know you better, it was a blessing that you didn't get the job." He rushed to stop the gathering scowl on Miranda's face as he explained his reasoning. "Listen, I don't say that to ruffle your feathers but it's the truth. You are not cut out to push paper behind the desk. And basically, that's what I do all day. I've had a lot of fun doing some fieldwork, in getting out there, but for the most part an administrator is a paper pusher. And that's okay for me. I enjoy budgets and spreadsheets and meetings whereas I think all of those things would just weigh you down."

Miranda lost some of her bristle as his explanation hit home. "You're right," she said with a bit of revelation in her voice. "I hate the idea of being stuck behind a desk."

"See?"

"But I have my son to think about, too," she countered. "I can't work the same job for the next twenty years, without any hope of advancement. Eventually, my son will have bigger needs than my meager paycheck can handle. How am I supposed to buy Talen a car? Or put him through college? Aside from the fact that my job is no longer mentally stimulating, it doesn't pay the bills. Don't get me wrong—I get by, but I'm tired of just *getting by*. I want to make a good living *and* make a difference out there in the world. I shouldn't have to choose between the two."

Jeremiah understood and made a sudden decision. "Then you should start looking for something else. Check the federal wire. There's always something popping up. You might have to move but sometimes relocating is good for a fresh start."

"Actually, I did look into something—it's my dream job. But I haven't applied."

"Which position is this?"

Miranda seemed reluctant to share until he wouldn't let it go. She relented with a sigh. "Mary told me about it and I told her it was a dumb idea but she got my mind to thinking that maybe…it might be possible…but now I don't know. To be honest, my application would have to cross Stuart Olly's desk and you and I both know how he feels about me."

Jeremiah swigged his beer and contemplated the validity of her statement. She had a point but he didn't like the idea of her quitting before giving herself a chance to succeed. "I don't deny that you're not Stuart's favorite person, but that's no reason not to apply. What is this job? Maybe I know a few people who could help. I have connections, too."

"The listing is for a Special Services Enforcement Officer. The position is a much higher pay grade, and a lot more responsibility, but it sounds exactly like what I'm looking for. Not only that, I'd only have to go into Anchorage a few times a month and the rest of the time I can work from home."

"I saw that listing on the wire. You're right— it would be perfect for you. You should apply."

"Stuart hates me. Even if I was the best-qualified person for the job he'd still throw my application right into the circular file and you know it."

"Don't let fear stop you. You don't know what's going to happen. Just do it."

"That's what Mary said, too."

"Then she's a smart woman."

Miranda regarded him with open vulnerability and he longed to pull her into his arms if only to reassure her that she was more than qualified to apply for that job. If she was hired, the enforcement division would be lucky to have her. But all he could do was offer the same level of friendly advice as he would to any coworker. He took a hard swig of his beer, hating how he felt inside, as if he were stuck on the outside of the glass, staring into a wonderful life going on without him. "When's the closing date?" he asked.

"Tomorrow."

"Is your résumé polished?"

She nodded. "Mary made me do it. But I didn't have the balls to send it."

"Well, tomorrow you're growing a pair, because you're turning in that application. I won't take no for an answer."

Miranda laughed but Jeremiah thought he saw tears glistening in her eyes. Miranda, so strong, so full of life, and yet she still needed someone to believe in her. Jeremiah was happy to be that person. It was the least he could do.

"Russ—" he gestured to the bartender "—two more over here, buddy."

He realized one drink was not nearly enough to dull the growing ache in his heart. In fact, there probably wasn't enough alcohol in the world.

CHAPTER THIRTY-ONE

JEREMIAH HAD HAD one too many beers and Miranda had decided it was time to put him to bed when Otter stopped them at the tavern door. Apparently Otter had also had too much to drink and suddenly felt it was time to get some things off his chest.

"My, isn't this cute?" Otter's voice was slurred as he lurched forward, gesturing to them. "Not even bothering to hide anymore. I guess no more sneaking around is required. Seems there are no rules around here anymore."

Miranda frowned at Otter, irritated at his sudden odd behavior and anxious to get out of The Rusty Anchor before someone realized how much Jeremiah had been drinking. She didn't want anyone to have cause to make another call to Stuart that might come back and hurt Jeremiah. "What are you talking about, Otter? You're drunk. Do you need a ride home? Do I need to call Mary?"

"I'm *fine*," Otter said with a sneer. "But what do you care? I'm just the friend who's always there for you and available to help whenever you need it. But that's not good enough for you, is it? You have to have somebody who you're not supposed to have. But then, that's always the case with you, isn't it? But I never thought you'd want to sleep with your boss. That's low, Miranda. Even for you."

"Go home, Otter." Jeremiah stared, his gaze hard as flint. "Don't be saying things you can't take back."

"You shut up. And don't call me Otter. That's only for my friends. I gave you a place to live and this is how you repay me? You move in on my girl?"

"I'm not your girl," Miranda cut in, shocked and growing beyond pissed, but as drunk as Otter was there was no getting through to him, no matter how Miranda protested. Otter suddenly jabbed a finger at Jeremiah, and Miranda had to hold Jeremiah back from punching out the drunk.

"If I didn't need the money I'd kick your ass out on the street. Well, and if I wasn't *legally* required to give you thirty days," Otter amended with a small hiccup. "I would totally evict your scheming, backstabbing ass. It's bad enough that you still have your job after what you've done."

Miranda did a double take and narrowed her stare at Otter. "What are you talking about?" Otter pressed his lips together, his bleary stare rebellious, and Miranda realized it was Otter who had made the call. "You were the one, weren't you? You ratted me out to Stuart, didn't you?"

"Not you, just him," Otter said plaintively, sounding like a child who'd been wrongly accused. "He's the one who overstepped his authority. It's all *his* fault!"

Oh, that's enough of that. People were beginning to take an undue interest in the scene and Miranda was ready to put the whole situation behind her. Otter was a grown man acting like a spoiled brat. If she'd ever had any inkling that they might be able to make something work, Otter's drunken display had just killed it.

"Your nickname ought to be *weasel* or *rat,*" Jeremiah shot back, and Miranda stepped forward and put a restraining hand on Jeremiah while she dealt with Otter before he got his ass kicked.

"Otter, I can forgive what you're saying right now because you are drunk out of your mind. I'm also going to try to forget that you're the one who tried to make trouble for me and Jeremiah when it was *none of your damn business.*" Otter blinked back mulish tears but she didn't feel sorry for him one bit. He'd brought this on himself and he was going to have to listen up and finally lose the dream that they were going to someday ride off into the sunset together. "Yes, you are my friend. I've never pretended to be anything other than that. But in case you haven't noticed, to be my friend is something I consider very special because I don't have many. But I can very easily remove you from that spot in my life. Is that what you want?"

Otter stared at Miranda until his lip began to tremble. Suddenly he was breaking down into a sobbing mess, and Miranda and Jeremiah had to rush to hold him up before he toppled to the floor. "Why don't you love me? I've always loved you. I would've done anything for you. I'd have bought you the finest house, cooked for you every night and never asked a single thing of you but to love me back. Why was that too much to ask?"

At Otter's impassioned plea, Miranda's ire dissipated. She stroked his cheek. "Otter, you have been my friend for as long as I can remember. You and I will never be romantically involved because I think of you like a *brother*. That will never change. I'm sorry if I ever gave you the impression that it might. But somewhere out there is a perfect woman for you. Someone who will love you for you. And I will be the first person to attend your wedding and babysit your children and invite you guys over for dinner. But I am not that girl."

Otter wiped his nose and nodded, all the fight leaving him. "Sorry, Miranda. I've been such a shit. I was the one who made the call," he confirmed with such misery that it was evident he'd been eaten by guilt for it. "I just couldn't stand to see you with someone other than me. I understand if you never want to talk to me again." He risked a glance at Jeremiah and added, "And you're a decent guy. I'm sorry for the things I said. Or, I will be sorry when I sober up but right now I'm pretty drunk and I'm still pissed at you for being so lucky."

"Apology accepted." He paused, lifting a brow with uncertainty. "Do I need to start looking for a new place to live?"

"No," Otter answered, wiping his running nose. "You're a good renter. You can stay."

Miranda chuckled. "Otter, go home and get some rest. I'll have Russ call you a cab."

Otter nodded and sat heavily in the nearest chair while Miranda talked to Russ. She and Jeremiah waited until Otter was safely packaged away in the cab and going home to sleep it off before they left the bar. She could only hope Otter wouldn't be too mortified in the morning but she felt better having said what had long needed to be said. Perhaps it'd been her fault for not setting Otter straight immediately. She just hadn't wanted to hurt him and then the rest of her life had imploded with different issues. By this point Jeremiah had sobered a bit and he could walk steadily but Miranda knew she didn't want to go home alone.

"I shouldn't want you," Jeremiah said, his voice a husky murmur. "I should say good-night and let you go on your way. But I want you to go home with me." Miranda didn't have to say anything, and he saw a mirror of his feelings in her eyes. "One more night?" he asked softly.

"One more night."

What neither of them wanted to admit was that one night was never going to be enough and they both knew it. Somehow to admit that they both needed each other in a deeper, more primal way, that their bodies reacted to one another on a cellular level, and that their souls felt intertwined, was just too much. To admit that would mean they'd have to answer some bigger questions and neither one of them was ready to do that.

So it was easier to agree—one more night.

MIRANDA RESTED HER head against Jeremiah's chest, the sweat drying on their skin. She could spend a lifetime lying in this exact position. What a difference. She never imagined she'd meet anyone who made her feel this way. Why did it have to be Jeremiah? It seemed a cruel irony that she'd gone and fallen in love with the one man who could not be the person she needed him to be.

"What's on your mind?" Jeremiah asked, his voice a low rumble in his chest. "I can practically see the tension rising from your shoulders."

"I think I am falling in love with you." Miranda held her breath, almost afraid of what that admission would do to their dynamic. When Jeremiah didn't say anything she squeezed her eyes shut and wished she hadn't said anything at all.

His arms tightened around her as he exhaled a deep sigh. "You know I'm not the right man for you despite how much I want to be. You need a man who can be a father figure to your son and I can't be that."

Tears stung her eyes. "I didn't say I wanted you to be my son's father. *I said that I loved you.* Does that mean anything to you?"

"If I said that I loved you back would it change anything? Each time I look at your son, I will remember mine and the fact that Tyler's gone. Every single day I think about how things might've been different if I hadn't bought him that damn ATV, so much so that it almost drove me crazy. The only way I've been able to shut off those questions in my head is by shutting down that part of myself, the part that had been a father. I won't know how to do that around your son."

Miranda rose, clutching the sheet to her bare breasts. "Life goes on, Jeremiah. It breaks my heart that you lost your son. I cannot imagine the pain that you have been through or how much it hurts every single day to know that your son is gone but I do know that you can't stop living.

Otherwise you might as well just climb into the ground with Tyler."

Jeremiah immediately bristled. "You don't know what you're talking about so I'd stop offering an opinion," he said sharply, climbing from the bed and jerking a robe on over his nudity. His glare said he blamed her for the sudden change between them. "This isn't the way I'd like to end the evening."

"Well, we don't always get what we want, now do we?" Miranda said, hurt and angry, but mostly hurt. She'd bared her soul to him and admitted her deepest feelings and he'd countered with "I can't be your son's daddy." If she were inclined to violence, she might be tempted to pitch something heavy at his stupid head. She scrambled free from the bed and quickly recovered her discarded clothing from the floor. She slid her panties and bra on, not willing to spend another minute in his miserable company.

"What are you doing?"

"What does it look like?" She pulled her jeans and sweater on and began looking for her shoes but Jeremiah grabbed them first. "Give me my shoes," she demanded.

"Just hold on a minute," he nearly shouted, and she crossed her arms and stared. "I'm just saying that it's ignorant of you to try and school me on how to properly grieve for my child when you've never been through what I have. You can't possibly imagine the horror and the pain of losing a child. And I hope you never do. But don't sit there and try to lecture me about living life to its fullest when you've never suffered such a huge loss."

"I'm not lecturing you. I'm just pointing out the obvious," Miranda disagreed. "You're choosing to cut yourself off from a new life with someone by refusing to take a chance."

"Don't you understand? I will never be the same. And I'm trying to do you a favor," he argued. "I'm not cut out to be someone's stepfather. You say you're not looking for a father for your son but how's that going to work out? Will we just continue to see each other on the side without allowing certain aspects of our personal life to mesh? That's no life. That's not a true relationship. That's a friendship with benefits or a booty call. And I'm not willing to disrespect you in that way. Don't you get it? I want better for you!"

"I don't need you to tell me what I need." Tears blurred her eyes. "I just told you that I loved you. That's it. If you don't feel the same then just say so. I didn't ask for an explanation of why you don't want to be with me. I don't need you to make excuses. I just had to tell you how I felt." She held his stare even though it hurt to look at him. "And I can see that I've made a huge mistake. Now give me my damn shoes or I will walk out of this house barefoot."

Jeremiah's arm snaked out and grabbed her before she could leave and pulled her close. "I do love you. Damn it, Miranda, I love you desperately." He ground his mouth against hers and she felt her body stirring with passion and bone-deep misery. She clung to him as their tongues twined with one another and their need reached a fevered pitch. "Is this what you want?" Jeremiah demanded to know between kisses, his touch becoming urgent and insistent. "Do you want to hear how much I love you and how it kills me to set you free? Because it does. It kills me to know that I'm not good enough. It kills me to know that the best thing for you is to get away from me. I will inadvertently hurt you and your son somehow because I'm not ready to face the grief that I've pushed so deeply inside of me." He buried his face between her breasts, squeezing almost painfully. But she gave herself to him as freely as she had admitted her love for him. He groaned against her. "I love you. I love you more than I have ever imagined loving anyone and it's killing me."

Tears rolled down her cheeks as they made love. Each thrust felt desperate, as if they both knew it was the end. They clung to one another as they rode out their passion until they were finished, gasping for breath, the smell of sweat and sex lingering in the air as they recovered.

She loved him. And he loved her. She'd be a fool to chase a man who'd already admitted he couldn't be the man in her life. She'd made a vow that she would never bring a man into Talen's life who wasn't going to be there permanently. Jeremiah had just told her why he couldn't be that man.

And she owed it to Talen to stick to that vow. Even if it cracked her heart in two.

CHAPTER THIRTY-TWO

JEREMIAH TRIED TO stay focused on his work but his attention kept straying to Miranda down the hall. He felt like a toad for shooting her down last night when she'd plainly bared her soul to him. Wasn't he doing her a favor by being honest? His intuition reassured him, yes, it was better to be honest and up front about expectations than to experience heartache later from disillusionment, but it hurt like hell right now and he even felt a little queasy.

He managed to stick to his plan of staying out of her hair for about an hour until he finally rose and strode into her office with a legitimate question.

"Did you turn in your application and résumé?" he asked.

She didn't look up from her task. "Yes."

"Excellent." He paused. "Did you see the letter of recommendation I emailed you early this morning?"

"Yes." She looked up. "I didn't send it."

"Why not?"

"Because I didn't want to worry about someone

saying that you wrote it simply because you felt guilty about something. With the recent situation with Otter, I didn't think it was prudent to send a letter where you sing my praises. If my application and résumé aren't sufficient, then I'm not cut out for the job."

"Miranda, that's ridiculous. There's nothing wrong with a superior sending a letter of recommendation for an employee he feels deserves it. I wouldn't have written it if I hadn't believed in every word."

"Be that as it may…in light of recent events…"

"You are the most stubborn woman I've ever met," Jeremiah fairly growled, irritated at her refusal to see reason in this one area of her life. "My letter could be of significant value. Particularly in Stuart's eyes."

"I don't care."

"You don't care," he repeated. "Then why'd you send the résumé and application at all? I call bullshit. You care plenty. You're just pissed at me, so you're cutting your nose to spite your face."

"Don't be stupid," she said, going back to her work. "Is that all? I have work to do."

She was done talking. He could see it in the stiff set of her jaw and the tension in her shoulders. "Fine," he bit out. "Be that way."

"I will."

"Good."

"Glad we're on the same page."

Jeremiah glared but his anger bounced off her like water on a duck's back. She'd effectively shut him out. He turned on his heel and returned to his office, steaming mad.

Of all the immature, reckless, stupid things to do... He fumed quietly, tapping his finger against his desk. She was perfect for that job. Her talents were going to waste in this old tin can of a satellite office. She definitely had what it took to do a good job in the other position. He hated the idea of Miranda wasting away, filing moose permits and languishing under sheaves of copy paper. He opened his email and quickly wrote a message to Stuart. If Miranda was going to be a pill, he'd just have to do what was right, whether she liked it or not.

Stuart,

I recently heard that Miranda Sinclair applied for the Special Services Enforcement Officer position. I've enclosed a letter of recommendation that I hope you will take into consideration for inclusion with her application and résumé.
Sincerely,
Jeremiah Burke, Director

She'd probably be furious when she found out, but he could deal with that. He was going to do what he felt was right and Miranda was right for that job.

Although he was relieved that Miranda had applied for the position, it didn't relieve his tension about how things had ended the night before.

As much as he hated to admit it, Miranda had touched on a nerve. It was true he hadn't dealt with his grief and he'd thought with time the pain would simply dissipate, and perhaps become like an old scar, visible but no longer agonizing. But he'd begun to lose hope that that would ever happen, because every time he thought of Tyler, it felt as if his heart were being wrenched out. But how did he know that he wouldn't be able to handle being around someone else's child? Truthfully, he'd never chanced it. He'd kept separating himself from children in general but he'd never thought about someone he cared about having a child. He loved Miranda. He knew that without a doubt. He wanted to see her succeed; he wanted to watch her soar. He wanted to sleep beside her every night. But she and her child were a package deal. Could he handle the pressure of reintroducing a child into his life? And was it possible for him to love that child as he'd loved his own? There were so many questions that he didn't know the answers to and he didn't have the luxury of testing out his theory because people could get hurt. He'd rather suffer misery without Miranda than subject her to any pain on his part.

But even as his good intentions seemed pure and grounded in sound logic his heart was in agony, calling him an idiot for letting her go. He and Josie had had a good marriage but in the end they'd been way too different to be truly compatible. He'd known that for a long time but he'd been committed to making it work because of Tyler. What he felt with Miranda was unlike anything he'd ever experienced. It was as if he'd suddenly taken a deep cleansing breath for the first time in the purest of mountain air. When he was with her he felt alive. So, if he felt that way, shouldn't he at least meet her son and test the waters?

The stakes were too high for *maybe,* he reminded himself. It was either yes or no. Either he had the balls to face his grief head-on and work to healing the hole inside of him or he'd accept that it was simply too hard and say goodbye to Miranda forever. Basically, it was a cut-and-dried situation. He could pretty it up all he wanted with reasons and excuses and justifications but it really boiled down to those basic issues. Either he was in, or he was out.

He already knew how it felt to say no. The minute the words had left his mouth he wished he could reel them back in. On the surface it seemed the right thing to do. He was being the bigger man. But everything in him screamed this was wrong. She belonged with him. And he would do anything to make that happen. Even if it meant dealing with his unresolved issues.

How long did he expect to keep running from his grief? He'd never really answered the question. Denial was a powerful thing. And it had a firm grip on his life. But he was tired of living a half life, of running away from his pain and being afraid of hanging his son's pictures on the wall.

His son's memory didn't belong tucked away in a box in a dark closet. He wanted people to see Tyler's picture hanging on the wall and ask about him. He wanted to be able to tell people how his son had been spirited, smart and athletic. He wanted to be able to share that his son meant more to him than simply a tragedy in his past. And that was where he'd relegated him to by refusing to face it.

He'd deal with the pain somehow because that was part of the healing. But he would also accept the joy that was waiting for him around the corner. His life didn't have to be over. Like Miranda had pointed out, if he wasn't going to live his life, he might as well have climbed into the ground beside Tyler.

And he wasn't ready to give up just yet.

He grabbed a phone book and looked for the first grief counselor he could find. Within seconds he had dialed and booked an appointment before he lost his nerve. He didn't know if he was ready but there was only one way to find out.

MIRANDA NEEDED SOMETHING to distract her from her heartbreak over Jeremiah, so when the weekend came around she decided she and Talen would go visit her parents. She hesitated a long moment. She hadn't wanted Talen to see the lifestyle her parents were living in but she realized she couldn't shelter him forever. Her parents had problems and the only way they were going to get through it was if the family came together to help them. Even if they didn't realize they needed the help. But even so, Miranda talked to Talen during the car ride to cover some bases.

"Hey, buddy, before we go visit Grandma and Grandpa we need to talk first." She took a deep breath before continuing. "Do you remember when I told you that Grandma has a hard time throwing things away? And that Grandpa likes to hang out in his shop a lot?"

"Yes. *Mamu* says that Grandma Sinclair has a ghost living with her. What does that mean?" Talen asked.

Miranda frowned. *Mamu* had never said anything like that to her before. In fact, she'd never offered much of an opinion when Miranda had shared her concerns about her mother's living conditions. She'd have to ask *Mamu* what she meant by that. "Well, Grandma is having a really hard time right now. And we need to try to help her see that the way she is living isn't good for her. You think you can do that for me, buddy?"

"I'll help Grandma. Do you think Grandpa will teach me how to carve like him? *Mamu* says I'm very good."

Tears stung Miranda's eyes. In another world, one where Simone was alive and well, her father would've been happy to pass on his skills to the next generation. In this world, her father hadn't picked up a carving tool in at least two years. "Maybe. But I think today we need to focus on Grandma. Okay?"

"Okay. How can we help?"

"Well, I thought we could offer to help her clean up a little bit. She has a hard time organizing, so I thought maybe if we helped her, then she would be able to get a start on a very big job. Now, here's the important part and I need you to pay attention.... Grandma's really sensitive about her house. So try to remember not to make a comment about if it smells or if it's disgusting. We don't want to hurt her feelings. Okay?"

"Does it smell like fish? Fish stink. *Mamu*'s kitchen always smells gross when she makes her fish stew."

Miranda laughed. "I don't know what it will

smell like but it likely won't smell good. But try to think of it as an adventure. A smelly adventure."

Talen nodded. "Okay, Mom. Maybe we'll find buried treasure."

Hopefully we don't find a buried body, Miranda thought with a mild shudder. There was no telling what they'd find in that mess.

They pulled up to the house and Miranda shot a quick look at the shop before heading to the front door and letting herself in. As before, the front door was nearly blocked by junk and she had to push to gain entrance. "Mom? Are you here? It's me and Talen. We've come to visit."

Her mother appeared from what used to be Simone's room and quickly shut the door behind her, a startled expression on her face. "You should have called. I didn't know you were coming."

"We wanted to surprise you."

"I'm surprised." Jennelle's eyes lit up with genuine joy when she saw Talen. "There's my beautiful grandson. Come and give your grandma a hug."

Talen walked tentatively over the mounds of stuff to his grandmother and gave her a good squeeze. "We've come to help you clean your house. It's a real mess."

Miranda winced when Jennelle arched her brow and shot Miranda a dark look over the top of Talen's head. "Oh, is that so? And here I hoped it would just be a visit for a visit's sake."

"It's going to be an adventure, Grandma. We might find buried treasure!"

Miranda smiled wanly and shrugged, and before her mother could shoot her down, Miranda jumped in quickly. "I thought about what you said and thought maybe I could be more helpful rather than critical," she added. "So, here I am with Talen, hoping we can help you get a little more organized. What did you used to say? Many hands make for light work," she reminded her mother.

Jennelle's gaze softened and she nodded. "Yes, I did used to say that." She glanced around, distress in her eyes as she struggled with her own issues, and Miranda held her breath until Jennelle reluctantly agreed to some help. "I suppose I could use some help organizing some of these things."

"Maybe we should start in the kitchen?" Miranda suggested, even though she had a sinking suspicion it was probably a hazmat zone.

"No, I'd rather stay in this room," Jennelle said. "Besides, I rarely cook any longer, so it's not imperative that it be in tip-top shape."

Yes, but shouldn't you be able to at least reach the stove without fear of toppling something over? Miranda bit her tongue and smiled instead.

"Okay, we can tackle the kitchen another time," she said, trying for compromise.

Armed with trash bags and plenty of patience, Miranda, Jennelle and Talen worked all day to clear a spot in the living room but it was painfully slow going as Jennelle was being an obstacle to their overall success.

"That's not trash," Jennelle said stridently just as Miranda was about to toss a magazine that was at least five years old and had water damage.

"Mom? Are you kidding me?" Miranda asked, losing her patience. "It's ruined and it's outdated. What could you possibly want with this magazine?"

"I haven't read it yet."

Miranda turned it over and glanced at the cover. "News flash—none of this is relevant any longer. In fact, it's so outdated that some of these people aren't even alive anymore!"

"Maybe I was going to clip recipes or coupons."

"Come on. You can't be serious."

"I *am* serious. Put it down."

"Where?" Miranda asked. "I don't have a pile for outdated, useless trash. Oh, wait, yes I do. It's called the *living room!*"

"And there it is. I knew your offer to help came with hidden agendas. You can't just listen to me when I say I don't want people telling me how to live my life. I think we're done tidying up for today," she announced.

"We still have hours' worth of cleaning to do," Miranda said, irritated. "We should keep going."

"I don't want to keep going. I want to rest. Being with you and your constant criticism is exhausting."

"I didn't say a word today until just now," Miranda pointed out. "And I thought you said you wanted to spend more time with Talen? Well, if that's what you want, then you have to clean up this mess because it's unsanitary."

Jennelle looked offended and her bottom lip trembled. Talen stood off to the side, his trash bag in his hand as he waited with a worried expression. Miranda drew a deep breath and knew if she didn't end things right now, a fight was going to happen. She backed down with a choked apology. "I'm sorry, Mom. I'm just trying to help."

"Yes, well…" Jennelle sniffed, communicating just how little she thought of her daughter's brand of help. She ignored Miranda and smiled for Talen's sake. "I had a lovely time with you, little man. Next time we'll have to meet at the park and have lunch." She shot her daughter a look. "If your mother approves, of course."

"That's not fair," Miranda said in a low voice. "You never stop hitting below the belt, do you?"

"I'm merely saying—"

"I know what you're saying and it's bullshit." Jennelle's eyes widened at Miranda's foul language but Miranda didn't care. "Talen, get your things. It's been a long day and it's time to go."

"But Grandma's house still stinks," Talen said, looking worriedly at the mess.

Miranda glared at her mother as she helped Talen into his coat. "Grandma likes it that way," she said with disgust. "Let's go."

They left and Miranda felt deflated. She'd tried to make her mother feel safe enough to trust her with the cleanup but each item seemed to have some special significance in Jennelle's life. Mostly all they'd done was move piles around. Jennelle had only allowed Miranda to throw away the equivalent of one garbage bag in an entire day of work.

What a waste of effort.

"Why is Grandma so messy?" Talen asked as they drove home.

"I don't know," she answered her son. "She didn't used to be that way. She's different now."

"Why'd she change?"

"I think when Aunt Simone died, Grandma's heart and mind changed," she said. "But only Grandma knows for sure. Thanks for all your help today. You were awesome and I think you deserve some hot cocoa for that."

Talen smiled. "I don't mind. Someone has to

help Grandma because she's all alone. Except for the ghost but I don't think they talk all that much."

Miranda didn't know if Talen meant a figurative ghost or a literal one. She hoped it was figurative. That was all she needed to deal with on top of everything else—a real ghost haunting her damn mother's house!

"Well, we managed to clear the sofa enough for people to sit somewhere," she said, trying to look for anything positive so it didn't feel as if the whole day was ruined.

"Yep. And now Grandma can stop sleeping in the bathtub."

"Bathtub?" Miranda was appalled. "Why do you think she sleeps in the bathtub?"

"I saw blankets and a pillow in there."

Miranda didn't know what to say. She swallowed and forced a smile. "Yeah, a sofa is probably far more comfortable than a bathtub to sleep." *Lord have mercy...* She hoped Trace got here soon. She was *this close* to turning her mother over to the authorities and letting them sort everything out. Somehow, she had to push from her mind the knowledge that her mother was sleeping in the bathtub because she'd been pushed from her own bed by her disease. If she didn't, she'd turn the car around and drag her mother out by her ear and demand that she come to her senses.

Not that it would work.

Her mother had a stubborn streak that was damn near legendary.

Kind of like her own, she mused.

She thought of Jeremiah and her stubborn refusal to send his letter of recommendation for her when she'd submitted for that position. He'd been right: she had been cutting her nose to spite her face but she'd been angry and hurt.

Now she just felt stupid.

How did she manage to keep making dumb decisions that could potentially affect her entire future? She glanced at Talen and felt an overwhelming surge of love and despair. She wanted the best for Talen…but so far she'd done a terrible job of providing it.

How was she supposed to fix that?

CHAPTER THIRTY-THREE

IT'D BEEN TWO weeks since Jeremiah and Miranda had said their piece to one another and in that time Jeremiah had done plenty of soul-searching. He'd vowed to make some changes in his life, starting with one very important thing.

As he pulled Tyler's pictures from the box, he was bowled over by the wash of emotions they stirred—both happy and sad. When he wasn't sure if he could suppress the sadness, he let it knock him down and he sobbed until his voice was hoarse and his nose ran with snot. It was an ugly cry, the kind they never show in the movies, because sometimes human biology was gross.

But when he emerged from that dark place, his soul felt light. He knew there would be more tears and more grief but each time there would be less. This was the process he was supposed to go through when Tyler had died but he'd run away from it, refusing to succumb to the natural stages of grieving. Perhaps by not grieving, his subconscious was made to believe that he could pretend that his son hadn't died. Who knew? All he knew was that it felt good to remember Tyler and look at his pictures without immediately shying away from anything that had to do with his son.

For the first time since Tyler had died, he wasn't afraid to think of the good times, which made him remember that he'd loved being a father. Did he have what it took to be someone else's father? He didn't know but he felt ready to try.

Of course, first, he had to convince Miranda, and after his grand and noble speech in bed that night, he might have to do some serious groveling.

Jeremiah drove to Miranda's house, and when he began to knock, he realized his palms were sweating. Miranda opened the door and startled when she saw Jeremiah. "What are you doing here?" she asked. "It's the weekend."

"I know. I'm here to talk. Can I come in?"

"My son is here."

He wasn't sure if she was saying that for his protection or to put a wall between them but he was ready to show her that he was making changes. "I would consider it an honor if you would allow me to meet him."

"Excuse me?" She eyed him suspiciously. "Have you been drinking?"

He smiled at her confusion, and even though it was freezing outside, he was prepared to stand there and explain himself even if it took all night.

"I said a lot of things and they were true at the time but I've had some time to really think about how I've been structuring my life and I realized I was being an idiot."

"It's only been two weeks. What kind of grand epiphany could you have possibly had in two weeks?"

"A big enough one to set some necessary changes in motion."

"Such as?"

"Such as finally seeing a grief counselor," he admitted. "I'm set up for regular appointments every week. I've already seen my counselor twice and I've made promising strides. I've even hung Tyler's pictures on the walls."

Her eyes widened and she lost some of her attitude. "Are you okay? That must've been so hard."

"It was. Hardest thing I've done since attending my son's funeral but you were right. I can't stop living. My son wouldn't have wanted me to curl up and die with him and that's essentially what I did. I mean, on the surface I seemed fine but deep down I was destroyed. I guess what I'm trying to say is I've begun the rebuilding process and I would like to know if you would be willing to rebuild with me."

He held his breath until it hurt. He knew she was struggling because he'd hurt her pretty bad but he could only hope that she sensed how serious he was about making things work.

"Why?" she whispered, tears glistening in her eyes. "And what if you change your mind? I can't put Talen in that position where someone comes and goes from his life. If you're on board, you can't jump off when the path gets rocky. There are things in my past—very unflattering and embarrassing things that you might not want to know. I was a different person at one time. I was self-destructive and did a lot of things that I'm ashamed of before I had Talen."

"No one is an angel and I would never put that expectation on you."

"My family is so screwed up. I tried to help my mom clean up her place but it didn't end very well. This isn't a problem that can be wished away or handled with a day of cleaning. Likely, this is something I'm going to have to deal with a lot in the coming months."

"I'll do whatever I can to help you through it."

She made an exasperated sound. "Stop being so accommodating," she said. "This is serious."

"And I'm being serious."

"What about my position? How are we going to get around Stuart and his stand on office dating?"

"That's not going to be a problem."

"Why isn't it?" She paled. "Are you firing me?"

He chuckled. "No, you goose. It's not official

yet but I have it on good authority you're going to get a call tomorrow with an offer."

"How do you know that?" she asked, her eyes wide. "Oh, my God, did Stuart say something to you?"

"Let's just say my letter went a long way toward pushing him in the right direction."

"You sent the letter?"

"I did."

"Even when I told you not to?"

"Are you mad?"

She allowed a tiny, giddy smile as she admitted, "I'm relieved. I was being stupid. Thank you."

"No, you were angry and hurt. Never stupid. I'll always have your back. Even when you don't want me to." Her smile warmed and he knew he was making the right decision. "I'm not interested in jumping anywhere without you. If you'll let me, I'll go the distance with you and Talen." He took a step toward her, and she flattened against her front door but gazed at him with longing. "We can go slowly. I want to spend time with you and your son. I want to ease into a relationship with him so he knows he can trust me, too." She smiled and a tear slipped down her cheek. He wiped away the moisture with the pad of his thumb. "Say you'll give me another chance...." he murmured just before claiming her mouth and pulling her to him. She wrapped her arms around his neck and leaned into him, her answer in her kiss. God, he loved this woman. He loved her more with every passing moment and the fact that she felt the same made him giddy as a teenager.

When they finally broke the kiss, her lips were swollen and reddened—and she'd never looked more beautiful. "I got the job?" she whispered.

"You got the job," he confirmed.

"Then it doesn't matter who sees us kissing right now?"

"Not at all. Unless your neighbors simply enjoy a show."

She giggled and pulled him to her for a second kiss. "All right," she said softly against his lips. "How do we start this?"

"You could invite me in for dinner...." A slow grin crept across her face and caused him to ask, "What's that for? You don't eat?"

"I don't cook."

He matched her smile. "Then you're one lucky woman. I'm an excellent cook. Show me what I have to work with and I'll knock your socks off."

She laughed and grasped his hand to lead him inside. There were pictures of her son everywhere, just the way a normal house with children should. He smiled privately when the anticipated painful zing was merely an echo of what it used to be and he knew for certain he was ready.

"Talen," Miranda called to her son, who was watching television. "Come here, buddy. I'd like you to meet a special friend of mine. Talen, this is Jeremiah."

Talen, a striking dark-haired boy, regarded Jeremiah with intelligent coal-black eyes. "Nice to meet you, Jeremiah," he said. "Are you here to have pizza with us?"

Jeremiah looked to Miranda and smiled. "I have a better idea.... How about we see what's in your kitchen and you can help me whip something up."

"I don't know how to cook," Talen said.

"You don't know until you know.... Would you like to learn?"

A slow smile crept across his young face and he nodded vigorously. As they headed to the kitchen, Jeremiah sent a warm look to Miranda as he mouthed, "I love you."

And his heart soared when she mouthed it back.

* * * * *

Be sure to look for the next book in
THE SINCLAIRS OF ALASKA *series*
by Kimberly Van Meter!
Available in 2014 wherever
Harlequin books are sold.

LARGER-PRINT BOOKS!
GET 2 FREE LARGER-PRINT NOVELS PLUS
2 FREE GIFTS!

HARLEQUIN

super romance

More Story...More Romance

LARGER-PRINT BOOKS!

HARLEQUIN *Presents*

PASSION
GUARANTEED
SEDUCTION

GET 2 FREE LARGER-PRINT NOVELS PLUS 2 FREE GIFTS!

YES! Please send me 2 FREE LARGER-PRINT Harlequin Presents® novels and my 2 FREE gifts (gifts are worth about $10). After receiving them, if I don't wish to receive any more books, I can return the shipping statement marked "cancel." If I don't cancel, I will receive 6 brand-new novels every month and be billed just $5.05 per book in the U.S. or $5.49 per book in Canada. That's a saving of at least 16% off the cover price! It's quite a bargain! Shipping and handling is just 50¢ per book in the U.S. and 75¢ per book in Canada.* I understand that accepting the 2 free books and gifts places me under no obligation to buy anything. I can always return a shipment and cancel at any time. Even if I never buy another book, the two free books and gifts are mine to keep forever.

176/376 HDN F43N

Name	(PLEASE PRINT)

Address	Apt. #

City	State/Prov.	Zip/Postal Code

Signature (if under 18, a parent or guardian must sign)

Mail to the **Harlequin® Reader Service:**
IN U.S.A.: P.O. Box 1867, Buffalo, NY 14240-1867
IN CANADA: P.O. Box 609, Fort Erie, Ontario L2A 5X3

**Are you a subscriber to Harlequin Presents books
and want to receive the larger-print edition?
Call 1-800-873-8635 today or visit us at www.ReaderService.com.**

* Terms and prices subject to change without notice. Prices do not include applicable taxes. Sales tax applicable in N.Y. Canadian residents will be charged applicable taxes. Offer not valid in Quebec. This offer is limited to one order per household. Not valid for current subscribers to Harlequin Presents Larger-Print books. All orders subject to credit approval. Credit or debit balances in a customer's account(s) may be offset by any other outstanding balance owed by or to the customer. Please allow 4 to 6 weeks for delivery. Offer available while quantities last.

Your Privacy—The Harlequin® Reader Service is committed to protecting your privacy. Our Privacy Policy is available online at www.ReaderService.com or upon request from the Harlequin Reader Service.

We make a portion of our mailing list available to reputable third parties that offer products we believe may interest you. If you prefer that we not exchange your name with third parties, or if you wish to clarify or modify your communication preferences, please visit us at www.ReaderService.com/consumerchoice or write to us at Harlequin Reader Service Preference Service, P.O. Box 9062, Buffalo, NY 14269. Include your complete name and address.

HPLP13R

ReaderService.com

Manage your account online!

- Review your order history
- Manage your payments
- Update your address

> **We've designed
> the Harlequin® Reader Service
> website just for you.**

Enjoy all the features!

- Reader excerpts from any series
- Respond to mailings and
  special monthly offers
- Discover new series available to you
- Browse the Bonus Bucks catalog
- Share your feedback

Visit us at:
ReaderService.com